No More Quests

No More Quests

CAL DORNE

First published in Hungary in 2001

This edition published in 2018 by iPon Computer Kft.

Translated by Gábor Cebe

Cover by István Kurdi

ISBN 978-615-00-2279-6

Contact: dornyeikonyvek@gmail.com

I, Triturus, master bard and chronicler, wanderer of worlds who saw the events unfold through magic orbs and listened into the pasts and souls of the people involved with the help of my familiars and the art of mind reading have written this tale down in my own style of storytelling, and now I am offering it to you my friend Horius, chief advisor to the King, so you can give an accurate report to your master about the demon lord that destroyed half the city, and all the incidents leading to its arrival...

There are many tales told about great heroes, adventurers whose glorious deeds didn't fade through the centuries. Quite the opposite, the stories were reborn again and again, being told from one man to another. Men prone to exaggerating always found a way to embellish the old legends, each adding their own tale to the original. These heroes guided by the grace of the Gods, Fate and Luck saved entire countries and nations from Evil, and deserve all the credit they get for their deeds.

Still we can't forget those who for whatever reason lacked the abilities heroes possess or their determination to devote themselves to the right cause. I am talking about everyday adventurers who had the opportunity to make their names part of History with their deeds but it never happened. Why?

For some it was their lineage. For others the lack of proper attitude. They were individuals who didn't trust themselves, never recognizing their own talents or underestimating them. They won battle after battle, but they could never defeat themselves. They hid behind the influence of different narcotics to live a life that lacks true emotion but is also uncomplicated and somewhat enviable.

There were some though who had everything to become a great hero - proper strength and determination; but their lives was shadowed by misfortune. They always picked the wrong choice when faced with a crucial decision or simply the odds were stacked against them. They became victims of the evil machinations of Lady Luck with failure as their constant companion.

Still others were simply too childish and too much of a fraud to become a true hero. They dabbled in everything, wanted to know it all. But their restless nature and impatience made them always itching for a change and never let them truly immerse themselves in a single discipline. Their knowledge - just like their power - was superficial gimcrackery.

They considered themselves heroes, like the child who managed to scare away a cat with his toy sword but they were simply adventurers, nothing more. Those who knew them well enough were laughing behind their backs.

These people, different but similar are the heroes of this story:

Weevil, the goblin cleric whose heritage presented an insurmountable challenge for his fame;

Zaislo Oakstool, the adventurous tavern brawler who sacrificed all his hard earned combat experience on the altar of the great deity of Wine and Debauchery;

The barbarian Behemor, once known as an dauntless warrior until he had a strife with Lady Luck, making her turn against him. After that, his good fortune left him, catching one bad break after another.

And lastly Yabbagabb, the meddlesome, childish, bumbling dilettante of a warrior-mage, a wild talent in psionics whose life was soured by his own unruly nature, frivolousness and naivete.

Though I find it improbable Horius, dear friend, but should you find yourself entering an old taproom, tavern or watering hole and meeting some unkempt figure sitting in a corner by candlelight smelling of several days worth of sweat and dirt - just like Behemor, Weevil, Yabbagabb or Zaislo - do not judge them immediately for it is possible for that man to have had a fuller life than yours who is chief advisor to the king. And if that guest honors you by talking, and telling you the details of his old, voluminous memories, it is entirely possible, that after the first few words of this seemingly pathetic creature you will stand there with your mouth agape, listening inspired to his astounding tales.

Perhaps remaining under the influence of the five dimensional magics of Arkania, is the only reason behind all these grandiose words of mine. Returning to my own meager world and birthplace, I did not let myself give into melancholy, choosing instead to immerse myself in the life of a randomly chosen tavern called the Yellow Serpent. I have to tell you, that I was touched by the events I witnessed there. Sometimes they made me laugh, other times they made me ponder the meaning of life, and the roles and places we fulfill as individuals in this world.

Chapter 1
The company gets together

The ancient city Karavan, once the most influential center of the Mongor Empire was showing signs of decay. All the rickety little huts, barracks and castles that remained were mere reminders of past glory. These buildings, all several centuries old, were on the verge of collapse, already fading from history, just like the war torn Mongor Empire itself.

Right next to the main gate, hidden behind the watchtower in the shadows of the crumbling, eroded city walls, was a sizeable inn, called the Yellow Serpent. A huge crowd was gathering in front of it. Humans were the most common people in Karavan, but this crowd had drawn several dwarves, elves and even a goblin!

The inn itself was a rudimentary two story building, built from wood and lacking any discernable ornaments. There were several chimneys on top, and despite the humid summer weather, thick columns of smoke were emerging from all of them. In fact, not only the chimneys, but also the oak planks serving as the roof were spewing smoke. This was due to the flames that were currently consuming the worm-holed planks from the inside. The inn was on fire!

Just a few minutes ago, the ragtag bunch of shady guests were fighting for the seats in the oppressive summer heat. The sun was shining stronger and stronger and as the temperature rose so did the temperaments of the guests. Different groups held different political and religious views which lead to spirited arguments. These went on for a while, but since the opposing parties never met with an agreement, they went for the easiest way of settling their differences – a bar fight.

Punches were thrown. Noses and windows got broken. Chairs and people were flying through the air.

Grog, the slant-eyed innkeeper with a yellow and somewhat scaly skin – one of his ancestors must have been serpentfolk – was shouting, trying to calm his guests down. He vaulted over the bar, brandishing an impressive looking meat-mallet in his hands. He thought it would be a sufficient tool for restoring order. But no matter how spirited he swung it left and right, the rioting failed to cease. Then someone hit him in the back of the neck with a chair-leg. This made him fall forward, smashing his head into a table and taking himself out of the fight for a while.

It was never found out who actually started the fire. There were many guesses, remarks and less than subtle accusations. These almost resulted in another brawl, but after the injuries they sustained, the guests have learned, at least for a little while the merits of self control. „It's better to stay calm" they thought, licking their wounds.

Everyone ran out to the streets, where they were joined by a small crowd to watch the building slowly succumb to the flames together. It's not every day one can see an inn burn to the ground after all!

The fire kept spreading.

A smoldering dirty-yellow form burst through the door of the tavern. He was cussing up a storm, cursing everyone in the vicinity, shaking one fist at the people, while using the other to massage his scalp. Using his characteristic rough hissing voice, he shouted at the crowd:

"Bucketsss here! My taavern isss burning! Aall I have! Breeng water!"

The innkeeper started to tear out his hair, even though there was not much to tear, the top of his head being already completely bald.

The crowd kept cheering and clapping.

"We should put it out as soon as possible. Unless we hurry, the flames could spread to other buildings. The whole district might burn down" The goblin mumbled, in the middle of the great riotous mob, but no one listened. Who cares about the opinions of a lowly goblin?

Seeing that cursing and ordering people around yielded no results, the innkeeper decided to employ a different method. He was a creative mind, a truly mercantile creature. He never faltered, not even in the bleakest of moments, but always found the right words to get him out of trouble. Just like now.

Addressing the simple folk gathered around he said:

"Thosse taking part in the doussing of the fire weell get a drink from a barreel of vintage Tokelnau wine. On the housse!"

This worked! But common folk are not devoid of common sense.

Many of them asked "What size is the barrel?"

Grog grit his teeth, pulling his lips apart. He was snarling, showing his tiny, pointy canines. Then he twisted his features into a smile. Airily, he announced:

"Feefftee galloouns!"

The crowd pushed him out of the way. Humans, and other creatures were pouring into the inn. The mob even swept away those who had no intentions of fighting the fire. The guests set to dousing the flames with a fanatical determination, some using their own cloaks in the process. Others decided to employ the water barrels in the room, or ran to the old well at the end of the street, returning with buckets full of water.

As you can see, fifty gallons of noble Tokelnau wine is capable of miracles. Even if we count it as five silver a cup, the mythical full barrel is still worth about three hundred gold pieces. A lot of people would turn on each other for a single gold piece or two. I don't think I have to explain what promising something worth three hundred - especially if it's an alcoholic drink - is able to do to those people.

The current situation produced several almost hysterical scenes in the crowd.

The noble people of Karavan were fighting the fire with a zealous soul, shoving, kicking and sometimes falling over each other.

Generals should have distributed Tokelnau red among their soldiers before leading them to battle. Soldiers, however, rarely saw wine on those occasions. Or even beer. What they had were mercenary clerics, who had no idea about summoning wine. They only gave blessings. It's no wonder the Mongor Empire lost the war. But enough about politics, let's return to the tavern.

The fire was smothered to ashes. The smoke was vented out, the tables and chairs were licked into shape and the bar was reinstated. They swept the floor and wiped down the tables. All in the time of fifteen minutes.

After they were done, the tavern was more orderly than it has been before the fire.

The guests filled up the chairs, the stools, all the space next to the bar and the entire floor.

Those, who haven't entered the tavern yet, were left out. The guests allowed no-one to come in. Fifty gallons is an impressive amount, but there were an impressive amount of people inside as well. Everyone would be able to get three pints at most. No need to divide it further.

Grog was giving the evil eye to the drunkards at the entrance, who prevented others from coming in, but he did not dare to speak up against them, fearing that he would be thrown out of his own tavern.

Had one of the oligarchs himself the idea of spending the night in the Yellow Serpent, he wouldn't have been allowed inside either. A true drunkard doesn't compromise. If it's about alcohol, he knows no gods or kings.

Ninety percent of the people currently in the tavern were such lovers of fermented beverages.

This is how a bunch of famous adventurers, returning from a long journey and wanting to get a room were prevented from entering the tavern. One of them was a quick tempered, grumpy dwarf who reached for his battle axe immediately. He was threatening to destroy the entire tavern unless he and his companions could go inside. But they couldn't. They couldn't destroy the tavern either, despite having a powerful half-elven mage, and an actual knight in their company. It just didn't matter to anyone at the moment.

"So can we go in or not?" The dwarf asked as the voice of impending doom.

The guests rushed him as one, trampling him down. The knight was smashed into the wall. The others were beaten up.

That's heroes for you.

When those adventurers still capable of walking managed to flee, taking their less fortunate compatriots with them, the guests calmed down again, returning to their seats. They could barely wait for the free drinks to be distributed.

The four main characters of the story were already inside at this point, and they have even participated in the events that happened thus far. There were some who were only taking an observatory role, and there was someone who shouted and bellowed together with the people. His curse words echoed through the tavern. His hands didn't stay idle during the fights. He even shined his boots with the hair of one of his fellow men.

The innkeeper had a barrel brought up from the

cellar, and ordered the servers to measure out the portions. The room fell silent, guests discreetly releasing wind could be heard from across the tavern.

No one had an opportunity to scrounge - to get in line twice for the expensive nectar. Everyone was watching their neighbours like a hawk. The servers moved through the room quickly and filled everyone's cups.

Grog himself helped in the distribution as well. He was very particular about giving everyone the same amount of wine. No less, no more. He was very good at that. His hands moved with an incredible speed, tipping the bottles over. The tokelnau red poured out in a thick stream, sparkling wondrously in the candlelight. It was red like a dwarf's blood at midnight.

The innkeeper had steady hands, not a single drop was spilled. This was true art, unlike swinging a sword! Grog took his trade very seriously. It could be seen in every single movement of his. How actually, deadly serious he was about it however, not many of the guests knew yet.

He stepped up to a table for four which had small benches on each side. Only three people sat there at the moment. This was not surprising, for these three were not exactly sympathetic looking, and on top of that, they were emitting a peculiar sort of smell.

These were all adventurers! They spent their lives going from town to town, searching for the unknown. They met new cultures, encountered new civilizations, races and people. They have traveled to places where no man had set foot before. Nature was both their companion with its rivers giving food and drink, its caves and forests providing shelter and simultaneously their worst enemy with its barren deserts, poisonous swamps and deadly cliffs and chasms.

They were used to hardship on their travels. Would they be unable to find water from stream or spring, they could very well die of thirst. If someone were to mention washing, cleaning or keeping yourself presentable to them, they would laugh in his face. Even if they had the opportunity to bathe, the only reason they would immerse themselves into the water would be to prevent a predator or monster from tracking them by smell.

They didn't care about how they looked. They only cared about one thing: to find more and more danger. They were fanatical in searching for life-threatening situations, letting impatient Death, their only true companion closer and closer to themselves.

Perhaps it was this peculiar, definitive type of smell, characteristic for unfastidious people, that made the three men sit down together, and made them look at each other with sympathy, even though they did not know one another. We will find out later, that they are fundamentally different people, but they were companions in spirit, this was instantly recognizable from their adventure-worn clothes and gear.

The one called Yabbagabb wore a crimson cape ornamented with runes over his simple traveler's clothes, making him appear as a magician, but the clumsy, spiked war-club resting against his seat implied that its owner was a warrior. The cape was a patchwork of mends and tears and sported a number of strangely coloured stains, which gave off their own, even weirder smell.

With his shifty eyes sparkling with childish mischief, Yabbagabb was examining his companions.

Next to him, Oakstool Zaislo was wearing a black robe, resembling the cloth of some clerical order. It was held together by a loose belt around his waist. The belt had a scabbard on it, serving as the home of an ancient sword, that has seen even more battles than its current master. Zaislo's face, reddened and leathery from constant drinking, was turned toward the innkeeper at the moment, he was watching him, excited and enthralled as the tokelnauian wine was pouring, from a bottle into his enormous cup.

Across them - taking up almost the whole bench - sat

the massive barbarian, Behemor. His unshorn hair and bushy beard both held uneaten food scraps, some several days old. He had thrown his weapon, an enormous, rusty battle axe leisurely under the table with his sabretache, and the backpacks of his companions. Behemor wore no clothes apart from a loincloth. His gigantic, ogre sized muscles, and his chest were both covered with thick hair. He was using one of his hands to scratch his armpit, and the other to hold out his cup. Once it was filled up, he raised it to his lips at once. The barbarian easily downed it in one go, obviously he was used to stronger drinks.

"This isn't much!" He burped. Zaislo voiced his support:

"Innkeep! Is this a child's portion? We were promised more than this! A promise should be kept, or by all the saints, I will set this tavern on fire!"

Grog gave him a grim look, but he kept his temper in check. He responded in a calm voice:

"Yess, not the whole feeftee gallons were disstributed yet. But I do not remember sstating the time when I will bee treeting you. I have dessided to disstribute the resst at meednight."

"That late? To hell with it! Why midnight? This makes no sense!"

"Iff you cannot weeit, you can go. Or you can buy another porteeon if you have the monee, and I will bring it to you right now."

"So that's what you are playing at." Zaislo grumbled. "I swear on all the saints, I am prepared to wait until the break of dawn if I am rewarded with a cup of Tokelnauer. But until then, bring me some more wine. It doesn't matter what kind... make it the cheapest."

"It will be right here." The owner replied, seemingly polite but a well trained observer could have recognized the murderous glint in his eyes. It was the look a wolf gives to the sheep he is about to devour.

Someone else approached the table after the innkeeper

left. This someone was so small that he barely reached the top of the table. A goblin. His yellowish-brown wrinkled skin and dog-like face made him repulsive to the human eye. His nose and ears were pierced with small bones and his body was decorated with runes and symbols. Apart from a torn cape he was completely naked.

"Can I sit here?" He asked in a rough voice.

CAL DORNE

Chapter 2
Getting to know each other

"Go to hell you hideous, mangy freak!" These kind words of greeting came from Zaisolo's mouth and to give them a little more weight he even rose up from his seat, flexing his muscles.

This kind of behaviour usually resulted in two types of response from fellow adventurers - at least those brave enough not to back down. The goblin wasn't a coward. The others sitting at the table were expecting the dog-faced creature to draw his tiny dagger, which would be coated with deadly venom and stab Zaislo in the gut; or perhaps pretending to let it go, playing the whole thing for laugh, buying a drink for the abuser and then stabbing him in the gut when he least expected it.

The goblin however did neither but replied in a calm voice instead.

"Hideous, mangy? Freak?" he asked himself, lost in thought for a minute. "Ugliness and beauty count for less than a single drop of water in the sea. The question should be wealth or poverty instead. With the help of the arcane, the wealthy could buy any appearance they desire for coin. But the thing that really matters is whether or not you are happy. Everything else is just extra."

Well this wasn't a reaction anyone expected. Zaislo and the two others at the table have all met goblins before. They knew them as a dumb and primitive slave-race, unable to form sentences with more than one or two words in them so they were completely dumbfounded by the answer of this tiny creature.

"Can I sit down?" The goblin asked again.

None of them answered.

"I will take that as a yes," said the critter and he climbed up to the place next to Behemor. He looked even smaller next to the hulking barbarian.

Yabbagabb was the first to wipe the oafish look of bewilderment off his face. He tried to put on a serious expression.

"Do you consider yourself happy then?" he asked bemusedly.

"Only those who can experience the joy of the moment can be truly happy. Do not look to the future, learn to appreciate the moment, because otherwise you are never truly alive. When looking at a young boy or girl I see their demise, the hopelessness of their future and I cannot believe in happiness anymore."

Yabbagabb was smiling. He found the whole situation of having a conversation with a goblin absurd.

"You are a strange one," Zaislo said, hitting the small creature in the chest with such force, that it almost fell off the bench. The goblin gave him a pointed look.

"What's your name?" Yabbagabb asked.

"Weevil. And who might you fine people be?"

"Behemor"

"Zaislo. Zaislo Oakstool."

"Yabbagabb" the fighter-mage answered, shaking his head in disbelief. "I don't believe you are an actual goblin! A goblin does not talk like that. Admit it, you are an illusionist who has taken the form of a goblin!"

"No, you are mistaken. I am not an illusionist."

"Then you must be the victim of some prankster magician who has turned you into a goblin to mess with you. I know goblins well; they are primitive, lowly creatures. You cannot be one of them." Yabbagabb insisted.

"I am a goblin." Weevil said calmly. "I was born a goblin. There was no spell or curse cast upon me."

"Maybe you just don't know about it. That ill-wishing magician acquaintance of yours might have also cast a spell on you to forget it after the transformation."

The goblin gave a long sigh. He was about to let the stubborn man think what he wanted but then he bristled up instead.

"There was no transformation or forgetfulness spell cast upon me. I remember my whole life clearly. I could tell you the story if you have the time."

"We have time."

"All right, I will tell it but first I will order something to eat."

One of the servers was walking toward their table. The goblin raised his arm to signal him.

"Excuse me, I would wish to order."

The server passed him.

Weevil took out his coin purse in response, spilling a good amount of silver coins onto the table. The sound of them clinking together made the server turn and walk up to the table.

"What can I get you?" he asked with a bored expression.

"Good man," the goblin began. " There is no sound more beautiful than the song of coin. Am I right?"

"Right. Money talks, dogs bark. Stop barking at me dog-face and tell me what you want!"

Weevil answered calmly. He was used to be treated like a dog. Those who didn't know him considered him an inferior being. Those who knew him a little considered him a comical and annoying weirdo. Those who knew him well... were non-existent.

"Bring me raw meat and some sort of woodland berries."

The man gave him a strange look and then shrugged, signaling that it might be possible. He was still examining the silver coins.

"Get a move on servant!" Zaislo shouted "And take a look at my wine order while you are at it! Or there will be cacti growing in my stomach soon. You do not want that do you?"

Chastised, the man almost ran to the kitchen to get their order.

"Will you begin your tale, Weevil?" Yabbagabb asked when the server was gone.

"Right, I will. The story of my life is long and can get quite boring sometimes, but I will try to make it shorter and more enjoyable. Where should I begin? Imagine a goblin village, a few ordinary hovels dug into the ground, pathetic little huts made from mud and loam. Little Weevil was born in one of these dirty shacks as the twenty-first child of his parents. My father - according to him - was different than other goblins once. He was smarter and wiser, and traveled through the world with open eyes. His curious nature - which I inherited from him - was overlooked by the others for he was a great warrior, with the bloody corpses of ogres and trolls at his feet and the knights of mighty orders kneeling in front of him, begging for their lives pathetically. His weapon of choice wasn't a blowpipe, a tiny dagger or even a short sword, he slayed his enemies with his dreaded morningstar. That weapon is still hanging on the wall of our hut, unless one of my brothers has stolen and sold it. My father won battle after battle, he had no match on the battlefield. Still, in the damned battle of Anthia he acquired a wound that made him a cripple for the rest of his life. It's a cruel twist of fate, that he wasn't struck by an enemy but a friend instead: a mountain giant, who failed to notice him. The giant trampled him in the heat of the battle, crippling one of his feet. My father was celebrated as a hero when he returned to the village, but he was never the same after that. He couldn't take part in any more battles, and his only remaining joys were feasting and siring children."

'I was born two years after the battle of Anthia which changed my father's life, and only heard of his glorious deeds from the tales and stories. By that time those memories of his proud fighting days were the only thing he could be proud of, for the years of indolence made him a lowly, pathetic, scheming, thick-headed goblin like all the others of my kind. The life of goblinkind is full of feasting, debauchery and cruelty. Even as a small child I have known that I am not like them. I had enough of my fellow goblins; hated the crumbling little hut I had to live in, the kind of building you humans wouldn't keep your pigs in. I despised our shaman preaching about worshipping demons and I hated the savage rituals, the sacrificing of humans, elves and pixies. I became jaded, and wanted a change for something more noble. Somewhere deep in my soul I knew that the world is different than this pathetic goblin settlement, that there is more to life than this."

'In the end, my eyes were opened by an old elven priest who was captured on a raid. He was the dangerous sort. They bound his wrists and ankles tightly, shoved rags into his mouth and tore off his holy symbol. They were frightened of his power and with good reason, forty goblin warriors were killed before they could capture him. Our tribal shaman wanted to sacrifice him that same night."

"Is this going to take much longer?" Zaislo asked yawning.

Weevil just shrugged. Then he took a deep breath and continued his tale:

"I still remember the cool night when the shaman approached me and said with a twisted but satisfied smile: 'Our lord, the demon will be content with the volume of this sacrifice. You will watch over the elf, Weevil, while the others are feasting before the ritual!'"

'When he left, I didn't say a world, just stood there in the cutting wind, examining the captive. I gazed into his eyes, and then I wished they have bound his eyes as well! For that look he gave me went straight to my heart, melting all the remaining ice around it, and there was so much wisdom, power, knowledge and experience in his eyes, that I simply couldn't look at him like the enemy of my people - the goblin people - anymore. The old priest saw the change inside me and wanted to persuade me with his eyes to free him from his binds. I didn't know what to do. If I do what he asks, I would have to leave the village behind or I would be sacrificed myself. I would become an outcast. What chances does a single goblin have in the world? None. Goblins travel in hordes. Even my father, the mighty warrior was always accompanied by at least a dozen of his kind. So what would I do all alone? But I found an answer in the eyes of the old priest. All my doubts went away when I saw his helpful, sympathetic gaze. If there was anyone who could drag me out of this muck, this soul rotting place where I have lived all my pathetic years it was him. 'Will you take me with you?' I asked him in the common tongue. I spoke Mongorian a little, thanks to my father. He nodded slowly, multiple times. I took the rag out of his mouth and unbound his limbs. Quickly, he jumped to his feet, and grabbed me like I weighed nothing. He jumped up, didn't say a word, but started to run with a speed that belied his age. There and then I thought he would smash me into a rock, taking the evilness of my kind for basis - that, and the fact that this stranger already defeated forty of my kind without mercy.'

'I thought he would kill me with clear conscience, but he did nothing of the sort. Once we got to a safe distance from the village he put me down and we had a long conversation, which ended with me becoming his apprentice. He was a disciple of the God of Knowledge, Pure Mind, Wisdom and Logical Speech and when he recognized my aptitude for his faith he decided to make me a priest despite my lowly heritage."

"This is how I was brought to the temple of the God of Knowledge, which to me was a completely unknown and amazing new world..."

Suddenly the innkeeper appeared with everything they ordered on a tray. "Thiss iss the Calquiaan wine, raww pork and we had sssome woodland beeries ass well. Ssomething elsse?" He asked, interrupting Weevil, while quickly taking the coins from the table, and setting down four wooden cups, a jug of calquian koboldmusher and a plate with berries and raw meat in front of the goblin.

As the adventurers ordered nothing else, the innkeeper quickly went on to take another order.

"I love the calquian koboldsmasher." Zaislo admitted, loudly slurping the reddish-brown drink. "Do you know how it's made? They add a few dead kobolds to the grapes before mushing them together, so there is plenty of kobolt blood in it. It gives the drink an easily recognizable heavenly bouquet."

The goblin, however, was looking at the berries instead, with amazement in his eyes. Then he sampled one of them and gave a satisfied nod.

"Just as I thought," he said." These are magical druidic berries. Our innkeeper is either a fool, or he did not know what he was giving us. A single one of these berries would be worth a whole gold coin. I wonder where he got them from."

"Let me have one!" Yabbagabb cried, already snatching it up from the plate. "This is indeed tasty," he added with a smug face, his eyes sparkling with childish glee.

Zaislo gave one a try as well.

"It's filling too. I feel like I ate a whole boar!"

"It contains druidic magic within. If we had any wounds, they would have closed by now," the goblin explained before putting the valuable berries safely into his satchel. "But I haven't finished yet," he went on, "will you let me continue my tale?"

"Wait just a second! Innkeeper!" Yabbagabb asked Grogg who just passed him by. "See if you have any more of these woodland berries! I would be interested in them!"

"No moore. I onlee had theese accidentalee."

"Couldn't you get more?"

"I don't think sso."

"Are you sure? I would pay you well. It's a very tasty type of berry."

"I am ssure. I could breeng you rootss, parteeally rotten pine coness or grass."

"Uhmm. A little early for those, barkeep."

The snake-faced innkeeper left.

"Continue your tale, Weevil!" Yabbagabb said "I can see you like to talk a lot."

"So...," Weevil went on, "I was brought to the priests, and spent ten whole years there. Every single day went the same way. I almost never left the temple. The first few months while I was an apprentice my day consisted of this: I spent four hours in a deep sleeping-trance, I prayed for two hours in the morning, then I took part in the communal breakfast after which a whole day of learning would began with lunch at noon. After that we had dinner and another two hours of pious prayer to end the day."

"I gained a scary amount of mental discipline from all this. I studied together with all the other priests and they helped me recognize the more complicated types of thought. I soaked up all available knowledge and felt myself closer and closer to the Ancient God of Knowledge. After a while the mental power I acquired became unmeasurable and unbelievably strong. This power, which comes from the God of Knowledge allows me to cast spells."

"I can do that too." Yabbagabb interrupted, "After all I am not just a great warrior but also a mage."

"When I said 'casting spells' " the goblin continued, "I didn't mean some childish cantrips but the higher spheres of magic: blade walls, mass suggestions, time puddles, gravity manipulation, plagues of locusts, mountain-moving, parting the sea, dimension deformations, planar shifts, extradimensional manipulations, demon screeching, the madness of the Dragon, upturning the rims of the skies and so on…"

The men at the table looked at each other.

"Impressive" Zaislo admitted, taking a big sip from his koboldmusher.

"I know spells just like those, "Yabbagabb said. "Thousand-year-old eyes that pierce the realms of darkness, the summoning of an ancient slave-race - extradimensionally of course, the unfolding of long lost magics, the learning about unknown magics and one of my favorites, Yabbagabb's Dreadful Burpmaker resembling the Rotten Swamps of Eternal Doom and the Living Dead of the Thousand Year War. The last one - as you can see by its name - is my own creation."

"I see you know the art of speaking ornate words. I have never heard such common spells described in such a beautiful way before by anyone else: darkvision, summoning a familliar, identifying and detecting magic are all simple cantrips, just like making people burp. " said Weevil with a solemn face, not letting Yabbagabb interrupt him. "I just wanted to say that I became an erudite scholar, knowledgeable in the workings of the world. My job is to observe and to find new knowledge, not to use it. I only use my power when I am directly threatened. Otherwise I am content with patience and humility as my companions. But now I continue my tale… I had many adventures, I have lived for a long time, have seen a lot and gained plenty of new experiences. Each one of my quests could be turned into a book on their own, and every single one of them could take from dusk till dawn to tell you about. But now I want to talk about the final station of my journey as a seeker. One day I had an epiphany about the reason for my existence, a kind of directive or life goal to share the knowledge I gained from my God with my people, the goblins. It was a dreadfully hard quest. In fact I can safely say it was the hardest one of my life. The idea that my goal was impossible and my noble ideas of converting my kind were doomed from the start due to their dismayingly widespread moral and spiritual desolation did not enter my mind yet…”

“After a long search, I found the perfect goblin village with a few hundred goblins. I quickly amazed them with my priestly knowledge, which resulted in their jealous shaman challenging me to a duel. He was sure in his power having been provided with unnatural strength by his demonic patron, but still he sensed that something wasn’t right about me. How right he was about that, he quickly learned during the duel. May the gods rest his soul. I became the new shaman of the village and carefully started reforming the faith of all those lambs lead astray. Sadly, the chieftain didn’t agree with my holy mission and tried to thwart my attempts whenever he could. He was a mighty goblin, protected against my magic by an enchanted stone constantly floating around his body. As my magic proved ineffective against him I had to find another way to continue the conversion of my people to the faith of the God of Knowledge. I soon found out that fate was on my side though. A terrifying monster has moved into a cave close to our village. We didn’t know exactly what kind it was, but the size of its footprints evoked dread in my people.”

‘Dragon’s feet - the goblins whispered with reedy breaths as the mountain shook and the trees in the forest trembled from the thundering roar. Fear held reign over the hearts of the goblins. First they ran to the chieftain, expecting help, but to no avail. Then they came to me. I told them that I would defeat the monster with the power of the God of Knowledge. And to stay true to my word I hit the road immediately, quickly reaching the foothills of the mountain. The cave there spewed the foul breath of the creature upon me. I did not hesitate but entered, and progressed through the tunnel until I found the monster, an enormous golden dragon! Still, it was powerless against me. I only had to look at it and it was dead. I cut off its head as a mark of my glory and returned to my village with a proud stride. Shoving my trophy into the face of our chieftain made him grovel at my feet with dread. He was swearing to the Gods of the Heavens and Earth to do anything I want. Finally, my time has come!"

"The goblin people obeyed my orders, and listened intently to my teachings about the God of Knowledge. My delight didn't last long. That joyous smile of mine withered away quickly when I realized that I was laying siege to insurmountable walls; the goblin mind is protected against the power of knowledge by unbreakable bastions of ignorance. All my diligence and determination were in vain, my mindless brothers and sisters simply weren't able to acquire the Knowledge I was offering them on a silver plate. In fact, I began to feel that they might compromise my crystalline faith with their primitive thinking. After the first signs of my deterioration I fled in panic, leaving my people behind before they could drag me to stupidity with their mental degeneracy. Now I sit among you, trying to forget the shortcomings of my inferior kind. This is the short version of my story."

"Try a little calquaian koboldmasher! It's the best thing if you want to forget something." Zaislo offered. No small thing, an alcoholic tavern brawler offering wine to a goblin.

"Someone else will tell us a tale while you drink," he went on. "Like you, whatsyourname...Yabbagabb! Gods curse the fool who came up with that idiotic name! What was your last adventure?"

"My last adventure?" Yabbagabb repeated, scratching his chin before a shifty smile spread onto his face and he rose from his seat a little.

"I fought a chimera, the strongest and most destructive

predator of the southern wilds... Do you not know what a chimera is? Imagine a monster the size of an elephant, with thick, barky skin and three heads! Don't even bother, I cannot imagine anything you could come up with would be even close to the truth. You have to see it as the enormous monster blocks out the sun, everything falls dark, and blood freezes in your veins as you look at your sword and realize that the hide of the creature is thicker than its length. The feeling that you are already beaten before the fight even began starts to overwhelm you. And then you pull yourself together, whispering 'Bravery!' to yourself as you charge at the beast with your toothpick of a weapon. The chimera strikes at you with all its heads, goat, lion and crocodile, as you..."

"Hey, that's not a head chimeras have!" a man at a neighbouring table interrupted the tale. "Chimeras have heads of a lion, a goat and a snake. I don't believe you ever saw a chimera. It is a much weaker monster than a dragon anyway. Don't you have a more believable story?"

People all around the tables began to laugh. Yabbagabb frowned grimly at the stranger. He made a grab for his spiked war-club behind his back but quickly pulled his hand back when he stabbed it on one of the spikes.

"What would a dumb peasant like you know about the deeds of adventurers?" He asked mockingly while rubbing his bleeding finger. The man was unarmed, so he decided to remain silent. Yabbagabb continued:

"But to sate your curiosity, I will tell you, that my chimera was stronger than the dragon the goblin defeated. This is how it had an enormous crocodile snout instead of some laughable snake's head. I doubt an ignorant peasant like you even knows what a crocodile is. Well I leapt at it with a daring, one-of-a-kind move, sliced up all its major organs and then cut off its heads. First the lion, then the goat and finally, the most dangerous of all, the crocodile head. I see that even you stare at me unbelieving, Behemor. So let's hear about your last adventure! What was it?"

"Dragon slaying." The barbarian answered curtly.

"Yeah, right. We already heard that one from our goblin brother here." Yabbagabb laughed in the barbarians face. Behemor slammed his fist into the table.

"Dragon slaying!" People at neighboring tables stopped their conversations, and stared at the barbarian.

Behemor pulled off his loincloth without any self-consciousness, and turned his ass cheeks, first toward Yabbagabb and then towards the other guests. A gigantic mark of a dragon's bite was clearly visible on his rump. No one dared to laugh.

"Wow!" Zaislo said. "I am curious about the details." Behemor put on his loincloth again. Slowly nodding, he stared blankly into space as he recalled the events.

"A sorceress hired me to free his father from the claws of an evil black dragon."

"Did she pay you with gold or something else, this girl?" Zaislo asked, licking the corner of his mouth. "Tell me, did she have big tits?"

"Be quiet while I speak! A sorceress hired me to free his father from the claws of an evil black dragon. She led me to the dragon's cave. She cast a protective spell on me. Then I fought the monster. I got my rump wound there. I needed twenty-two stabs to kill it!"

"You must have pretty weak stabs then." Yabbagab laughed but the barbarian paid no attention to it and continued his tale:

"I saved the girl's father. When we bid farewell to each other the old man told me to take the black coins from the black dragon's hoard for they might come in handy later. He must have been a man of great wisdom and kindness for the coins turned into gold after a while."

Hearing this, the goblin grabbed his head and started sighing and wailing in despair. The others looked at each other, confused.

"What's gotten to him? Is he going mad?"

"I think he just realized what a pitiful creature he is." Zaislo said.

"Where and when have you slain this dragon?" Weevil asked in a peremptory manner.

"It was four weeks ago, to the southeast of Kalmir inside a barren mountain surrounded by an oak forest."

The goblin was now smashing his head into the heavy oak table as a change of tactics.

"Are you alright?" Yabbagabb asked as Weevil smashed his head into the table again with an even greater force.

"Harder!" Zaislo cheered but Weevil was already done. He has calmed down, sitting there silently like nothing happened.

"You want to tell us something?" Yabbagabb tried. Weevil was obviously debating whether or not to speak but decided on the former in the end.

"Behemor, you have made a grave mistake. You have been horribly deceived! It wasn't a protective spell the daughter of the old man cast on you before fighting the dragon but an illusion spell. You saw gold as black. That wasn't an evil black dragon imprisoning an innocent old man but a gold dragon guarding a prisoner from escaping. That's why you saw the gold coins as simple black pennies for a while. I have no idea who it was you saved but I am sure that you have unleashed a dangerous villain upon the world, someone rotten to the core."

The locals were giving angry looks to the barbarian.

"I have no idea what you are on about." Behemor was blinking rapidly in confusion. "The dragon I killed was gold instead of black and it wasn't evil but good? The one I freed was evil instead of good? And I did a bad thing and not a good thing? Pah! How did you come up with this nonsense?"

"Because last month I was there myself. It was the cave where the monster terrorizing the evil goblin people resided. But when I reached its lair it was already dead. I only found the corpse of the golden dragon in that cave. It was you who has been there before me and slain the creature you thought was a black dragon!"

"But a few minutes ago you were saying the dragon was very much alive when you entered its cave and that you defeated it in a battle!" The barbarian objected.

The goblin shook his head.

"No, I didn't. To quote myself precisely, I said 'I only had to look at it and it was dead'. If you misunderstood my words, you only have your own stupidity to blame."

"Who are you calling stupid?" Zaislo asked, his features twisting into a frown as he balled up his fists.

"The one who wants to solve everything with a brawl." the goblin replied instantly and without any sign of fear. Yabbagabb put his hand on Zaislo's shoulder in a calming gesture.

"Take your hand off me or I will break it." growled Zaislo Oakstool with murder in his eyes. People who knew him called him an alcoholic tavern brawler for a reason.

Yabbagabb quickly removed his hand from the man's shoulder and then, with sudden insight, he filled up his companion's cup with wine before pushing it towards him.

Zaislo grabbed the cup instinctively then he took a large gulp and calmed down. Behemor didn't even notice the developing conflict. He grumbled, irritated:

"It doesn't matter if I killed a good dragon or an evil dragon! A dragon is a dragon! What matters is that I have killed a dragon but Weevil didn't. And I got a bunch of gold in the process."

But a transient at one of the tables was shouting at him:

"It was you, you scoundrel! You were the one who set Cornutor, the dreadful wizard free and you killed our protector and benefactor, Admanatus, the golden dragon! That's how Cornutor and his devil-worshipping hellspawn of a daughter were able to return! That's why they could slaughter my village!"

"Well, it's a small world," Yabbagabb sighed.

"Everything there is is connected by cause-and-effect"

a careworn Weevil added.

Zaislo just kept drinking. He had done it in moderation so far.

"Say something!" The agitated stranger was shouting at the barbarian as he approached with determined steps.

"I thought I did good by slaying the dragon." Behemor burped. "I am sorry, pal."

"That's not enough!" The commoner was half-mad, shouting into Behemor's ears. He drew a tiny dagger and put it to the barbarians throat with a speed almost too fast to follow.

"Bring my poor wife and innocent children back from the dead or I will slit your throat, right here, right now!"

After all this Behemor was starting to get a bit cross.

"Look, pal! A simple stab with a knife or a dagger won't be enough to kill me. Even if you managed to slit my throat, I would have at least ten heartbeats to retaliate. And even after that I would have half that time to enjoy the sight of my retribution. Put that pathetic knife away."

The man didn't move.

"If you kill each other who will punish Cornutor and his daughter?" The goblin was attempting another line of reasoning. The knife was pulled away by a few inches from Behemor's throat but the man wasn't convinced by Weevil's argument.

Yabbagabb, however, sighed in relief and said:

"It's fortunate that one of us is a mighty cleric who would have no trouble raising your wife and children from the dead." Even though Yabbagabb was looking at Weevil as he said it, the stranger turned toward Zaislo, fooled by his black robe resembling the frock of a priest.

This single second of confusion was enough for Behemor. He took a swing…

"I do feel kind of sorry for the guy." Yabbagabb admitted as he watched two bouncers grabbing the unconscious man and throwing him out the door. The bouncers didn't care whether someone was knocked out by alcohol or someone else - every case fell under the same scrutiny. Those who stopped drinking had to go.

"Maybe one day he will get his revenge on Cornuton and his hellspawn of a daughter," Yabbagabb went on moonily.

"At least he has something to live for," Behemor grunted.

"By the way, would you have been able to bring his family back from the dead?" Zaislo asked Weevil mockingly.

"Of course," the goblin priest answered with a serious face, "provided they haven't been dead for longer than sixteen days."

Some time has passed, before Yabbagabb said:

"Now it's your turn, Zaislo. Tell us your latest adventure!"

Zaislo looked at the ceiling, pondering.

"Recently, I have set fire to an inn... but that's not something you can call an adventure. Let's see… Before that I have slain twelve dragons but that's a boring story."

"If this goes on much longer," Yabbagabb interrupted, "dragons are going to be extinct in a few years. Maybe a thousand years from now, no one will believe they even existed."

"What the hell should I talk about? I will go bald before I think of something, "Zaislo began, and then took a sip from his wine. "My hair needs watering from the inside you know, better not let all the roots dry up! And now I know what I will talk about! It happened exactly two weeks ago. Me and my enemy, we were standing, face to face in a cavern. She was a horrid beast. Thick hair covered her entire body, her skin was bare only at a few places on her stomach and shoulder, you could see her calloused skin there. She snarled at me with yellowed tusks then roared and started to approach - first with small steps, then speeding up and finally breaking into a run." Zaislo shuddered, but continued.

"Her wizened breasts, resembling an empty wineskin made a loud smacking noise as they hit her stomach. She lunged at me! Blood froze in my veins as the haze of intoxication enveloping my brain lifted and I realized the horridness of what I agreed to do. The laughing, salivating jowls of the robust orc female got closer and closer to my face and I could do nothing to prevent it, for she pinned me to the ground with her weight so effectively that I was barely able to breath let alone move. I tried to get free fiercely to avoid my horrible fate but the louder I shouted and objected the more the bloody orc bitch enjoyed it. She was completely aroused by my opposition, she burped into my ear in her primitive orcish language something about how she has never met a man who said no to her and that my resistance wakes up unusual wild urges inside her so she is going to reward me with a present that I will not forget as long as I live. I thought I was going to die right there for sure! Sadly, I didn't. If only I had lost consciousness or drank more than a barrel of moonshine before but no. I had to suffer through the whole bloody night. I will truly never forget it. A hideous, drooling face with a tongue covered in warts. Uuugh! Festering boils, yellow carbuncles..."

Zaislo stopped his tale, and not even the enthusiastic pestering of the others could convince him to tell more about what else he had to endure during that night.

"Tell us about the prelude then!" Yabbagabb asked.

"If you want an entertaining little story you will be disappointed. There is none. I simply got drunk and was dumb enough to tell my friends that there was no enemy that could scare me. Then they winked at each other - obviously thinking the same - and asked me if I dared to take on an orcish female in bed.

'Why not?' I answered like the idiotic moron I am. One of my friends ran to the nearby stone quarry and recruited one of the orcish miners for the task. The rest you already know..."

The others around the table sighed in commiseration as they tried to imagine the tumble between Zaislo and the orcish harlot in bed, then as soon as they succeeded they tried to get rid of the thought.

A few minutes later an unexpected event happened in the Yellow Serpent. Maybe it wasn't that unexpected - a majority of adventures starts like this after all. A wizard wearing a black robe materialized in the middle of the room. The gust of wind that accompanied the teleportation upset several cups and ruffled the hair of a few people. It was the former which angered the guests more.

"Damn you, idiot wizard! You spilled my drink!" Zaislo shouted.

"You just had to teleport, didn't you, you retarded cripple?! Walking is not good enough for you is it?" Yabbagabb enquired.

The goblin only mumbled "Usually tavern guests do not to leave the place using their own two legs but to not arrive using them either?"

"Tell me you didn't came for the free tokelnauer!" Zaislo prompted with suspicion in his eyes.

But no matter how upset the guests were with the stranger they didn't dare to confront him physically. After all, someone who knows teleportation might have many other dreadful spells at his disposal.

The wizard ignored the drunken mob completely. He started walking toward the table of Yabbagabb and company.

"Well it's time for adventure I think." Behemor grumbled.

"I already had seventy-eight of my adventures start with a wizard in a black cloak appearing in a tavern, commissioning me to do some sort of quest." Yabbagabb said. "Although only on four of the seventy-eight occasions had the wizard arrive by teleportation." Then he mumbled:

"I hope he doesn't want to hire us to killing dragons."

The wizard was getting close to their table. When he was only a few feet away Zaislo whispered to the others.

"When it comes to payment let me do the talking. I am good at negotiating."

The wizard reached them.

"Greet…," Zaislo started as the man with the black robe went past their table"…ings!"

With a disbelieving frown on his face Zaislo watched the wizard moving on.

"He went past" the surprised alcoholic brawler mumbled.

"He didn't even notice us!" Yabbagabb stated angrily.

"He went past."

"He didn't even greet us!"

"He…went past." Zaislo repeated.

"Hey, wizard! We are here!" Yabbagabb waved, but the black- clad stranger paid no attention to them. He stepped up to a table, that also had four adventurers sitting at it. Judging by their looks, one of them was a warrior, another a wizard, the third one looked like a cleric and the fourth one was a guy with no armor but daggers on his belt, possibly a rogue.

"I have a quest for you!" said the black clad wizard in an authoritative voice.

The four adventurers were looking at the stranger excitedly.

"There is a tower, for you at an unbelievable distance, far beyond the sea, where trees are black, wild dwarves dig their burrows deep into the ground, beyond the obsidian mountain and the prison of the demon Ismordan, not far from the Valley of Death, quite near to the Chasm of the Planes on No man's land. The ruler of the tower and the owner of the item I want you to get is a former black knight who became a death knight. I do not care whether you destroy him or not, but you need to get the fiery red medallion he constantly wears around his neck on a white gold chain. All the knight's other treasures you can keep. I will get you to the tower with teleportation. Once you completed your task I will know it and return you from No man's Land the same way. Do you accept?"

"Yeah, we accept!" The warrior of the group said.

"Yeah, yeah…" The wizard of the group said.

"We hit things, we gain experience." The cleric of the group rejoiced.

"Do you have any questions?" The black clad figure asked. The adventurers looked at each other, confused.

"If you don't then we can start right away. I will teleport you to the tower," he said, and started chanting the magical words at once.

"Just a second! I have a question!" Zaislo shouted. "Why do you trust these greenhorns with your quest when you have us here?"

The wizard turned around and looked at Zaislo, making the lantern on the wall shed light on his deadly pale features just for a second. It was Pentelor, the archmage, though most guests could scarcely recognize him for he hasn't left his hiding place for seven centuries. He looked at the alcoholic brawler with disdain on his eyebrowless face.

"I do not employ drunks," he said with simple scorn.

Zaislo blew his top immediately.

"Who are you calling a drunk?!" he growled, and hurled his cup at the mage with force. He jumped up from his seat, to grab the man by the throat.

The wooden cup hit the stranger in the forehead but he must have been protected by magic for he showed no sign of pain and was even able to finish retaliating by chanting a magic spell.

A spectral hand the size of a bear's paw appeared in the air, right in front of Zaislo. The hand rose up a little and then it struck him. It was a smack of epic proportions, the sound made frightened pigeons take flight four houses away from the inn.

Zaislo felt as if a bunch of the armored war elephants from commander Sarlat's regiment had trampled on his head. He fell back to his seat with ringing and roaring in his ears and for a few minutes he wasn't sure he even had a head left or if it was chucked into one of the corners by the blow.

The wizard paid no more attention to Zaislo. He was looking at his hired adventurers and started chanting the words of the teleportation spell.

After a minute or so, he and his companions popped out of the inn like soap bubbles, leaving another gust of wind like the one when the mage first arrived in their wake.

The empty table left behind was quickly seized by a few drunk locals.

"Are you alright, Zaislo?" Yabbagabb shook Zaislo by his sleeve. The brawler looked at him with a confused, oafish face.

"...e...went...past?" he asked, muddle-brained.

"He teleported away with the other adventurers."

"Is that so?" The man hissed, slowly recovering from the daze caused by the slap. He was getting angry. "He ran away, the slimy cockroach, hopefully into the arms of that orcish hag! The worm scarpered! If only God would grant me the favour," Zaislo raised his hand high, "of running into him again!" He was roaring with spittle flying from his mouth. "I would bash his bloody head in! I would wish him a good night and punch him in the face so he would never get up! Who does he think he is?! An archmage? So what? I couldn't care less! Should I just kneel down in front of him? I will stab him instead! He doesn't know who he is playing with! I have connections! I will send the local Assassin's guild after him! He made me so bloody angry!"

Yabbagabb grabbed a cup of wine and set it in front of

his companion. Zaislo drank it in one go. He grumbled on for a while before calming down.

"Well, I will be damned." This time it was the goblin. "The quest was snatched from us by a bunch of greenhorns. One of them says 'Yeah, we accept' and the other 'Yeah, Yeah'. Are they mad? Did they have no questions? Like, why the mage needed that fiery-red amulet that badly or why he didn't get it himself if he is so much more powerful than them? Or who this death knight is? What his weaknesses are? Who his minions are? Or if there is some information, maybe even a map about the inside of the tower, the rooms, the secret doors, the traps? These are all things they should have asked!"

"Well, what did you expect?" Zaislo asked crabbily, "They didn't even ask for any down payment or inquired about what other treasures this knight has apart from that medallion. He may have none." "And we have been left without a quest." Yabbagabb added with his voice trembling.

"Without a quest..."Behemor repeated bitterly.

"Not so fast!" Zaislo cried, jumping up from his seat. "The inn is the center of the city and the innkeeper is the center of the inn. An innkeeper must know about everything. If there is anyone who knows about a quest it's him!"

He stepped up to the bar.

The center of the center of the city was cleaning a dirty mug. He spat at it then spread the spit around with a rag that was dirtier than the mug itself.

"What you want?" he growled at Zaislo. He was starting to get fed up with this unruly guest, and the suspicion that this is the one responsible for his inn almost burning to the ground was getting stronger by the minute.

Zaislo smiled his friendly smile at him. Were there any small children in the room, this smile would have surely made them cry.

"Innkeeper! My friends and I had enough of loafing around. Is there a task worthy of us that needs to be done?"

The owner thought about this. First he pouted and started to shake his head left to right then something came to his mind.

"I could geet sssome work for you, your brootish friend, and the sheefty looking babyfassed man but I don't eemploy ssscruffee goblinss."

"What did you have in mind?"

"There are logss lyeeng in the backyard that need to bee cut and dissed, and once you are reedy, you ssshoud put the wood in the sshed. If you fineessh by dawn I will give you three sssilver piesses and free breakfasst." He offered with eyes sparkling from mirth, obviously pleased with himself.

Zaislo's face turned red with anger.

"Who do you think we are?!" He shouted, smashing his fist into the bar. "You want us to clean the latrine as well while we are at it?"

"Weel, now that you ssaid eet... ," the innkeeper began but quickly stopped for Zaislo kicked the bar with such force that it almost broke to splinters.

"Remember this if you want to live: we are adventurers! Warriors and magicians not some filthy starving bums!"

"Sssorry, I did not know that, I sswear it on my poor old mother, the innkeeper said. "But eet changess notheeng. I have no otheer tassks for you."

"Pour me another jug of koboldbasher, and give me another cup!"

Affronted to his very core, Zaislo returned to his companions through the crowd with the jug and the cup in his hands. All he said was:

"We are left without a quest."

There was a lot of sighing, disbelief, shaking of heads, hitting of tables, cursing and crying. Well no actual crying, but still, the news made them mournful.

"You know what?" Yabbagabb said."If there is no adventure to be had then who cares? We are fine without a quest. Personally, I felt so insulted that the cowled wizard didn't choose us for his quest that I don't feel like adventuring anyway. If a wizard came up to me right now asking to get some enchanted plant from whatever swamp I would tell him just where he could shove his request. And even if he offered more gold than I could imagine - and I have a great imagination, believe me - I would still only laugh at his problems."

"Yeah!" Zaislo was inspired. "If someone came to ask me to search for something or another of his I would tell him to go to hell! 'It's your problem,'" I would tell him. "Solve it yourself, bub!'"

"That's right." The barbarian growled, mauling a piece of raw meat he got from the goblin's plate with an uninterested expression. "We are on a holiday! No quests for a whole day."

"No quests for one day!"

"We do not accept any tasks! We don't interfere in anything! We don't recognize any requests!"

"Without a quest! Let's drink on it!"

"Glory for the Wine!"

"Without a quest!"

"Just so!"

Four cups clinked and the four men officiated their solemn statement with the calquan koboldbasher.

Chapter 3
Quarantine

It was starting to get dark. Most of the guests had to work the next morning but few of them were able to bring themselves to leave. People drank peacefully and the inn became unusually calm, only a slight murmur could be heard from the guests.

The goblin was busy cutting the remaining meat to smaller pieces. Yabbagabb was playing with a cockroach that was trying to crawl across the table. The eyes of the barbarian were moving up and down at a steady pace as he was mapping out the curves of the barmaid moving past him. Zaislo was searching for happiness in his cup of wine.

Weevil started to talk for not hearing his own voice for several minutes made him a bit dispirited. He started a long monologue, which his companions followed with interest for a while but then Yabbagabb returned to playing with the roach, Zaislo drank and amused himself by recalling pleasant old memories of carousing and Behemor - after his busty vixen disappeared into the crowd - put his face into his hands and fell asleep as the goblin droned on.

"We deserve being ignored by the black-clad wizard

when he was hiring people for his important mission." Weevil started. "In my opinion, we might have been overqualified for the task but the wizard did not know this for he didn't know about our power. None of us spends enough time and effort improving our renown. Has any of you known the name Weevil? No? Of course not! That's just my point! For me, the names Behemor, Yabbagabb or Zaislo didn't ring a bell either. And this is because we don't care about our reputation enough. And because we don't care about it we cannot take our pick of assignments."

"We don't have impressive backstories as Borg Whitebeard, Anal Natreh and Agay the Dreadful, for example, people who planned their adventuring consciously and spread the rumors about their successful endeavors all around the world."

"Otherwise who would still remember after four hundred years how in the year 4120, the first day of the frost month, Agay, the human priest, Natrah, the elven wizard and Borg, the dwarven fighter completed their first mission together successfully."

"Slaying Gryphonsegg, the evil wizard of Whisperhill, and freeing beautiful Chelonia, true Empress of Shador, was nothing but a clever ploy on their part. They raised awareness of their deeds right away. Breaking the dominion of an evil wizard, who oppressed the weak and the poor gave them the sympathies of the common folk. Freeing the Empress was the icing on the cake, gaining them the interests of higher circles as well. Their early success made them bond quickly. A fighter, a wizard and a cleric - they complimented each other well. They made a pact in Abrak always to adventure together from then on."

"Their next quest came from a rich animal merchant who was robbed of his most expensive specimen by an evil ranger who wanted to sell its expensive organs to a witch doctor as spell components. Tracking down and reclaiming this extraordinary creature was a clever move on their part.

They gained the approval of the Ranger Fellowship, the Royal Animal Protection Society and the druidic orders."

"They took part in the Imperial Games in the year 4121 as well where people from all corners of the world could admire their combat prowess in the arena. The warrior dwarf, Borg claimed second place, and the dark skinned elven wizard, Natrah came in third. Rancorous gossip actually stated, that Agay, the Dreadful refused to take part in the Games so he could use his divine magic from the auditorium to help his companions from the outside - which is of course completely against the rules, and in my opinion impossible to do unnoticed. However, despite these small needlings two places on the podium did a lot of good for their reputation. Only the stone giant of Shador proved to be more powerful than them in the contest. But even then, Borg Whitebeard stomping his boots repeatedly on the blood-stained stone floor of the arena shouted into the faces of a thousand spectators that he will be back in four years and he will take the title of Champion from the stone giant then."

"If I remember correctly the three adventurers headed to the north after the Games to fulfill the request of a frost dwarf by destroying the dark spirit of Ice Peak Canyon, an undead servant of the sorceress Zynorra and saving the villages of the frost dwarfs. Of course they were successful in this endeavour as well and it earned them the appreciation of all the northern small folk. They left the cold northern land with the cheers of the frost dwarves and the blessings of the dwarven priests cast upon them, returning to the city of Abrak where they were immediately greeted by a new quest."

"They had to reclaim the magic orb of Great Din, master of Anal Natrah. The artifact was stolen by a sorceress named Drochryssa. Drochryssa fled to Shador with the orb, to the dreaded bandit lord El Harad, the King of the Desert. The group followed the tracks, reaching the hideout of the bandit lord, but their mission was unsuccessful - El Harad remained true to his infamous reputation; the daring adventurers almost perished there, they were lucky to be able to flee in the end. El Harad chased them right back to Abrak."

"They had no time to sulk about their unusual and unexpected failure, however, much larger and much darker clouds than El Harad were gathering on the imperial sky in those days. The dragon army of the archmage and archbishop Grimbundle Khenarr breached the imperial borders on the east, leaving horrible destruction in its wake. They transformed villages and cities alike into haunted ruins in a manner of days."

"The group decided to take on the dragons. On their journey many selfless souls joined them for this noble cause. One among them was special, he ...I have his name right at the tip of my tounge, a dwarf... Trumpeteer Tark who was slain in the battle against the dragons. The group discovered the dragon's nest, and destroyed hundreds of dragon eggs. They saved the seven kingdoms! Had they been unable to do it, there would have been no Mongorian Empire there would be only grim piles of rocks and dragon's nests would be where our cities are now. I think we should be thankful, even after four hundred years for them driving the dragon army back to the east. "

"As a reward, King 'Hair-raising' Klosh the Fourth gave the Whisperhill to the group. At that time they were often called heroes by the common people and they were greeted with the respect they deserved wherever they went. The heroes didn't rest however, and after learning that the master wizard Great Din was captured in the far away Bo Empire they immediately set out to free Natrah's old mentor. Their journey through the dwarven mountains was long and full of perils. The clues of Great Din's capturing led to the pyramid of the sorceress Zynorra. Even though they managed to slay the hobgoblin sorceress with the aid of the knight Sir Langvartel Gart and master Palladios, an extraordinary painter with a magical pencil, they only managed to recover the ashes of Great Din. They returned to the seven kingdoms, bitter and low-spirited, and no one heard anything from them for a while."

"They only resurfaced at the Imperial Games in the year 4125 again. Borg and Natrah both had the opportunity to test their strength against the 4121 Champion, the Shadorian stone giant in the arena. Borg managed to keep his promise by taking his revenge, knocking out the previously unbeaten stone giant in front of everyone. He managed to win at the greatest and most important competition in the world!"

"After this - as if they were playing with fate itself - the group sought more and more dangerous challenges for themselves. They quickly killed El Harad who was previously thought to be undefeatable and disbanded his bandit army. Anal Natrah managed to acquire the dreadfully powerful magic orb of the late lich Voöl."

"They set out to visit far away lands and many companions joined them for a short while but they never stayed. The smart ones left quickly, the stupid ones were slain in the chaotic whirlwind of daring adventures. Still, the three of them survived every quest: they found the Peach of Youth, they reached the innermost circle of Gelirdol's forest, raided the temple of Senar, archpriest in the service of the gods of evil, killed Urathos, a dark lord ruling over half an empire, and after all these they took on an even greater challenge. They broke into a city that had been inhabited by half-demons for centuries and drove out all the dark demon spawn, freeing the city. "

"They heard about Red-handed Drago, the illegitimate ruler of Shador attacking the seven kingdoms with his army. Returning there they started raising an army of their own. Old friends all joined them: frost dwarves, brownies, clerics and elves and in the final battle they managed to claim a devastating victory against Drago's forces. They restored order to the empire, bringing about a period of peace."

"Still, their restless nature didn't allow them to relax, it drove them across the seas and oceans, to strange far-away continents throwing new obstacles in their way. They never lost, winning one battle after another. They never knew why they started adventuring, why they accepted that first quest, if they made the right decision by taking it on, whether or not they have regretted anything they had done, if they should have done it differently... better even, if it was worth sacrificing their happy, carefree youth, the joys of family and fruitful labor, the peace of old age for constant insecurity, unforgettable adventures, friendships forged in mortal danger, disappointments, the taking of all those lives however rightfully. They didn't know if it was worth it. Was it? The last quests they took were not for us, mortals to evaluate. They didn't even take place within the confines of this world. They became favored tools in the games of the gods, serving and entertaining them. They disappeared from us like a rainbow behind dark clouds. Have they died? Have they become immortal maybe? Who knows?"

The goblin fell silent, looking down morosely for a few seconds then he roused himself again.

"Is any of you even listening to me?" Waking up from his doze, Behemor rubbed his eyes.

"What? Did you say something?"

Weevil gave him the evil eye.

"Don't look at me like that, just repeat what you said. This wine made me weary a bit, and I dozed off a little."

Weevil sighed.

"I was telling the tale of three actual heroes in relation to furthering our own reputations. Namely about Borg Whitebeard, dwarven fighter Anal Natrah, the elven wizard and Father Agay, the dreadful. They met each other at a tavern in Abrak on a night uncommonly cold even for the season. Their first quest was against an evil wizard of the Whisperhills called..."

Zaislo reached for his sword. The goblin started to hesitate.

"...Grypgonsegg, who..."

"If you dare telling the tale of those three goddamned people again" Zaislo growled with a crimson face, "I swear to god you won't sit on that bench anymore but the bench will sit upon you. I cannot take these 'he did this, saw that, went this way, went that way' stories anymore!"

"As you wish, "the goblin replied huffily, "we could discuss something else. What do you want to hear about?"

"I want to hear about who is going to buy the next jug of calquan koboldbasher!" Zaislo replied without hesitation. The goblin spread his arms dismissively.

"You bought the first one from my silver." As Zaislo also purchased one, everyone looked at Yabbagabb. The fighter-mage, however, pointed his finger at Behemor.

"He is the one who gained a bunch of gold from the black golden dragon.

"I saved that for my retirement." The barbarian growled.

"Surely, you can spare a few silver coins" Zaislo prompted him.

"I don't want to use my gold coins."

"Just a single one!" They pleaded, but he shook his head.

"No."

"Server!" Zaislo shouted. "One jug of calquan koboldbasher here!"

"So you are paying?" The barbarian inquired.

"The hell I am! But I cannot wait until we decide who will. Are you sure you won't change your mind, Behemor?"

"Completely sure."

"But you have so much gold! I can't believe you are this stingy about a few pieces of silver."

"I don't have any gold on me." The barbarian hastily stated. "I have a habit of not carrying my money with me.

Whenever I get a large amount of treasure I always hide it somewhere. My closest hiding spot is more than a hundred miles from here. I don't want my money to run out until I reach it. I hate it when I fall on hard times."

As the barbarian was obviously stubborn as a mule and stingier than a banker Zaislo turned his attention to Yabbagabb.

"Pay for this one, pal!" He asked nicely. "Somebody else will get the next one."

But Yabbagabb could be stubborn as well.

"I won't! I will not let you exploit me, don't take me for a fool! This is about principles! And you drink more than the three of us put together."

The server was approaching the table with a jug of wine on a tray.

"Pay up!" The alcoholic tavern brawler kicked Yabbagabb threateningly.

"Why, have you run out of money?" Yabbagabb objected.

The server arrived right at this moment. He put the jug on the table and was waiting for his three pieces of silver.

"I have not." Zaislo answered and then continued without paying any heed to the server. "Although I have been much richer than I am now. I got thirty-five silver a week when I was serving in the army."

Behemor, trying to avoid an uncomfortable silence, in which someone might try to make him pay again, quickly countered.

"So what? One and a half years agowhen I was the bodyguard of Count Gormack in Naggakar, I got paid seventy silver a week."

The goblin joined in as he saw the man bringing their order looking his way, starting to extend a hand for his money.

"Thirty-five or seventy silver? It matters less than a drop of water to the ocean! Look further! One would have a hundred years of hard work before collecting enough money to enjoy himself, the other two hundred."

The server brought his hand in front of Zaislo, awaiting payment. The alcoholic tavern brawler, however, gave him an uncomprehending look and turned toward the goblin.

"It matters a lot whether I can afford five or ten mugs of wine a day and whether I can lie with an ugly or a pretty wench!"

The young server was shifting around uncomfortably but did not dare to speak. Zaislo snapped at him.

"Why are you still loitering around here, mongrel?"

"The jug of wine costs three pieces of silver, sir." The young man finally dared himself to answer.

"Give him five!" said Zaislo, waving at Yabbagabb in a generous manner.

The warrior-mage looked at his companion with a dumbfounded face then glanced at the server. The man's face already split into a happy smile as he realized he was getting a two silver tip from him.

It would be very awkward to get into an argument for mere five pieces of silver right now, Yabbagabb thought. But if he pays it, he would be the loser of this little intermezzo. He couldn't let his reputation suffer such a blow.

"Uuuh...five silver? Five silver...I'll get it, just a second..." he mumbled, while rooting through his pockets. But where the hell have I put my coin purse? I just can't find it right now."

"It's on your belt, under your cloak" Weevil told him helpfully.

"No, that... that's not it." Yabbagabb told him with a scowl, before pasting a forced smile on his face. "That's where I keep my lucky stones. Ummm... here and there I collect a piece of stone from places where I go. It helps me remember, making it easier to recall my adventures. But let's not make this poor young gentleman wait! Weevil, pal, give him his five silver pieces, I am sure my coin purse will turn up shortly."

With a hopeful expression the server turned towards the goblin. Weevil was starting to feel uncomfortable. He had enough.

"Here you go!" he said defeatedly, counting five silver pieces into the waiting hand of the man. The server left with a relieved sigh.

"Show me that purse!" Snarled Weevil at Yabbagabb who was smiling a self-assured smile.

The warrior-mage took it off his belt, opened it and then made a surprised face. The purse was full of gold and silver coins.

"This actually is my coin purse!" he exclaimed happily then he quickly made a sad frown after glancing at Weevil's beastly face. "But then where the hell could my lucky-stone purse be?"

"Give me my five silver pieces!" The goblin raised his voice. Yabbagabb was barely able to contain his laughter.

"Why would I give you five silver? Zaislo ordered us a jug of wine. It's your own fault if you decided to pay for it. Nothing would have happened if we didn't pay."

"You told me to pay for it and that you will pay me back later!" The goblin argued.

"I said no such thing. I told you to pay for it and that my coin purse will turn up shortly. But I never said I am going to give back your five silvers. If you misunderstood my words then you only have your own stupidity to blame."

Behemor and Zaislo were laughing as they quickly distributed the wine among the four cups before Weevil could grab the whole jug in his anger. The goblin was looking at his companions silently, obviously plotting revenge. If the thing I am about to describe happened a second later, it's quite possible the goblin would have tried to murder Behemor, Yabbagabb and Zaislo for his five silvers worth of grievance and since this would not have made those three happy and also because they did have a few tricks of their own up their sleeves they most likely would have taken their goblin associate to the afterlife. And they would have had quite a lot of trouble continuing their conversation, there being uncomfortably cold, or - according to others - unbearably warm there.

But the following happened instead:

A sickly looking fellow stumbled in through the door of the inn. He was swaying like a drunk but it wasn't alcohol that gave him trouble coordinating his limbs. Even though he could barely hold his own weight up there were no tough guys brave enough to escort him out. Quite the contrary!

As the stranger approached people scattered like the pigeons from the rooftops when they heard the slap on Zaislo's face a few minutes earlier.

The man's pale skin was peeling away from his rotting, bloody, pus-leaking body. He looked like a zombie. Were he to partake in the yearly contest for the Ugliest Creature of the Empire, held right here in Karavan, he could have easily given the crippled halfling and gnome freaks a run for their money, claiming his own place on the podium or at the very least an audience award. The man, however, seemed untouched by the competitive spirit.

"You are not here for the free tokelnauer, are you?" Zaislo Oakstool grunted at him with darkened expression.

The man with the rotting skin and signs of leprosis on his body looked at the alcoholic tavern brawler with murky eyes then threw himself in front of his feet, grabbing the hem of his black robe with a desperate expression on his face.

"I am begging you good sir, help me! Hide me! They will kill me if they find me but I swear on Almandarr I did nothing wrong!"

As he was tugging at the robe, one of his fingers tore off by itself and was left behind on Zaislo's clothes.

Zaislo threw up on the man and kicked him with such force that the unlucky guy flew to the middle of the inn and lay motionless where he hit the ground. Whether he was unconscious or dead no one dared to check it out.

Zaislo shook the rotting finger off his clothes, grabbed for his cup and drunk all his remaining wine in one go.

"What the hell is wrong with this bloody hick?" He raged.

"He has leprosy if I am not mistaken." The goblin said matter-of-factly.

Panic and anxiety spread through the inn's guests like wildfire, people were starting to whisper about infection, epidemic and death among themselves. The simple folk wasn't prepared for such an unusual turn of events, they came here to rest and have a good time and if they ever wanted a thrilling experience, that was fulfilled by a little tavern brawl or by employing the services of a more generous tavern wench that weren't advertised on the menu. The appearance of a possible leper filled them with dread.

The man was lying on the ground, seemingly dead.

Behemor, Weevil, Zaislo and Yabbagabb on the other hand were unaffected by this turn of events. They have lived through plenty of strange adventures and saw many horrible things. This occurrence wasn't enough to disturb their idea of a peaceful drinking time.

Many were rushing toward the exit, thinking they could outrun the infectious disease.

They thought wrong.

An arrow hit the floor, mere inches from the first man after he opened the door. It came from the outside, accompanied by a militant yell:

"Back off, all of you! No one is to leave to Yellow Serpent! Back off!"

Keeping a large distance, a line of soldiers made a choke-hold around the inn. They were fighters wearing chainmail and wielding longswords with crossbows strapped onto their back - members of the capitol's regiment. A lieutenant, forming a funnel with his hands was shouting:

"Guests of the Yellow Serpent! Stay where you are! Those trying to escape are going to get killed! I am serious! Everybody, go back inside! Right now!"

White-robed priests were starting to appear behind the privates, forming another line of the quarantine around the inn. They were clerics of Almandar the Protector, powerful combatants owing their well-deserved reputation to a dreaded arsenal of combat spells.

That this is no laughing matter occurred to the guests when they spotted the Almandar priest wearing a golden girdle among the crowd. The golden girdle was worn only by the Grandmasters of the Protector. The high ranking priest was flanked by two centurions wearing golden breastplates and crimson cloaks and he was engaged in a fierce argument with them. Even though the people stuck in the tavern could not hear it the dispute was about their lives. The two centurions, in a complete agreement with each other, were demanding the immediate destruction of the tavern.

"We need to set it on fire and raze it to the ground, Father, " one of them argued, "it's the only way to make it secure for the city. We cannot risk the disease spreading. We need to have everyone in that tavern killed, right now!"

The older centurion wasn't as rash as his companion but he held the same opinion.

"I know it is painful for you, father... It is the same for all of us. My heart is heavy as well, but we have to make this sacrifice for the city. The demonic plague of your fellow cleric would have infected the entire tavern by now. The guests in the Yellow Serpent are already dead. We would only prolong their suffering by letting the disease feast on their bodies for days. They should probably thank us for helping them avoid the long, painful torment by a benign flame strike."

"Flame strike?" the priest startled. "What... flame strike?"

Right at this moment people started to appear on the square. They had red faces with black stripes and there were about two hundred of them.

At once the Alamandar master understood what the centurion was talking about.

The closed formations of the well disciplined red-robed figures stopped in the middle of the square. The older centurion exchanged a nod with their leader, prompting the formation to disperse and the men creating a third ring around the tavern, the guardsmen and the clerics.

The guards and the clerics backed off even further away from the building. They were looking behind themselves, knowing what the newcomers were capable of.

"Centurion Farberg! You called the fire mages here, without asking me?" The Alamandar master asked, shooting an accusatory glance at the officer. The centurion, however, did not back down.

"I thought this the best solution. My superiors gave me a free hand in handling this matter. The fire mages are good at what they do and we are in dire need of their talent at the moment. By the time they are finished nothing will be left of the Yellow Serpent. All you and your clerics will have to do is prevent the fire spreading further. The mages await my command... So now I ask you, Father: Can I order this flame strike or do you have any actual arguments against my decision?"

The Alamandar master was rubbing his sweaty forehead, clearly conflicted.

He was thinking about Father Bakefiel, once a fellow member of his order, now awaiting his death sentence behind the walls of the tavern.

'Why did it have to be this way the master thought with a sudden stroke of despair. Why did you search for forbidden lore, Bakefiel? What malignous idea drove you to contaminate your knowledge with the hideous spells of warlocks, imps and kobolds? Where did you get the courage from, trying to bring a demon under your control?

How could you be so reckless and foolish? You should have known your magic will not be powerful enough to hold the demon at bay yet you still summoned it. You were always a fool... a power hungry fool. The demon cursed you before you could banish it. Your malediction is rotting away, more horrid and devastating than any plague or leprosy. Anyone you get close to will share your fate and then spread the disease further by infecting others. Maybe you deserve what you got. I know you well enough; would you have been able to control the demon you would have used it for evil. You deserve death and you can only blame your own selfish and feeble mind for it but those inside the tavern do not deserve to suffer.

'I have to despise you, Bakefiel, for not accepting your fate, for not going into a lonesome exile with the dreaded disease inside you, for keeping the botched invocation a secret as long as you could and for infecting dozens of innocent people in the process. Just this once you could have been selfless but you were too much of a coward to confess or to hide away and die. Now the game is over and the circle is complete. The fire mages are here to execute you... and everybody else in that tavern. The fire mages of Karavan, they are quick and merciless. Should I... Can I give them the lives of the many citizens inside the tavern?'

To make this decision, the Alamandar cleric needed but a single second.

"Centurion! For these unfortunate turn of events, the church of Alamandar is to blame. I ask you to give us time to remedy the problem. I will ask for an audience of the patriarch, and try to persuade him to join us down here. The divine might of His Holiness would be enough to break the curse of the demon and to purify the tavern. All I ask of you is a week!"

The younger centurion was shaking his head, but his companion replied:

"Taking the gravity of the situation into account, I shouldn't allow your request. If even a single person escapes from that tavern Father, the consequences would be unforeseeable. The whole city could get infected! But I do not want to invoke the wrath of your church either: you can have one day to resolve this."

"One day?!" the cleric and the younger centurion asked in unison, both angry. While the former thought it too little, the latter found it too much.

"One day? One day is dreadfully short" the cleric argued "I need more!"

"I am sorry Father. One day, no more."

"A mere centurion shouldn't make decision in a matter of this importance!" the cleric was shaking his fists by now "I am going to have a word with your superiors!"

"Do as you wish. You should know however, that my superiors are actually trying to keep their distance from this sensitive matter, that's why they gave me the right to make any decision as well as all the responsibility… You have your reprieve until the next midnight, I will issue the order to the fire mages after that."

The cleric of Alamandar saw that the centurion could not be swayed, and knew time was running out, so without further delay he turned tails and hurried for the patriarch of his god.

The centurion turned toward the Yellow Serpent, and shouted loud enough for everyone to hear:

"Citizens! I am Centurion Ibrak Farberg, commander of Opolk! I am sorry for what happened, but I wish to ask for your understanding and cooperation! We are pursuing an outlaw suffering from a serious infectious disease who fled into the Yellow Serpent as a last desperate resort, infecting the entire tavern in the process! Exercise caution, and do not approach him! We have the patriarch of Alamandar arriving at midnight tomorrow at the very latest, and he is going to heal everyone while also performing a local purification! Until then remain calm, and refrain from doing anything foolish! To avoid any confusion in the matter, I will state that we are going to kill anyone who attempts to flee the scene! The good of the city commands it! I thank you for your understanding! And now, please close all doors and windows leading to the street, to decrease the risk of infection further!"

For a while, the guests stared at the centurion, the crossbowmen pointing their weapons in their direction, the clerics of Alamandar, and the silent, red faced fire mages. Many were shaking - some from fear, some from rage and some simply from the oppressing feeling of helplessness.

The servers closed the doors and barred the windows.

A dark, grim atmosphere settled over the tavern, with the rotting pile of flesh in the center as a source - you couldn't call it a human anymore at this point.

"We are going to be set free soon" someone whispered hopefully "the man outside promised it!"

"I should have been at work tomorrow!" an angry local grumbled.

"My wife is going to kill me!" another added."

Not far behind them were two traveling lowland dwarves, maybe a yard tall, and just as wide. One of them was so busy berating the other, he didn't even notice the pickaxe in his left hand scraping the floor as he was waving it around.

"Didn't I tell you to go to the Smiling Spirit, you pearhead?! I did! But no, you had to visit the Yellow Serpent at all costs! And now we are stuck here! I wish your pickaxe would break! A whole day of delay! Do you realize what this means?"

The dwarves were gold diggers. Keeping their trade and their destination a secret, they were heading toward south, to try their luck at a rich gold deposit recently discovered by their brethren - and many others since.

"We will get out somehow. We are going to be outside of Karavan's walls, just as we planned." his companion was whispering to the dwarf. "Just calm down! I will find a way to get out of here!"

"This is the last time I come here." the man sitting at the table behind Yabbagabb grumbled. "Even if the patriarch himself purifies the place, the atmosphere of the tavern will never be the same again."

"What could that man's transgression be?" Yabbagabb asked, pointing at the man lying on the floor. "What has he done, and how did he catch such an ugly disease?"

"Who cares?" Zaislo answered. We agreed not to care about anything for a whole day. We should avoid getting involved in this as well. Let's drink instead!

"You are right" Behemor agreed. "Wine is the best medicine. It prevents all sorts of diseases. Let's order another jug of calquan!"

Yabbagabb nodded in agreement and then asked:

"But who is going to pay?"

Chapter 4
The first murder

"Et ermo de vino" Weevil chanted, holding the empty wine jug in one hand while making circular movements in the air with the other. Finally, he pointed his index finger at the jug, creating a wild gust of wind inside which filled the container with blood red liquid.

All around the table people stared unbelievingly at both each other and the goblin.

"This might be a stupid question and maybe I am going mad but did I just see you summon wine from thin air?" a confused Zaislo inquired.

"Yes, calquan koboldbasher" Weevil replied with a bored expression on his face. "There is nothing to it, really. I only did it to prevent another 'I will pay, I won't pay' argument."

The alcoholic tavern brawler was so astonished that he couldn't utter a single word, only blink uncomprehending. He was pondering if it was possible that the goblin told the truth when he was listing his powerful spells earlier.

"You are skilled in summoning wine?" Behemor asked in disbelief.

"As you can see. But there are drinks, like the noble

tolkenauer wine, that not even I can summon."

"How can you summon wine?" Zaislo asked once he was able to talk.

"I am a cleric. It's simple emanation..."

"Something is not right here" Yabbagabb interrupted "You serve the God of Knowledge, right?"

"Right."

"Then how is it possible that your god grants you a spell which makes you dumber if you use it? And more importantly, I would also like to ask how a cleric of the God of Knowledge can allow himself to drink wine?"

Before the goblin could answer however, Behemor grumbled the following question:

"Wait...wait just a second...Let me ask something first! We have paid for the wine thus far, a few minutes ago we even almost went at each other's throats about who should pay for our order, and now I see that our goblin pal is able to summon wine?! Are you playing games with us, goblin drinking buddy?"

Chafed, Weevil answered promptly.

"You cannot be foolish enough to think that I would waste my divine magic on summoning wine! The God of Knowledge wouldn't be happy about using his gift for such a lowly purpose often and without a good reason. This was a single unique occasion, focused on preventing us from arguing aimlessly about who should pay the next round. Knowing your characters, the argument would have ended with you angering me and in my incited state, influenced by my wine-addled brain I would have been forced to slaughter you all."

"Hahh!" the barbarian replied "just because you know about summoning wine, don't think we will grovel before your feet! Brute force is worth more than any magical humbuggery!" Raising his voice, he stealthily pulled his battleaxe resting under the table closer with his feet.

Zaislo was slowly getting over the shock the goblin caused in his spirits by his miracle. His deadly pale complexion turned rosy again as he was sniffing at the magically conjured wine. Looking at the goblin, he smiled a foolish smile.

"It seems real!"

"That's because it is. It cannot be distinguished from traditionally made wine. Don't be shy, taste it! It won't bite!"

Zaislo didn't need to be told twice, he was already pouring the liquid into his mouth, straight from the jar, not wasting any time with cups. When he drank his fill, he emitted a satisfied burp of such proportions that it made some large, decorative antlers fall off from the opposite wall.

"Hey, little goblin!" he exclaimed happily "have you ever thought about opening a tavern? You could create the wine, and I would be the barkeep. Since we wouldn't have to purchase anything, nor would we have any material costs, we could offer our drinks at a lower price so sooner or later everyone would come to us for boozing. Then when all our competition went bankrupt we would of course raise our prices and become rich in a year or two! By all the saints, it would be an enormous business opportunity. What do you say? Let's shake on it!"

"My God, where did I go wrong?" Weevil asked, looking up at the ceiling with a loud sigh, then he collected his wits and spoke in a calm voice:

"Previously Yabbagabb asked, how the God of Knowledge could have granted me the wine summoning spell. I will answer now. The spell was given to me because people become talkative when drinking wine, and they might disclose things they would not speak of otherwise. I have uncovered the secrets of many different creatures like this, acquiring valuable pieces of information which not only furthered my own knowledge but the might of my God as well. This is the singular reason I was granted this spell and not so I could barter with it."

"So you don't want to be partners." said the alcoholic

tavern brawler grimly He raised his arm threateningly but did nothing apart from a wave. Sitting there with a sour face, lost in his own world he looked like he might cry but then his features hardened and raising his eyes higher, he started to cuss angrily:

"My God, Lord of Wine and Debauchery! Your name be damned! How can it be that a simple goblin is able to summon wine, but not me? Even though I am not your cleric, only a follower and warrior but still, you could have granted me this miraculous spell...damn you! How could you do this to me?!"

However the God of Wine and Debauchery was not yet drunk enough to comment on his followers lament. Zaislo's question went unanswered.

The four of them continued to drink.

When Weevil set his wine cup on the table, Yabbagabb asked him:

"Are the clerics of the God of Knowledge allowed wine?"

"No."

"But you are drinking it right now!"

"There are rules which don't get you expelled from the order if you break them. This is one such rule." the goblin said, then after a short hesitation he continued:

"I will quickly tell you the tale of how I began to like drinking. A few years ago I was on a quest in the dark forests of southern Mongor. My mission was to find and recover a religious artifact of a magical nature. I will not go into details. Sufficient to say, that I was able to locate the desired object, albeit with some difficulty. There was only a single hurdle left between me and a successful mission: the owner of the artifact. It was a strange, freakish creature. I have never seen anything more disgusting in my whole life. Still, I hadn't thought that it would pose any challenge. I was sure I would be victorious in the battle which seemed unavoidable. Sadly, I underestimated his power. My demonic enemy struck me with his left arm first, which produced an unforeseen side-effect. His touch made forget all of my more complex and powerful spells for a whole month I could only use the weakest cantrips I knew! Then before I could gather my wits, he already hit me with a magically empowered right swing, which first made my mouth bleed, secondly - and this is the interesting part - made me fall out of the world! Because everything was spinning around me, first I thought his punch sent me to the ground and I am on my way to unconsciousness but then I was amazed to learn that this is not the case: the powerful magical attack of the creature made a hole in reality itself, and I flew out of the world. Don't look at me with such a stupid expression Behemor! For a while I was spinning as the prisoner of an extradimensional vortex and to my great fortune when it released me I didn't end up on some bizarre plane of existence like the Nine Hells or the Elemental Plane of Fire, but remained within the boundaries of my own material plane, only I was sent far away from Mongor, into the middle of an enormous desert.

Happy to escape the battle with the monster with only minor injuries, I started chanting a mighty spell to escape from the sea of sand and the piercing rays of the sun as soon as possible. That's when I realized that since the hideous creature siphoned my powers with its touch, my remaining magic is only enough for activating a few pathetically weak spells. Like summoning wine. To my deepest regret, I wasn't skilled in summoning simple water at that time so I had to quench my thirst with the disgusting smelling and tasting drink I conjured and which I in fact had a great trouble swallowing in the first few days, several times it actually came back up to see where I was going.

Then as the days went by, I have grown to like my new companion and I didn't even vomit that much anymore. The drink helped me to endure the cold of the nights and during the day to pass through the heat spewing desert, driven mad from the tragicomedy of my situation, sometimes singing marching songs as loud as I could, sometimes spontaneously laughing so hard, I was frothing at the mouth.

You could imagine how hard it was for me to drink the wine. If you get really honest-to-god drunk, you desire ice-cold water the next day, not wine, lukewarm from the fiery sun. But I had nothing else to drink. I had to make due with it for a month. By the time I emerged from the desert, thank God, wine was my actual life-saving pal, a loyal friend in need, a true companion, never to part with."

"By all the saints, you speak very nicely about wine" Zaislo perked up, before adding "I forgive you all your previous dumb blethering."

"We will drink to it!" the goblin cleric smiled.

"Will do!" Zaislo agreed.

They toasted and drank. They drank a lot. Weevil was stretching his limbs contentedly, closed his eyes and smiled again, inhaling the smoky, wine-addled air of the tavern before emitting a big, pleased sigh.

A dwarven company was smoking their pipes nearby. Coils of smoke, waved languidly through the still air, fusing together in a billowing, mystical cloud above the room, seeming to form a magical, peacefully dozing but always changing ghost-monster, a tired air elemental. The speech of the dwarves and the other guests sometimes resembled a softly flowing mountain stream, other times - when the flow strengthened - a chaotic turmoil, a rushing rumble which either brought the wine-soaked souls harmony or sent them into wild, intoxicated madness.

The whole building, the simple nobility of the worn furniture, the tiny blinking lights of the lanterns on the wall, the sad eyes of the monster and animal trophies staring at the guests, the rotten, dangerous, trollwood passage upstairs - in dire need of repair - the steep stairs leading to the dark and ancient cellar, the ornate tapestry resting behind the bar were the keepers of a thousand tales and secrets.

The Serpent was an enchanted place, just like all true inns.

"It won't be hard to keep our promise" Behemor started "we will not escape from here before midnight tomorrow. They will only let us out once the patriarch disinfected the place. We have no chance of getting involved in some sort of quest. We don't have to do anything."

"Being idle makes me happy, as long as it is accompanied by having fun." Yabbagabb stated.

"I think we are going to be bored to death…"

Right this second an agitated man appeared on the top of the trollwood stairs and shouted down:

"Citizens! There is a dead dwarf in my room! He has been nailed to the wall!"

For a few seconds, a frozen silence enveloped the tavern. This silence was a herald to the upcoming chaos.

Plenty of the guests in the tavern already suspected that all hell is going to break loose soon.

"There was a murder!" Weevil jumped up.

People gasped.

Scared and confused faces could be seen in the crowd. Everybody was trying to speak all at once, they offered advice, shouted, walked and ran in all directions. The cacophony made it almost impossible to understand each other.

The goblin jumped onto the table, waving his hands toward the guests in a calming manner.

"Remain calm! Everyone, stay right where you are! We will try to get to the bottom of this! My friends and I will sort this case out!"

Despite him having adventurer blood flow through his veins and determination to do something in his soul it was just not enough for the guests to pay him any heed.

"Sit down!" Behemor growled at him.

"Have you forgotten our agreement, Weevil?" Yabbagabb chastised, "We are not going to get involved in any quests for a day."

The goblin stared at his companions unbelieving.

"But there has been a murder here! A dwarf was killed. And since the tavern is closed down, the murderer is here among us. His identity needs to be found out!"

"So that's how much our agreement is worth to you," Yabbagabb said, turning to Zaislo "Do not forget, that we sanctified our vow with wine!"

"By the gods, we did sanctify it with wine!" Zaislo cried before grabbing the goblin and putting him back to his seat. "None of us is going anywhere! By the God of Wine and Debauchery, each and every one of us will stay at our places and we will not get involved, no matter what happens."

"We won't get involved in anything." Yabbagabb repeated.

Barely audible, the goblin was grumbling about how a carelessly stupid declaration made in an elevated moment shouldn't result in such illogical steps taken, like retreating into full passivity. But if all the others insist on ignoring the occurrences, he too will honor his word and keep himself to their agreement.

"Let's not worry about it then! Pour some more wine Zaislo, and tell us a tale to distract us from these chaotic events unfolding around us," conceded Weevil with an uneasy smile.

Zaislo poured him some from the calquan koboldbasher, and immediately scoured the weirdest parts of his brain for a fabulous and not very believable story completely unfitting for the oppressive mood ruling over the building, a tale which - according to him - happened to him a few years ago on the dangerous waters of the Merian sea.

He was serving as a warrant officer in the armed

attachment of a merchant vessel. His duties among others included making sure the ship docks safely in the harbour of Calqua, the city famous for its wine. Come pirate fleets or sea monsters, he, Zaislo Oakstool, God as his witness would have performed admirably but he could not fight the unpredictable weather conditions of the Merian. They got swept away by a horrible storm. It was as if the sea went mad, the wild, unfettered waves were dancing a dreadful macabre dance. The ship was thrown around fiercely by the wrath of the God of Storms. The old wooden planks croaked and screamed until one of the support beams were crushed by a titanic wave. Water rushed in, the ship sank and was swallowed by the sea. The bottom of the Merian almost became his grave as well. His survival he owed to the coincidental arrival of the enchantingly beautiful sea-fairies.

The goblin was only half listening to Zaislo's tale, he was more interested in the guests reaction to the murder in the tavern.

Most of them were standing around dumbfounded. Shuffling in one place, they were sharing their theories about the murder with each other.

The dwarven company sitting at the large table, who have been peacefully sitting and smoking their pipes for the whole afternoon and the evening seemed to go berserk. Their seventh companion recently went up the stairs to lie down in the room they rented. Worry, and anger were slowly overtaking the dwarves that it was their adventuring companion hanging dead on the wall of the room. They wanted to go up and make sure.

Grog, the slant-eyed innkeeper stood in their way, saying no one was allowed upstairs. Heeding his call his large bouncers - brandishing short wooden truncheons - rushed up the trollwood stairs to herd the inhabitants of the upper rooms down to the tavern.

"There are rooms the people don't want to leave. They either shut the doors, sent us away or didn't even answer.

What should we do Gorog? Break their doors down?"

The innkeeper was unable to answer because the dwarves were getting louder and louder with their threats.

"Stand aside, big man," one of them said "we will go upstairs to see if it's our friend that died. Do not dare to stand in our way!"

The innkeeper glanced at the three armed bouncers standing behind him, and their presence instilled some courage into him.

"Noobody goes upstairss. Evereeone stayss here! We wait teel the caranteen isss lifted, and pressent the casse to thee citee watch!"

The dwarves stepped closer to each other, grabbing small battle-axes, waraxes and throwing axes - looking like an enormous hedgehog together.

"You didn't understand us, big man! We will go up, and see who died. And if that somebody is our companion then we will find the one responsible and deliver justice!"

The innkeeper replied angrily.

Thiss iss Karavaan, not ssome filthee dwarven citee! You cannot do thingss your way heere. Obey the lawss and ruless of the citee, unlesss you want to get into trouble!"

The dwarves looked at each other.

"Out of our way, innkeeper!" The leader growled scornfully, and he started to advance.

Grog cursed, but he had no intentions of letting himself slaughtered - he stepped aside, and waved his servants to do the same. The three hulking bouncers, never breaking eye contact with the dwarven warriors and snarling like fighting dogs, backed up slowly.

The dwarves rushed up the stairs, and disappeared into the corridor.

A young man among the citizens present spoke to the innkeeper.

"Innkeeper, sir, if these few dwarven hicks are making too much trouble, you can count on us - he was pointing at three other similarly confident and daring young men.

My friends and I - although simple tradesmen - have been known to put tougher lads than these to their places."

"Thanksss, but I weell not need your help. I want no altrecationsss. I want my inn in one piesse tomorrow." Grog answered before turning to the bouncers. "Wheech roomss were the guessts unweelling to leeve?"

"Rooms two, four and twelve," the bouncer answered. "The people in two said, they won't come down until they are allowed to leave the inn. In four, someone just grunted from behind the door, and we had no answer from twelve. It's either a heavy sleeper renting it, or they have been killed as well."

"No, it wass the drueed in number tweelve."

"Oh, right. He already...moved out."

"Numbeer two wass rented by a lardass of a sspisse meerchant. He wass sspending the night with hiss weakling aprentiss. I don't know what ssort the man liveeng in numbeer four iss. He wass ssome primiteev, ssilent lonessome persson."

"What should we do?"

"Notheeng! We wait! One of you weell sstand at the ssellar door. I don't want aneeone to go down. The otheer two sstay here where they can ssee you, and make ssure there iss no ruckuss, and the sserverss sstay at the bar and the wine barrellss. Drink iss still not for free! Watch out sso no barrelss go missing in thiss gigantic mess, becausse I will beat itss prisse out of you!"

"Are you even listening to my story Weevil?" Zaislo was chastising the goblin. "Why do you care so much about the death of a lousy dwarf? So, the island of the water nymphs is an amazing place, like some sort of heaven on Earth. Those women...they are fearsome beasts. The pampered me to the max! By the Goddess of Love, I am not a romantic sort but bloody hell, I fell in love with all one hundred of the beasts. No human woman is able to make love like them, with such desire, lust, magical endurance, pulse, full devotion, relaxation, such artistic expression, knowledge and instinct, such force and gentleness...they are maddening little tadpoles!" He swallowed the drool threatening to escape his mouth and sighed contentedly.

"My hand wandered for hours on their perfect fish bodies, on the tiny, reflective, blinding and burning scales, the dangerous, strong, and firm dorsal fins, the playful pectoral fins, the dorsal fins trembling with the finest of touches or softest of breaths...not to mention everything else. No human woman comes even close, I, Zaislo gurantee it!"

The sound of a crash filtered down from upstairs, and then nothing could be heard for a while. A few seconds later someone was banging on a door followed by cursing and shouting. A loud smack, the noise of running feet, and some struggle. Then silence again.

The dwarves appeared on the trollwood stairs, grim determination on their faces. They escorted a fat albino in a silken robe, a frightened, emaciated, half naked boy, clearly on the verge of tears and a harassed middle aged man with an unshaven face and shoddy clothes. The man was very agitated, and was grumbling continuously.

"You shouldn't have broken my door down. There are going to be dreadful consequences."

One of the dwarves turned to the innkeeper.

"The dead man in the upstairs room is our brother-in-arms. We will not rest until we find his killer! We gathered these people upstairs. We brought them down here, so everyone is in one place until we investigate the matter. This man," he pointed at the unkept, middle aged guy, "tried to resist. When we broke his door down, he almost stabbed me" the dwarf gave a push to the man. The middle age guy hissed at him, annoyed:

"You broke my door down in the middle of the night! You rushed in brandishing weapons! What the hell were you expecting from me?! I asked you to leave me alone, but you broke the door instead! What sort of behaviour is this?"

"Dwarf warriorss," the innkeeper said, "You have no right to desstroy my inn, or to harass my cusstommerss! Put your weaponss awaay!"

There was a kind of self-assured confidence in his voice which made the dwarves put their murderous instruments back in their backpacks and halters.

"We don't want to cause trouble," one of them said, "all we want is the killer!"

"You broke my door! Thiss cossts you two gold piecess!"

The dwarves stared astonished at the innkeeper for a second, before one of them counting two gold pieces into his hand without a comment.

"And what are you gooing to do now iff I may assk? How weell you begin your invesstigation?"

The dwarves looked at each other with worried faces. They had no clue.

Help came from a table with five adventurers sitting at it. A veteran soldier with a chainmail and a handlebar mustache, a ranger with leather armor and a childish face, an elven warrior wearing elven chainmail, a human female sporting an athletic body and a grim, hardened but beautiful face and an older elf wearing a grey cloak but no weapons.

The woman who was a follower of the God of Life judging by the circular medallion on his neck spoke to the dwarves:

"I am Schiza, priestess to the God of Life. You could get closer to catching the culprit if you discovered who was inside the inn, who left for a short while, and weren't here at all. Is there someone, who cannot prove where he was at the time of the murder. Obviously you need to question everyone for this. Also it wouldn't hurt to know when the murder was committed."

"The murder must have happened a short while ago," a dwarf said "our friend only went upstairs a short time before that guy started shouting about finding a corpse on his room. Who hasn't been in the tavern at that time?"

The dwarves started questioning the guests systematically.

"Where were you during the time of the murder?" One of them asked in a commanding manner, while staring at Weevil.

But it was Zaislo who answered instead of the goblin:

"We were sitting here the whole time, having a conversation. It's what we would be doing right now if you let us be, for the gods sakes!"

For a while the dwarves went on interrogating the guests, but they gave up their fruitless endeavours quickly. They were simple warrior, and had no idea about investigating. There seemed to be no chance of finding out who was where at the time of the murder. Plenty of people have been alone, sleeping in their rooms, using the bathroom or just walking up and down at the crucial moment and there was no-one to verify their whereabouts.

While the dwarves were trying to narrow down their circle of suspects, Behemor, Weevil, Yabbagabb and Zaislo were talking about the Gods.

The subject came up when Zaislo - after the dwarf left - began an ungodly cussing and cursing for being interrupted with his tales and fantasies about the water nymphs.

"Aren't you afraid Zaislo, of being struck by the anger of the God of Wine and Debauchery one day, for involving his name in such ugly curses?"

Zaislo emitted a guwaff.

"Don't be ridiculous Weevil! Wine and debauchery go hand in hand with swearwords. Believe me, when I curse, it is worthy of a prayer and I gain the favor of my God. Of course your god of Knowledge and Wisdom and...whatever else expects another prayer from you obviously."

"The God of Knowledge, Pure Mind, Wisdom and Logical Speech does indeed answer to a different prayer. And what about you Behemor? Which God do you praise in glorious hymns?"

"I follow the Lord of Storm and Lightning but I don't pray to him. My God is a God of pure strength and just like me he cannot suffer moronic chanting. He prefers deeds, sacrifices of wild animals and monsters. Standing on the plains in pouring rain and winds roused by a bellowing typhoon below the skies besieged by thunder and lightning, becoming one with the rage of the elements as you bathe in the blood of your prey - this is the greatest joy for Him, and for me. Then the storm goes, the land calms down, the only things remaining are trees brought down, the birds killed and the remains of your blood sacrifice and then spiritual peace is restored."

"A barbaric ritual," the goblin said, condescendingly, "still better than the worship of demons and totems though."

"My god is mightier than yours." Behemor growled.

Weevil pretended not to hear it, for he knew from experience, that if such a 'whose god is greater' argument like this gets going, it could easily end with the loss of lives.

He diverted the conversation quickly and efficiently instead.

"And you, Yabbagabb, which god do you follow?"

"Actually, I follow them all."

The other three all gave him unpleasant stares upon hearing this.

"Even the God of Knowledge?" the goblin asked, unbelieving.

"Yes, even him."

"And the God of Storms?" Behemor inquired.

"Him as well."

"The God of Wine and Debauchery?"

"He is one of my favorites, Zaislo."

"But most Gods are at war with each other!"

"I don't care about that."

"But still, who do you make sacrifices for?"

"None of them."

"None of them? You are a fool! The wrath of the gods will strike you down."

But Yabbagabb answered:

"It hasn't yet. Why would they do it now? And anyway, had I made sacrifices for all the Gods, I would have gone hungry already. And if I only took an exception for a few of them, I would have angered all the others. It's perfect just the way it is."

"But still, even you don't follow Lady Luck, right?" the barbarian asked in such a threatening tone, that Yabbagabb thought wise not to make hasty statements. And he thought well for had he admitted following her as well right away, he would likely be dead already.

"Why do you ask?" he inquired instead.

Behemor gave a giant huff, took a huge gulp from his wine cup and started to talk:

"The source of all my woes, the sourer of my life, the cause of all my misfortunes is that filthy bitch! Just thinking about her makes my hands shake, my mouth froth, my eyes go red. It makes me go berserk with hatred and I cease to be human!"

Weevil shifted further away from the barbarian.

The dwarf approaching the table to ask if they heard anything unusual, or noticed any other guests behaving suspiciously changed directions and went to another group.

"By the God of Storms" Behemor swore, thumping his chest "I hate no-ones God, apart from this one. She is a pathetic two-faced whore! I, Behemor, the barbarian claim it!" He was shouting at the top of his lungs, uncaring of the weirded out stares of the other guests.

Spitting onto the ground, he continued:

"That filthy snake, that pathetic, petty, lowly louse! If she ever ended up within my reach I wouldn't hesitate for a second to gut her. I would treat her like all my other sacrifices. I would offer her soul to the God of Storms!"

"What has she done to deserve such hatred?" Yabbagabb risked the question, happy about not standing up for his beloved Godess and denying to follow her instead. This gigantic, neurotic barbarian would have torn him apart with bare hands if he let it slip.

After all, Yabbagabb was a spineless sort, maybe that's why he never became a true hero.

"Lady damned Luck ruined my entire life! I don't usually tell this to anyone, even now it's mostly the wine talking, but since you brought it up, Yabbagabb I will tell you why I hate her so much, that I wouldn't hesitate to fight her if she appeared to me, despite her being a Godess.

It happened a long time ago, when I was but a young lad. I was brought up in a far-away village in southern Larkin…"

"You are a Larkinian?! I thought you Mongorian." Zaislo interrupted, and an angry frown appeared on his face.

"What does it matter? I am Larkinian. I don't hide it."

"I wouldn't go around telling it to people in Karavan if I were you," the goblin whispered into Behemor's ear, "Larkinians are hated even more than goblins around here. Past wounds heal slowly. The country ending up in the state it is now is largely due to Larkin."

"Larkinian!" Zaislo growled "Had I known that you are a Larkinian, I would never have sat down here! I am drinking at the same table as a Larkinian filth! The shame! I should have realized where you came from from your accent but who would have thought? No one could tell that you aren't a Mongorian barbarian by looks alone. To hell with all the petty despots for putting up with such scum. It's high time we had a strong handed ruler on the throne. You had the nerve to show your face at my table?!"

The barbarian tensed his arm muscles, and clenched his fists.

"Are you drunk or simply mad, allowing yourself to adress me like this? Just this once, owing to our previous conversation I will forgive your hasty words."

But Zaislo, the alcoholic tavern brawler was not the sort to back down once he got himself going. A few hours ago he had thrown his wine cup at an archmage. What does a mere towering barbarian matter after that?

Zaislo wasn't a spineless coward, he wore his heart on his sleeve.

"Larkinian buffoon! Three times we beat you and chased you off till the Day of the Alliance."

"Or you could say that we managed to conquer you three times you pathetic drunk."

"Yeah! After the monsters broke through our borders from the South and destroyed everything. It wasn't hard like that! Still, we always managed to beat you! And anyway, gods damn it, the last time it wasn't even you who conquered the empire but Imp Khelben! You were just the cannon fodder lackeys of that demon-spawn wizard."

The barbarian huffed.

"But it wasn't you that liberated the country either, instead what couldn't be accomplished by your whole people was done by a single damned priest of death."

"Moronic oaf! Aren't you afraid of dying by my hand?"

A heatbeat later Zaislo had a sword in his hand and Behemor his five foot long, two handed battle axe.

"There is a pentagram painted in blood around your companion nailed to the wall?" asked the grey-cloaked elf, the wizard of the adventuring party who has been silent so far, "Why didn't you say this before?"

The dwarves looked at each other, confused.

"We didn't think some smears on the wall had significance." one of them admitted.

"A pentagram, a five pointed star might be a magical symbol," the wizard chastised them, "You should have told us at once! Your dwarven companion might be the material component in some dreadful spell!"

The dwarves had no idea what their friend being a material component entails, but they did not like the idea.

"What could this mean?" asked the one who has spoken earlier.

The wizard, accompanied by his four friends started to ascend the trollwood stairs.

"We might be up against a magician. I will examine that pentagram. Has any of your friend's valuable equipment or money disappeared?"

"No" the dwarves shook their heads.

"So we can exclude robbery. He wasn't killed for his money."

"But then why?"

"We will soon find out."

One dwarven warrior followed the adventurers upstairs the rest stayed below. The innkeeper was glaring daggers at those leaving. He didn't like people searching his inn. There was no time for him to sulk however for he already had other things to do.

The two pickaxe wielding lowland dwarves currently in the inn were in about to smash in the head of the bouncer who was standing at the stairs leading to the cellar.

Grog took a club in his hand, called one of his servants to him and walked up to the dwarves. On his way he noticed two of his guests berating each other with sword and axe in hand a hair's width away from attacking one another. He apprised the situation and decided on the dwarves being more important. He approached them.

"What iss the probleem?"

The dwarves - swinging their pickaxes around - were

shouting with the man guarding the way down so vehemently that they didn't even hear the question of the innkeeper from behind.

"Iss there a probleem?" He repeated his question.

"There is one indeed! Tell this hulkling to drag his fat arse out of the way at once unless he wants a pickaxe sticking out of his head."

"What buissiness do you have in the cellaar?"

"We will not stay here any longer! We will look for a spot to breach the wall and dig our way to the sewer system. We will reach the surface following that."

"You may no go! I weell not alloww eet!"

"We did not ask premisssion!"

"Thiss iss my inn, and you weell do what I ssay!"

The dwarf turned red with anger, his veins bulging out of his forehead. He was hitting the floor of the tavern with his pickaxe repeatedly.

"We have to leave! We are already late! We are taking part in a risky business. We will run out of time unless we hurry. But you know what? You would be wise to come with us. Who knows what bloody plague that man-shaped smear is spreading in the middle of your inn. It would be better to haul ass as soon as possible. I have no desire to look like a cow patty. Hope you agree, innkeeper."

"I think wee are already all contaminateed. The onlee thing to do iss to wait for the patriarch."

"You would only spread the disease around the whole city if you managed to leave the inn," a Karavan citizen added.

"You won't go anywhere until we have found out who killed our brethren!" one of the dwarven warriors was shaking his fist.

The lowlanders were examining the odds. An innkeeper, two or three bouncers, half a dozen armed dwarves and a few locals - it's too much, they would be biting onto more than they can chew. They lowered their pickaxes and slunk away. Not too far though. They thought, there will definitely be some hubbub around which will allow them to sneak down the cellar easily. Thy were not mistaken. The innkeeper didn't take their pickaxes away and with that he made a grave mistake.

They stared at each other for a long time. Zaislo's face held a mix of anger and determination. Truth to be told once he jumped up, the ungodly amount of wine he consumed went to his head, and he didn't actually know what his quarrel with the barbarian was about. But he hid his confusion well, and his anger haven't lessened a bit.

Behemor held his gaze with a wild, mocking smile while twirling his battleaxe around in the air a few times. The gust of wind he produced then brought out cool, rigid features on his face.

"Feeble human beings, surely you won't go for each other's throat?" the goblin wondered, "Think of the agreement! Until the deadline, you cannot engage in any quest. You said so yourself, the agreement was made under the name of the God of Wine and Debauchery, it must be honored and you cannot break it! No quests!"

Zaislo was swinging his sword leisurely from one hand to another.

"Let's not exaggerate. This is no quest. This is fun," he said as he swung his weapon to attack.

The barbarian grunted. He wasn't surprised by his opponents move, and retaliated with a forceful blow. The two weapons met each other above the table, a few inches from Yabbagabb's face. They almost cut off the head of the warrior-mage.

Yabbagabb made an observation to the others with almost childish glee:

How old are your weapons? From this distance, they seem to be covered with rust!

The combatants ceased their fighting for a second. They were surprised by the weird exclamation of the warrior-mage.

"My weapon is so shitty because I always lose it when I get drunk anyway," Zaislo explained, "there would be no point in buying a more expensive one for they always get lost in two or three weeks."

Behemor, resenting Yabbagabb's words was looking at his battle axe.

"This is a very good weapon! Trustworthy! It might be old and rusty but I am no longer young myself. It had a lot of storms pass it by. Windorian steel is durable but it cannot be as resistant to the forces of time and nature as me."

"Surely you don't want to continue your battle?" Weevil asked.

"Why the hell not?" Zaislo laughed, "I will just pop out to the outhouse. When I return, be gone, barbarian or I will end you!"

With that, Zaislo turned his back to Behemor, and started to walk to the door leading to the yard.

"Do not be angry at him!" the goblin said to Behemor, once the door slammed shut behind Zaislo, "this is his nature. He is a harried soul. One day he will grow up and settle down. Be the bigger man, and put the weapon away. You cannot fight each other to the death just because you have a different view of things."

"This Zaislo is a dirty, booze-addled worm. If my ancestors could pummel the Mongorians then why shouldn't I do the same to him?"

"Behemor listen to me! Look into my eyes! You are not actually angry at Zaislo. The change of your so far flawlessly calm demeanor can be attributed to the mention of the name 'Lady Luck'. You were talking about her when you lost your temper. This is why I advise you to put your weapon down and think about who you are angry with, Zaislo or Lady Luck?"

At the mention of Lady Luck, a muscle started to twitch on Behemor's face.

"Thet dirty bitch! Of course it's her I am angry with!

Who cares about Zaislo? I don't give a damn about pathetic nobodies like him!"

"Then please sit down, calm yourself and continue where you left off. Why do you hate Lady Luck so much?"

For a while Behemor stood still and wordless like a statue then he sat back down, gave a curt nod in agreement and put his battle axe under the table.

"Damn your silver tounge, Weevil, I would have loved to see the two of them fight!" Yabbagabb whined, like a kid who was taken to a puppet show by his parents, but wasn't allowed to watch the performance to the end. He was clicking his tongue, disappointed while shaking his frowning face left to right.

"I was sixteen," Behemor said, lost in past memories, "when I killed a brown bear armed with a single dagger. A single dagger and something the tribe didn't know about: my berserker rage, which made me a possessed, bloodthirsty beast. The chieftain made me a warrior. There were plenty of kobolds swarming around the village those days. Babies and small children disappeared at night. They were eaten. One day, my little cousin was eaten. He was four. The next day we met a lone kobold on a patrol. He tried to flee, I pursued. The others shouted that it's a trap but I didn't care. When my brain gets flooded with rage the world goes dark around me and I become a murderous unstoppable monster. It's better if no-one is around me at those times. I rage and destroy, dancing a deadly dance. I am worse than a werewolf. This is what happened to me that time. I wanted nothing else than to have that kobold's throat in my hand, to tear it apart alive, to tear off its legs while it is screaming and to squeeze its guts out and eat them. I ran like the wind. I rushed through thorny bushes which ripped my skin to shreds but I felt no pain, the only thought in my head was that I had to catch the kobold. I don't even remember entering the cave system. I faintly recall climbing a crumbling loamy hillside, getting cut by rocks, but my first clear memory is the cold, dark cave tunnel, and the warm, stinking, sticky and hairy paste in my hands and mouth that used to be an ugly kobold.

After my rage ended, I realized that i have no idea where I am, and which way I should go to reach the surface. I wandered through underground tunnels in the dark for days on end, without food or water. The situation was getting more and more desperate as the days went by. Hopelessness grew inside me. I made my peace with death. I offered my soul to the Lord of Storm and Thunder and that's when a miracle happened. I saw light in one of the tunnels. I followed it and it led me to a very large chamber. What I saw there...was unbelievable. Thousands of sparkling objects, weapons, shields, armors, necklaces, colorful vials, rings, ornate books and scrolls were lying around on the floor, they must have been collected by dragon kings. Rulers of any empire were pitiable beggars compared to me at that moment. Needless to say, a maddening magical power was radiating from these objects, and as a young barbarian spirit the head-splitting invisible force drove me completely mad. So frightened was I of the unknown auras of the magical artifacts, that I started to destroy them, one after another.

I raged for hours, smashing the magical weapons, jumping up and down on the helmets and armors, tearing up the books, breaking the potions, cracking the shields and rings with a battle axe and eating the magical scrolls. There were artifacts that blew up when they were destroyed, or like one of the rings shot lightning at me as I approached it with a grim look on my face but I still stomped the beastly thing it into the ground. As time went by, I got more and more into the destruction, and as the number of artifacts dwindled all around, their otherworldly powers was transferred into me. This power and experience I had a great need for indeed since one of the swords - when I picked it up to smash it into a rock - tried to gain control over me and wanted to force me to cut my own head off. For a single hair-raising moment it seemed like I would obey its order but then as a stubborn man I followed my first intention instead: I smashed it into the cavern wall with such force that it broke into tiny pieces, emitting a whining noise like a slug thrown into the fire."

The barbarian pondered for a second, then continued.

"I needed a few hours to calm down. I just sat on the floor, marveling at the beauty of my destruction. I felt very tired but very strong at the same time. The power of the destroyed artifacts became mine. The change I experienced was scary. I felt faster than ever before, I could have snached a fly from mid-air, ran faster than wild horses, bowl over a war-elephant with a charge. The strike of my weapon was deadly like the bite of a snake and there was indescribable vitality coursing through my veins. In that moment, I felt unbeatable, the most powerful man in the world, and I gave thanks to the Lord of Storm and Thunder. This is where I made my mistake according to the damned Lady Luck, if only she could die, the dirty bitch! Why didn't I offer her my thanks? Why - the worm asked. No mortal had ever met with such fortune and I still wasn't kissing her leprous feet. How can this be - she didn't understand.

I told her, I follow the Lord of Storm and Thunder, fortune or woe I will turn to no-one else as long as I live. Then she said in her whiny voice: 'So be it' and I even sassed back 'It will be so, damn your eyes' not that I knew if a goddess had eyes to damn or not. And after this my luck ran out. The Goddess never showed herself to me but I always felt her presence, her shadow was upon me sending me misfortune and damnation. Whenever I had to make an important choice, I choose wrong. Emerging from that cave, I was the most powerful adventurer on the continent, my strength rivalled that of armies, I could have decided the outcome of wars, fought demons and fallen angels and never lose a battle. And now I am standing here as a miserable puppet, moved by the strings of Lady Luck.

My vitality was siphoned by vampires, wraiths and dark

spells. Cursed objects sapped my combat prowess and a ghost stole half my soul. I always made bad decisions. In my last quest, I thought I would do good to kill the dragon. Then it turns out that monster was the protector of a village, and dozens of people died because of my action. It's hard to bear, but what could I do, Lady Luck will not fight me, at least not until she has weakened me considerably..."

He fell silent, staring gloomily into nothing for a long while, his soul as empty as his wine cup.

"Aren't you the barbarian, who set the temple of Lady Luck in Trakar alight, and who had a bounty put on his head by her clerics?" Weevil asked.

"I am."

Yabbagabb filled his barbarian companion's cup and added:

"It's weird how everyone shares what ails their hearts. Weevil and Behemor both shared an important aspect of their lives and I think Zaislo would have done as well had he any. Maybe we should adventure together from now on?"

"You are mistaken Yabbagabb," the goblin answered, "what I told you so far was only the surface. Muddled water, nothing else. What lies below the swamp is what's important, believe me."

Chapter 5
Slaughter

The door swung open. Zaislo was returning to the tavern with confident strides, albeit swaying from side to side a little.

Four men were having a dice game at one of the table. They were trying to lift the oppressive atmosphere of the inn with some playing. Their eyes were glued to the turn of the dice. Silver coins were scattered all over the table.

One of the players was a large man with a face like an ape. He threw the dice…

Zaislo miscalculated his next step, his legs got tangled and he stumbled into the table so hard that he almost flipped it. The dice rolled off the table and disappeared among the guest's legs.

The people at the table gave an annoyed hiss and the ape-faced man stood up, fixing Zaislo with a murderous stare.

"How dare you?!" he growled threateningly. "I lost a sure game because of you, you limping swine!"

"Call your orc of a mother swine, not me you scum!" Zaislo hissed back and hit the ape-faced man in the head with such force that he first fell back into his chair, then he flipped over with it, ending up on the ground. There he rested.

The men around the table gave another hiss but did nothing else.

"Lowlives!" Zaislo grumbled before returning to his table.

"Did you manage to calm down?" Behemor asked him.

"Let's continue what we started!" the alcoholic tavern brawler angrily replied and he reached for his sword but it was nowhere to be found.

He looked at the barbarian uncomprehendingly, and several seconds passed before he actually said:

"Damn it to the troll's gullet, I lost my weapon! How the hell will we fight now?"

"You can use my spiked club" Yabbagabb offered his own weapon helpfully.

"I cannot use such a clumsy instrument! I need my sword! I won't fight without a sword!"

"Just wait a moment then! You must have left it in the outhouse. Stay here and don't move a muscle, I will get it for you. I need to relieve myself anyway."

"You are a good man Yabbagabb. At least I can have some wine this way. I see you have barely left any."

With fast strides Yabbagabb ran to get the sword. He entered the inner courtyard, finding himself in the garden surrounded by the inn's walls, full of bushes and trees. He used his psionic power, focusing his inner energies to switch to thermal vision granting him better navigation in the darkness.

The outhouse was a wooden shack in the middle of the garden. Under the watchful eyes of the stars Yabbagabb entered one of the doors of the building reeking with an unbearingly foul smell. He did his business, and then started searching through all the other rooms. He only got to the third before backing out.

He has seen plenty of corpses in his day but the body in front of him still froze him in his tracks for a few seconds.

"Oh, Zaislo! Why do you drink if you can't keep it together and end up doing all kinds of crazy shit?" asked Yabbagabb rhetorically while examining the corpse.

The man was struck in his back by Zaislo's sword so the tip of the blade peeked out on the other side, somewhere around his stomach.

The victim was one of the innkeeper's bouncers.

Yabbagabb didn't know what to do. He looked around and saw no one. Closing the door carefully, he returned to the inn as if nothing had happened.

Looking at Zaislo he had a sly grin on his face. This grin was a trademark feature of Yabbagabb. No matter what mood he was in, what he thought or felt this grin was shadowing him, betraying his base nature.

"Did you find the weapon?" Zaislo asked.

"I did indeed! A man has it in the third room of the outhouse.I tried talking to him but he won't give it back. I think you will have to convince him."

"If that's what it takes" Zaislo said, slamming his fist to the table "I will find out how he got hold of it but he won't get to see another day, that's for sure!"

"Oh, I am pretty sure."

The tavern brawler stood up from the table.

"Hey Zaislo!" Yabbagabb called after him "How much do you need to drink to forget something you did?"

"A huge amount. Four or five times as much what we had so far" he stated and went to leave the room but an unexpected event interrupted him.

The five adventurers and the dwarf appeared on the stairs leading up. They had two things in common. A frightened pale face and shaking like a leaf.

"You mustn't let anyone leave the room!" the elven wizard of the adventurers shouted.

"Do as Dragwaren says!" the dwarf agreed.

Even though no one knew yet what this was about, the

dwarves moved to block the exits of the inn.

Dragwaren, the elven wizard stopped on one of the lower stairs, and started to speak in a firm and serious voice:

"Please be quiet citizens! I have an important announcement to make. Please be seated! Our situation hasn't exactly been rosy before, being exposed to an infectious plague of an unknown origin. Unless the patriarch arrives in time we will rot alive just like this man - he pointed at the heap on the floor. Or perhaps there is something even more horrid in store for us. I don't want to waste any more words and what I am about to say won't make you happy in the slightest. A bloodthirsty demon lord will arrive in this inn within a day."

Many guests gasped, unbelieving, but the elven wizard didn't let his words to fade into the starting murmur. He strengthened his vocal cords with magic and continued with a booming voice.

"It was proven without doubt that the pentagram drawn around the victim is of the demon summoning kind. The ritual was done by someone in here, risking all our lives in the process. The demon is raw dark power and absolute evil itself. If the beast manages to materialize it will kill everyone in the inn, no one will be able to stop it. I don't know who the summoner is, a cleric, a mage or perhaps a warlock. I don't understand the reason behind his foolish behaviour. What made him conjure up a demon? Even worse, a ruler of demons, a demon lord! Why does he think he would be able to get it under his control? The chance of that happening is extremely low… But the summoner does have the heart of the victim, to try and control the demon with. But an enormous amount of magical power is needed to succeed which I doubt he possesses. I ask him now to step forward, give us the reason behind his deeds and hand the heart over. My magical power might be enough, if I have the heart to send the demon lord back to it's horrid native plane, to the nine hells… Who is the summoner?"

The guests of the yellow serpent stared at each other with suspicion. No one said anything, except for Zaislo cursing in the background because of two dwarven warriors standing in his way. They did not let him visit the outhouse and tried to tactfully invite him to return to his table and since he had no weapon unlike the dwarves, the tavern brawler returned to his seat "nicely."

"What's up with the mongrels? They won't let me out!"

"You should pay more attention Zaislo! Soon a hulking demon will appear from thin air and kill everyone inside the inn" Yabbagabb shared enthusiastically.

"You don't say!"

"Our status haven't got any worse" Behemor grumbled "and anyway let's not pay any attention to what's happening around us! You were the ones who said we should keep our promise. Let's have it your way! The demon can go to hell and all the dumb, boring and useless quests can be damned as well! I might never adventure again!"

"If that demon arrives, you surely won't adventure any more" Weevil mumbled.

"Don't concern yourself with what the future brings!" Behemor answered.

"He is right" Yabbagabb agreed "summon a little more wine instead, my goblin friend!"

"Good idea!" Zaislo grunted.

The drinks started to shake in their containers as the elven magician spoke again with his magic-enhanced voice.

"Because no-one assumed the responsibility for this ungodly deed, I hereby order a search for everyone present. For this I ask for assistance from my companions, the dwarven warriors as well as the owner and his bouncers."

A disapproving murmur started up among the people, guests were starting to fidget.

"They want to search us?"

"Can they do that?"

"I won't let them search me!"

Grumbled phrases like these started to fill up the room.

"Please remain in your seats! We are starting the search. Please realize that it is in all our interests to find the dwarven heart! We need to search your equipment for that!"

One of the citizens tried to object:

"You have no right to do this elf! The city watch has to be notified about this so they can act and have time to prepare. The arrival of the demon lord is a problem for the whole city not just for this inn."

Many were nodding in agreement to show their support.

Two young citizens - without waiting for any other opinions - ran to the exit, pulled the latch and opened the door.

Outside it was already a cool and dark evening with a strong wind blowing and storm clouds wreathing through the sky.

The inn was lit by the magical lights of the fire mages.

The soldiers, clerics and mages standing guard stared grimly at the opening tavern door.

The second the head of the first youth appeared from behind the door it was gone. Not gone as in back into the inn, but gone as in remains found on the otherwise yellow but now red walls of the Yellow Serpent inn.

The poor sod was first struck by two arrows with arrowheads so large that they almost tore his head off. But this was only a taste of things to come by the men surrounding the inn. The main course was a group of magic missiles bouncing into the apprentice's face then came the dessert from the clerics. They combined their powers to conjure a bolt of lightning which blew the young man's head off.

"Bastards!" his companion shouted from behind the door. "He only wanted to warn you that a demon is going to invade the city!"

"We are following our orders!" a warrant officer answered from the blockade. "We cannot make contact with people inside the building. Close the door before the breeze brings the plague out! Do you understand, or will I have to make them kill you?"

The youth got scared. He jumped to the door and tried to quickly swing it shut but he couldn't because his headless companion was lying in the way. He struck it twice with the heavy oaken door before he realized why it didn't close. He grabbed the headless corpse by its legs, pulled it inside the inn, shut the door, closed the latch then slumped to the wall breathing heavily.

This tragic fold of events plunged many into lethargy. People sunk into themselves, filled with melancholy. They saw their own future in the death of the young lad which made the wine taste sour in their mouths.

"He was still a child." Behemor grumbled.

"Yes, my barbarian brother," the goblin replied. "He could have become a great man or a villain who laid waste to multiple cities."

"He was a foolish creature," Zaislo spat, before taking a swig from the wine Weevil summoned. "That's how it ends for those who cannot stay in line."

The guests in the inn fell silent for a minute, only a dog lying in one of the corners gave a sad howl. You could hear the wind and the evening prayer of the blockading clerics outside.

"Eventually a separate room should be found for the dead," Yabbagabb whispered into Zaislo's ears. "A big one, for their numbers keep increasing."

The elf, Dragwaren stepped down from the last stair and went back to the guests.

"Elves, dwarves, humans...citizens! We cannot count on the city! We need to solve the problem ourselves. The demon lord can arrive at any time. We might only have minutes left! We cannot tarry any more. Please, I ask you to cooperate with us! The search would mean only a few minutes of discomfort. Let's start! Let's get it over with!"

He signaled his companions and they started searching the guests with the priestess Schiza taking the lead. The dwarves accompanied them.

The innkeeper remained behind the bar. He thought himself safer there. His bouncers didn't take part in the search either. One stood by the stairs leading upstairs, another at the stairs leading to the cellar and the third was lying in the third outhouse to the left, at least as far as physical bodies are concerned. His soul has already left this mortal realm. The fact that he was dead was only known to himself, other dead souls, a few otherworldly deities, Yabbagabb and the person who was wicked enough to stab him in the back with a broadsword while he was doing his business.

Grog had a good idea taking cover behind the bar. There were two many powerful guests staying at the inn - perhaps by chance, perhaps by intent - who had things to hide so they weren't exactly delighted with the search to put it lightly. Where this leads, I will tell you in minute:

The adventurer Drgwaren and the dwarves went through the tables one by one. Many people grumbled, cursed or made snide comments but at first everyone let them sift through their bags and backpacks. Only those patted down by the priestess Schiza were happy about the search.

One of the bouncers realized that his companion is taking too long at the outhouse. Approaching the innkeeper, he asked permission to check up on him and left the room at the door leading to the inner courtyard.

The search was going along at a good pace until they reached a guest sitting alone at one of the side tables. It was far from the wall lanterns, and the candle at the table wasn't lit so he, and his surroundings were enclosed in darkness. Someone put a lantern in front of his face, but it didn't do much. The stranger was wearing a robe that covered his entire body and face. Only the hand he used to hold his cup was uncovered but he pulled that back into its sleeve before the light could reach it. He must have been a cadaverous old man. He was hunched over, holding his head just inches above the table. Having no equipment on him, the dwarf doing the search only asked him to remove his robe.

As if he haven't heard the words of the dwarf the stranger continued to sit there wordless and motionless.

Were it not for his head held a few inches above the table, the guests could have taught him dead.

"Didn't you hear what I said?" the dwarf snapped "Take your robe off!"

The stranger did not respond. His passivity was starting to draw attention.

Dragwaren's adventurers and the dwarven warriors formed a circle around him with weapons in their hands.

"Has any of you interrogated this one about where he was at the time of the murder?" asked the dwarf. His companions all shook their heads.

"Doesn't matter. We will have that conversation now. You won't take your robe off? So be it!" he added raising his axe to strike as he reached to tear the man's clothes off with his free hand.

This is when the thing happened that none of the people present could explain. Something moved in the darkness. No one knew whether it was the robed man, or something else. The dwarf collapsed, dead and covered in wounds made by acid and fire.

Uncomprehending, the people surrounding the stranger took a few steps back. Dragwaren himself was confused. Had the stranger killed the dwarf with magic, he would have known, but he haven't felt the presence of magic. But then how did he kill him? What kind of enemy are they facing here?

His train of thought was stopped by the bouncer stumbling in the courtyard door, holding a bloody broadsword, raving like a lunatic.

"Talak was killed! Stabbed in the back with this sword! He lies dead in the outhouse! Another murder! Grog, what do we do? What's happening?"

Zaislo recognized his sword in the hand of the bouncer. He put on a very ugly face and he was in the process of standing up to reclaim it, but then he stopped, realizing that he would be accused of some newfound murder. He thought for a second about what exactly happened when he last went to the outhouse. He recalled nothing unusual. He did his business, came back and he left his weapon there.

Yabbagabb blinked at him conspiratorially, which made him shiver with dread. To get rid of his bad mood and to avoid organizing his scattered thoughts he drank all the wine left on the table in a single gulp. This made him drunk for a while.

"Whoossse ssword iss thiss? Whatss hapeening in that corneer?" the innkeeper asked. He was so confused, he didn't know where to look.

"Isn't that your weapon that guy is holding?" Weevil asked. Instead of answering, Zaislo emitted a deep burp and fell drunkenly onto the table.

The five dwarves stopped their retreat a few feet from the killer of their companion. The pulled themselves together and put on an angry face. Forming a semicircle, they advanced on their unknown enemy slowly and cautiously.

The lone man in the robe continued to sit there like a statue. He was obviously unconcerned by the dwarves armed with handaxes, war axes and greataxes who were preparing to cut him into pieces.

You could feel the tension mounting among the guests. They sat up in their seats rigidly, not daring to talk. It was as if time itself had stopped inside the inn. Nothing happened. And then the bell in the tower on the Peace God's temple started to chime. It was midnight. The cyclopean eye of the full moon watched the Yellow Serpent interestedly.

The dwarfs started to shout. With a loud war cry, they charged their enemy.

The robed man laboriously stood up on wobbling legs and started to shuffle toward one of the dwarves. Everybody was waiting for the battle but before it could start a commotion erupted among the spectators.

The source of this commotion was the man in ragged clothes who was dragged down from upstairs a few hours ago by the dwarves. They could not drag him so easily now for he was undergoing a remarkable metamorphosis. This change was brought on by the combination of midnight and the full moon which was no wonder since the man was a werewolf.

His limbs elongated, he hunched over but he still grew taller than he was as a human. His whole body bulked up and grew. His bulging muscles were covered by thick hair, his jaws grew long and his teeth got larger and pointy. His eyes darted around madly as he turned left and right among the people. An animal roar left his throat and he leapt at the shocked audience.

Throats were torn, hearts were ripped, heads were bashed in and they disappeared inside the werewolf's gullet.

He didn't slaughter the guests of the inn haphazardly. It was commendable that he left no wounded or crippled, anyone he got his paws on died a quick and painless death.

He didn't want a massacre in the Yellow Seprent tonight! He had no such intentions. Whenever the full moon came, he always left in time to bear the short-time transformation and the madness that came after far from civilized lands so only forest animals would fall victim to it. He was out of luck today with the quarantine preventing him to leave the city.

His bad luck was shared by the guests. Heads and headless bodies were flying left and right. People didn't know where to run in their panic. Some fled upstairs and some hid below the tables.

One of the guests choose an unusual method of staying in the background. I don't think many could have done what he did.

He leapt up the wall with a backflip and instead of falling down or breaking a leg he pulled himself up to the ceiling using the small cracks and trophies on the wall as leverage before settling down up there in one of the corners like a spider. He shifted around until his loose black velvet trousers, fashionable dark shirt and black vests hid him perfectly in the shadows.

The souls of the dwarven warriors were full of combat spirit and their brains filled with bloodlust payed no heed to what was going on behind them. They struck at the hunched man in the robe.

The leader of the dwarves used his momentum to swing at the enemy with an enormous greataxe. He was aiming for the head.

Another dwarf swung lop-sidedly with a twisted smile on his face expecting to cut the stranger in half.

His companion on the left had a throwing axe in his hand, and when he was only two yards away he threw it before dropping to the ground and rolling ahead like a massive barrel, intending to push their physically weak enemy over and pin him down.

Before he hit the ground, the dwarf behind him also threw his axe and leapt into the air as high as his stocky form allowed him, to flatten the enemy - who will surely fall to the ground after this - from above.

The last dwarf stopped, believing he won't be needed after seeing the coordinated attacks of his companions.

The innkeeper called to the remaining two bouncers. They reached him behind the bar in seconds.

Grog opened a secret door on the cupboard then

searched around frantically before pulling out three chest plates, two bucklers, a longsword, a flail, a morning star and a crossbow.

"Heelp me put thee armour on!" he ordered while picking out the morningstar and the crossbow from the weapons.

While the bouncers were busy with arming themselves, the two lowland dwarves loitering around the cellar door left the scene of chaos behind and started moving down on the currently unattended stairs swinging their pickaxes.

"Dress moore quicklee!" Grog hissed at his servants "I ssaw the two lowlandeerss going to the ssellar. We need to sstop them!"

Dragwaren and two of his companions, the veteran warrior with the fu-manchu and the elf in an elven chainmail went to help the guests. As they got nearer to the werewolf, a glowing red quarterstaff came to life in the hands of the elven mage.

Schiza, the priestess stood her ground for the time being, watching the attack of the dwarves instead. The ranger of the group stayed to protect her, a man with a childishly young face, wearing hardened leather.

The wrath of the dwarves reached the stranger like a raging hurricane.

The cloaked man sensed the first axe heading toward his face, the second one aimed at his waist and the two thrown in his direction followed by the pair of heavyweight dwarves. Still, he wasn't afraid. Neither him nor his partner!

Because he did have a partner…

Although to be more precise it wasn't a partner. When you say someone has a partner, it is assumed that its treated as an equal. Here this wasn't the case at all. For the cloaked man was a mere puppet, a slave to a greater force that was with him…on him.

The dwarven leader's axe struck, cutting the victim's head in half. At least the dwarf thought this would be the case, because he delivered his carefully planned attack with masterful precision. The axe did indeed hit the stranger and the man did stagger for a second but in the meeting between the metal and the cloak the axe was the weaker one.

The clothes of the stranger must have been made from a considerably durable material. Not a scratch was visible on it. On the other hand the edge of the dwarven weapon was chipped and ruined.

The fighter attacking from the sides encountered a similiar problem as his boss. His axe glanced off the cloak drawing sparks.

The first throwing axe struck the man below his shoulder but seemed to have no effect on him. The second projectile got better results, finding its way to an area unguarded by the cloak and embedding itself into the skull of the stranger.

The man said nothing, just went on fighting with an axe sticking out of his head.

These unnerving facts however did not prompt the dwarves to retreat. When a human encounters a wall, he would find a way around but a dwarf will just lower his roboust head and smash into it again and again, until he finds out if the wall is stronger than him. Stubborn, bull-headed people the dwarves!

The dwarf rolling on the ground hit his foe. Apart from wiping some dust from the tavern floor with his clothes he could boast no results. The stranger stood firm like a rock.

The dwarf clung to him, trying to shake him, break his shins and finally in his desperation he even tried to bite him.

His battle brother flew above him, hitting with a force

that would have destroyed a smaller hovel. He hit the mysterious cloaked figure like a boulder from a catapult, making him stagger for a second. The dwarf started pummeling him, flailing with his hands.

"Tear his robe off!" Schiza shouted from the background "That's why you can't hurt him!"

The dwarves attacked the stranger like a pack of rabid dogs, growling, gritting their teeth and barking. The combatants fell to the ground and a desperate brawl was starting. Bones cracking and breaking by the dozen on both sides.

Suddenly one of the dwarves managed to yank off the hood from the stranger's head. The sight greeting the guests was not the most pleasant one. Many thought it was better before they knew what they were facing.

The skull broken by the axe was covered in dry, yellow shriveled skin. The wound didn't bleed but oozed a bile-coloured puss. But the most shocking and nerve wrecking effect was coming from the eyes or the lack thereof. There were gaping holes in the place of the cloaked man's eyes.

One of the barmaids gave a loud shriek. The next second her neck was broken by the werewolf who then went on searching for another victim. He spotted a group of guests hiding below one of the tables.

The guests jumped up from their hiding place and rushed toward the door at a panicked pace. The werewolf was nowhere near them when they reached the door. They got outside.

The city guards, Alamandar clerics and fire mages were ready for their arrival. No heed was paid to their cries, the storm of arrows, magic missiles and lighting bolts came down. They all died.

Behemor, Weevil and Yabbagabb were looking at their empty wine cups. They only cursorily followed the events unfolding around them. Theirs was the only group still in their place, not hiding below the table, moving to the background or running off somewhere.

They sat there like a group of weary oldsters, at least a hundred year old each.

Yabbagabb, as always could not take what was happening in the inn seriously enough. He never really had a firm grip on reality. Zaislo was dozing off, resting his head on the table - he was only interested in wine and debauchery. Behemor, an experienced man knew that whatever he did, he could not raise his chances of survival. Whether he got out of this building alive was not up to him, but dependant on outside forces at this point. He didn't see a whole lot of hope for himself. Weevil also sat in his seat with a calm that indicated he made his peace with death a long time ago. Shaking his head, he spoke in a melancholy tone:

"The stupidity of man knows no limits! They just saw what happens to those attempting to leave the inn. I can't understand why they had to run for the door? Why didn't they try for the stairs? Why? Why can't they think? Why do they have to be so stupid? Why can't they use their brains? It is devastating to see the death of so many young souls."

"There are still some left. Should we save them?" Yabbagabb asked.

"What's the point? If they don't die today, then they die a day, a week or a few years later and if not them then others. It is human stupidity that should be eradicated, but my power isn't great enough for that. Humanity does have wisdom in its reach but it never allows itself to grab it. Why must stupidity always reign? Let me tell you a story that I experienced recently! It made me so furious that I had trouble sleeping for a week.

I wish to talk about the great massacre in Rotmar, but only a few sentences for it is not worth wasting more words on it. The Lord of Rotmar laid devastating taxes upon his people, his peasants were toiling day and night, and still it was barely enough to provide for their families the bare necessities. I was the guest of this man for several days after I saved him from some bandits. Fearing a continuous assault from highwayman, he decided to introduce a new defense tax to increase the number, pay and loyalty of his mercenaries. This was the straw that broke the camel's back. The peasants losing their patience and goodwill but lacking any weapons, decided to revolt by collective suicide. The Lord was not moved by the threats made by the common folk. No matter how hard I, a cleric of the God of Knowledge wanted to persuade him, he did not listen to me. He said that he cannot appear weak in front of the people, he will not change his word and anyway, he is a good card player and won't fall for a bluff. He didn't heed the demands of the poor people. And he suffered for it.

By the next crow of the rooster his peasants - no matter how hard I tried to persuade them otherwise - committed suicide one by one. They killed their families, wives, children even their draught animals to deny them to their Lord and then they hanged themselves. When I told this to the Lord, he would not believe his ears. Not a single peasant was left alive. The yearly crops were there on the fields and there was no one to harvest it. And then the Lord of Rotmar went mad. He exchanged the weapons of his soldiers for farm instruments and sent them to the fields to do the work of the peasants. He even expected me - a cleric and a guest - to work on the fields. When I denied his request, he shouted that he didn't need useless parasite clerics and threw me out of the castle. His mercenaries escaped the fields at the first opportunity, later joining up with the highwaymen to return and besiege his castle which did not prove to be a hard task. The Lord had a dozen soldiers left at the most, all of them his most loyal servants and closest relatives. They could not last a day and were all killed. The Catle of Rotmar has been a nest of bandits evere since." Finishing his tale Weevil let out malicious a parting strike:

"After all that forgive me for doubting the place of humanity among the sapient races."

Zaislo was lying on the table, resting so he had no way of strangling Weevil. If he was conscious he would have surely done it. A goblin belittling the intelligence of man - he could not let that go for sure.

Yabbagabb grinned, then loudly - to be heard among the fighting and dying noises of the inn - said:

"I remembered a story as well! I just don't know if I should tell it. Were I less drunk I wouldn't have mentioned it. But well, now I will tell it! Or should I? I just don't know..."

"Tell it!" Behemor said.

"Telling it would lessen my fame."

"Then don't." Behemor sighed.

"You have no fame." Weevil mumbled.

"But I think I will tell it anyway. Would you like to summon some more wine Weevil before I start?"

"No! No more wine! Look around this inn man! There is a werewolf slaughtering people here and some zombielord - like creature over there. I don't want to disappoint you, but I do not want to waste my magical powers on summoning calquan koboldbasher especially since I sense a much greater dark power in the inn than a pathetic werewolf or zombie."

"Where?" Zaislo raised his head as if he hadn't been sleeping a second ago.

"I cannot pinpoint it exactly. Evil lurks here in the Yellow Serpent!"

"Who gives a damn about evil?" Zaislo punched the table, annoyed "Did you just mention calquian koboldbasher or were I dreaming it?"

"Argh! I will not summon any more wine, it would decrease my magic abilities!"

"A last barrel?"

"No."

"A last bottle!"

"No!"

"Just a last cup then!"

"NO!"

"C'mon!"

"No!"

"Just a little?"

"No!"

"Why not?!"

"Just because!"

Zaislo would have continued this clever debate with the cleric of the God of Knowledge, Pure Mind, Wisdom and Logical Speech but Yabbagabb interrupted them.

"I think I will tell the story after all. It's a tale about how the most intelligent people can be really stupid sometimes."

"Let's hear it!" Behemor seized the opportunity, because Weevil and Zaislo were slowly driving him mad with their conversation.

"Have you heard about the fall of the dark mage in Cork-oak Forest?" Yabbagabb asked "Well if you haven't then I will tell it as it actually happened..."

Meanwhile the werewolf was searching for another victim frothing at the mouth and red in the eyes. He saw no living people around apart from Dragwaren and his two companions. He wanted to tear some unarmed victims apart as sport before fighting them. Raising his snout, he smelled the air for a while, attempting to scent some guests hiding smartly behind the furniture. He had a keen nose like a hunting dog. He smelled something but his grin froze on his face. Bafflingly he sensed the creature in the corner of the ceiling. He squinted, but couldn't make out the person among the shadows or if there was even anyone there. There must have been for he smelled it but he could see no one. He huffed angrily, beeing sure that the stranger hiding in the shadows was looking him in the eye. He gave an ear-shattering howl and prepared to pounce up and grab the hidden figure but he was prevented from doing so by a glowing red staff.

Dragwaren, the elven wizard raised his weapon filled with magic and hit his enemy in the head as hard as his feeble strength let him.

The werewolf howled in pain, a long streak of blood trickling down from his forehead to his mouth. Swallowing his own blood, he turned around facing his foe and attacked as if possessed.

The two fighters attempting to protect Dragwaren stepped between the wizard and the werewolf. They were trying to keep the long, clawed paws of the enemy at bay. They did not bother with attacking. As experienced adventurers they knew the abilities of lycanthropes well, until the transformation ends only silver or magical weapons can harm them. They couldn't do anything but defend while the wizard fought with his enchanted staff.

The werewolf pushed their weapons aside and would have been at the throat of the elven wizard but one of the fighters prevented it.

Dropping his sword, the veteran with the fu-machu and the chain mail jumped onto the beast using both his arms to grab on. He came from the sides and worked his way to his back while using his arms to grab onto the throat - he was hanging there like a cloak.

The werewolf shook his head angrily, trying to shake off his enemy.

The fighter - despite being well above six foot tall and weighing three hundred pounds with his armor on - were swinging around like a piece of cloth as the werewolf swirled him around. He hit the supporting columns, chairs, tables even his own companion but he did not let go of the throat.

Dragwaren was standing behind the other elf so he could not attack with the staff. Touching the ground with one end, he propped it with his shoulder, raising his hands up to cast a spell. He was chanting quick, firm magic words, having no time for more powerful but time consuming spells.

The werewolf lunged to make a dash at the man crouching in front of him.

The elven warrior could have evaded the attack, but he hesitated. He had one heartbeat to make the decision. If he dodges, he survives but the beast claims Dragwaren, the only one who can harm it. If he stays put, he dies, but Dragwaren can finish his spell.

Having no more time...he made his decision.

He would have liked to look at the faces of his companions one more time, saying a few parting words to the always cheerful ranger, the stubborn and haughty Schiza who seemed kind now in this moment of death - they had so many adventures together.

'Kavak, so proud of your facial hair, be blessed! And honorable, wise Dragwaren I will meet you at the gates of Anavrin, in the elven paradise. 'These were the last thoughts going through his head before the werewolf struck.

Schiza, the priestess of life was trying to make the battle easier for the dwarves. Holding her holy symbol in her hands she was chanting divine words at the zombie-like creature. An ordinary zombie would have already fled. But this enemy was no ordinary zombie. She could not turn it. And then, as if she sensed the doom of one of her companions he glanced at the battle with the werewolf. She saw the elven warrior collapsing.

"Help them!" she shouted at the ranger standing next to her.

"Who will guard you then?"

"I can take care of myself! Save the others!"

The young ranger hesitated. Schiza grabbed him at the shoulders and pushed him toward the werewolf.

"Help them already! Kill the beast!"

The ranger glanced back at the priestess annoyedly, but he faltered no more and went to get slaughtered by the werewolf. Schiza already started chanting a new spell which reassured him somewhat.

The clothes of the dwarves was painted with blood - their own blood. They ripped, tore, hit and bit their enemy the best they could, but the zombie-like abomination always retaliated. The dwarves were shouting, screaming and roaring. The zombie-like creature fought silently.

After a while the dwarves managed to pull the cloak off their enemy and then using a few blind axe-swings they chopped his arms, legs and finally head off. The crippled body turned around a few times and then laid still. The dwarves - deadly tired - laid on the ground breathing heavily and trying to get themselves together.

Dragwaren closed both his fists and for a second he looked like he wanted to try and fight the beast with his bare hands. Then he opened his palms. Glowing purple missiles emerged from them. Without fault the small magical bullets hit their target, embedding themselves into the werewolf's gut, causing serious injuries.

The monster howled wildly in pain and fell to his knees grabbing at his wounds. Dragwaren picked up his staff and hit it in the head. The werewolf fell backwards, burying Kavak under his body. The mustachioed warrior felt as if the sky itself had fallen on him. He released the werewolf, gasping for air.

Dragwaren fought on determinedly. He struck with his weapon again, but it was no use. The monster stood up despite his onslaught.

In the far away corner of the room, Schiza had finished her spell which resulted in a warhammer appearing above Dragwaren's head, glowing with a dim, ghostly light.

"Fight with the hammer!" Schiza shouted after the

ranger, forming a funnel with her hands.

The young ranger ran across the room with frightful speed and graceful movements. When he heard the shouts of his companion, and saw the weapon materializing, he jumped up onto a table, leapt into the air and grabbed the hammer sailing above Dragwaren's head. He struck the werewolf while still in the air, and landing on his feet he stood elegantly in front of his foe.

The werewolf glanced at his broken shoulder. He commented on the recent events with an furious, throaty growl and then swiped at the ranger with his right arm.

The man leapt back, doing a backwards somersault then stood right next to Dragwaren.

The bloodlust of the werewolf did not lessen in the slightest but the surprising turn of events made him adopt a more careful fighting style. His left arm was hanging numb next to his body, he could not move it no matter how hard he tried. Swaying his head and hips left to right, he creeped up on his future prey.

"For Timarkhausozar!" shouted Dragrawen and he attacked. The ranger wielding the warhammer did as well.

Their foe roared into their faces.

Dragwaren hit him in the gut, but the strike had no strength behind it. He was fatigued, barely standing on his feet.

The ranger, although he preferred swords did make due with the warhammer. The werewolf dodged his swing, but he struck again with an almost untraceable move and hit his foe in the kidneys.

The success however was fleeting.

The werewolf clawed at the ranger and dislodged the hammer from his hands.

The magical hammer hit the ground and disappeared as if it never even existed.

The disarmed ranger lost his balance and stumbled into his friend. They tried to stay on their feet but the beast lunged, pushing them both to the ground. Dragwaren had no strength left to stand up and the ranger hit his head going down, he had no clue about what's going on for a few seconds.

All the werewolf had to do is choose from the three people lying there. Which should he tear apart first? The old elf, the young ranger or the mustachioed warrior?

Schiza ran to the dwarves shouting hysterically.

"Get up! We need you!"

One of the dwarves, blood on his face, with a broken leg, arm and face nodded sympathetically but did not move. His friends payed no heed to the priestess of life, just took deep breaths and clutched their wounds.

"Get up warriors!" Schiza shouted, kicking the dwarf lying closest to him. "Stand up! The fight is not over yet!"

This last sentence of Schiza was worth a true prophecy - the fight indeed was not over yet.

The cloak of the zombie they cut into pieces started to move!

"The dark mage of Cork-oak Forest" Yabbagabb began "was a terribly depraved, horribly mean blackguard of a man...a monster! His evil deeds and scheming made the people of Cork-oak Forest live in terror. He was damnation itself. Grass withered beneath his feet, flowers wilted and yellowed leaves began to fall from the trees when he approached. He gained his evil powers from sapping nature, every single spell he used for his selfish, cruel shenanigans made the forests, meadows and the animals, creatures, teeny-tiny monsters living there die."

"What a horrible, despicable beast this mage must have been" Zaislo interrupted Yabbagabb's tale by laughing in his face. Evil did not start like this for the alcoholic tavern brawler.

Yabbagabb just waved his hand.

"So anyway I only wanted to cross the forest to reach the games in the arena in time but the sad fate of the creatures in the forest made me so miserable that I could not say no, I offered my help. I promised them that I would have a talk with the cruel lord of the forest and I will try to persuade him to abandon his evil ways."

"I am glad there is still someone concerned about protecting the environment." Weevil said "Ever since humans appeared, drastical changes have been happening in the structure of nature. It is important to keep our sense of duty. I am happy you tried to make the mage see it your way instead of trying to kill him. Obviously you told him about how it is our responsibility to end the destruction of nature, to protect the endangered plant and animal species and the beautiful and essential lands, forests and meadows. About how we must think about the future and preserve the traditional values of nature for generations to come. That's what you told him right?"

Behemor and Zaislo shot weird glances at the goblin. Yabbagabb shrugged.

"I wanted to tell the mage of the Cork-oak forest to behave himself and to stop casting spells like a madman, oppressing the creatures of the forest because otherwise I will beat him to death with my spiked club. But there was no civilized conversation to be had after all. The villagers told me not to even try for there was no point. Then I offered to chase him away. Then they told me that was no good, he would just return after I left. So then I asked what the hell they expected of me. All together they told me to kill him. 'Hmmm' I frowned 'Are you sure he deserves it?' They all replied 'Yes!' Apparently their children could not sleep from fright. The black mage has made pacts with dreadful demons to strengthen his power. Fields were ruined, streams run dry, cattle were dying and the trees were rotting away. Cork-oak forest was starting to disappear from the face of the earth. 'Oh well' I said 'let's have it your way, I will kill the magician.'I was always easy to influence. 'On my way here I saw a large clearing with a huge old oak tree in the middle. Send a messenger immediately to the black mage of Cork-oak forest that I want to fight him there, right now.'"

He took a short pause for effect and then went on.

"The mage had a frightful appearance, his skin was covered in demonic symbols, tattoos and stigmata, his skin black as night, his eyes white dots, like the stars in the night, his hands a bunch of sharp claws. And indeed flowers wilted where he stepped. Because of my blessed good heart I gave him a chance to stay alive, to see the light. I told him that scheming with devils is a bad idea, that his spells ruin the nice flowers, to think about the other denizens of the forest, how much better it is to live in harmony and so on and so on…

My speech made him so angry that he started speaking the names of all kinds of demons and devils. When his rage subsided, he started at me with his cold, dark eyes, smiled gleefully and began chanting a brutal attack spell. He was speaking the words of the Prison of the Living Rot. This sadistic spell teleports the victim deep into the earth, and keeps it alive for a long time, it cannot move and has to stay in the dark as maggots chew on its flesh - so it not a pleasant spell to be targeted with. Long suffering and death awaits.

Well this was when it occurred to me that I have miscalculated something about recognizing our power levels. Well we are only human, we make mistakes. We have to deal with the consequences. 'Goodbye world!' I said stolidly. The black mage of Cork-oak forest was at the finishing words, all around him the grass shriveled up, the bushes died, the ground started to crack and even the great old oak was shaking as the spell drained its life-force. Finally the shriveled up roots could not hold this giant of a tree any longer and surrendering itself to decay it fell, burying the black mage of Cork-oak forest under itself with a large crash. For I while I just stood there uncomprehending - the mage of Cork-oak forest knocking himself out? Damn! Good show! How much learning and experience he needed to learn all his powerful spells and master the highest levels of magic, and how stupid he had to be to ignore a triviality like the huge oak. Well it did not matter in the end. I told the tale to the people of the forest as if I had defeated the black mage of Cork-oak forest in a terrible magical duel, and that's how everyone else heard this tale as well, only you know the truth. I hope I can trust you not to tell anyone what really happened."

"An interesting story." Behemor said.

"Nature always gets her revenge for the wounds inflicted upon her." Weevil was summarizing the moral of the story. Zaislo just laughed and then added:

"This tale of 'Little Yabbagabb versus the great wizard' made me remember something. This happened when I still served in the army. We had a horrid battalion commander, always tense, annoyed, stern, snapping at everyone, giving unreasonable orders, so to keep it short, he was a huge jackass and everyone hated him of course. We had a great laugh when he was killed by a mosquito. Just as I said, a tiny little mosquito..."

Zaislo had to stop for a laugh but he quickly got himself together and continued.

"It was a humid summer evening. We were hiding in our dugouts for four weeks with the combined army of the Maiir against us in their well-built fortress system outnumbering us two to one. We were hiding behind barricades made of sandbags and overturned carts to prevent anyone from leaving the enemy camp. Neither army dared to attack the other's fortifications, both were waiting for reinforcements. We were living on one forth of a ration, we haven't been paid for months, our only consolation was some diluted wine, it was the only thing that made the endless waiting bearable. The two armies were within shooting distance of each other, there was an ever-present tension as archer-assassins were constantly claiming victims on both sides. I was drinking that sour pig's wash resting my back on the sandbags and thought about what the hell I, an adventuring warrior with superior fighting skills was doing in this rotten army when my deeply hated battalion commander crawled up to me, kicked me on the sides with a kind roar and then asked me to collect stones to strengthen the barricade accompanied by a long string of curses. I jumped up immediately, and after barely half a minute I was on my way back with a freaking huge rock in my hands to bash his bloody head in. No one can kick me around! As I walked up on him I saw that he was furious about something different now, cussing up a storm and flailing around like a madman to boot. That's when I realized that it was a cheeky mosquito that made him lose his temper: it bit his face and left arm, and he cannot catch it no matter how hard he tries. It landed on his nose and he tried to kill it, but he hit himself in the face with a force that made his nose bleed. I was laughing at that point. The mosquito changed its mind and flew up. The battalion commander jumped up, grabbing at it then fell back with an arrow in his head, ceasing his cursing. Gods bless the sharp eyes and sure hands of maiir archers!

This is how a ridiculous little mosquito defeated the battalion commander. I kept laughing through that whole night, indeed my entire battalion had after I told about the death of the commander everyone hated. What's even better, the enemy didn't know what to do with the unusual merriment in our camp and thought that we were getting news about our reinforcements. They tried to break through the next dawn. Needless to say they were all killed. We won the battle."

"This is priceless!" Yabbagabb laughed. The goblin only shook his head. Zaislo was also chuckling as he looked at the far corner of the inn.

"What the bleeding hell is attacking the dwarves now?"

"It's a blanket...or maybe a cloak?" the barbarian was startled as well.

"No, no..." the goblin squinted "it's a black death if I

am not mistaken." A dangerous parasite, which looks like an ordinary cloak while it clings to its victim. It takes control over its wearer, preventing them to make their own decisions, and feeds on them. Their body withers away and dries out, and when it's completely used up the black death leaves it to find a new victim. These creatures reside in hidden far away places like swamps, caves and abandoned ruins and only go to populated areas when they need new victims. This must be the case here. Let me tell you just as we are among us that the dwarves have no chance against the creature!

The black death attacks with an almost untraceable speed, its touch has special properties: it burns and stings at the same time and it also has an advanced defense mechanism, being resistant against spells and only vulnerable against magical weapons.

I sort of pity the dwarves. They will realize how useless their struggle is. That's a horrible thing. When someone realizes their own confines, finds the limits of his own abilities and sees that he hasn't got enough power to fulfill his mission, it's a dreadful encounter with one's own self, with the cruelty of the world and the unfairness of fate…

The dark cloak lunged forward, attacking the dwarf closest to it. The dwarf was sitting on the ground, breathing heavily and haven't even noticed that his life was in danger. He was pondering their victory over the zombie and collecting his strength to face off against the werewolf. He was completely unprepared for the attack. His opponent was so quick that the dwarf didn't even realized what has attacked him and from where. The black death glided across the floor as if it was flying, jumped upon him, and embraced him like a constrictor snake. The spine of the dwarf snapped at once. The monster wasted no time leaving its victim to seek out new prey. The burnt, squished, oozing body of the dwarf fell to the ground behind him with shattered bones.

The dwarves jumped up from the ground. They could not believe their eyes. They lost another one of their brethren.

"By Ballagar, God of Dwarves what the bleeding red battleaxe is that!?" one of them groaned.

Never before have they seen such a thing. Though they were all bleeding from dozens of wounds and could barely stand from fatigue they attacked the dancing black cloak.

They fought it tooth and nail.

The only thing keeping their hopes up was that they outnumbered their enemy four to one. One of them, holding his small battleaxe in both hands lunged and struck the monster. The black death dodged the blow easily, then leapt after the dwarf backing up.

Axe hit the strange silky black skin - without effect. The dwarf looked at his chipped-off weapon, realizing he might as well tried to punch through a castle gate, he actually might had a greater chance succeeding with that. They won't be able to wound their opponent! They cannot hurt it!

The dwarf started shouting and instead of retreating he jumped at the invulnerable monster as a man possessed by madness.

The black death sensed that something got on its back and that something is slowing it down. It had many different ways of executing the dwarf and instinctively choose the easiest one. As if the warrior was a tiny insect landing in the middle of a carnivorous plant, the petals of the black death closed around him.

The cloak only held its victim for a few seconds and the terrible shriek emanating from inside died down in the blink of an eye. The black cloak spread out on the floor again, sweeping the remains of the dwarven warrior off its back - acid-burnt bones, a skull and pieces of stinking flesh.

Then the black death started moving toward the

remaining three dwarves. It seemed it won't stop until there are living people remaining inside the inn. Although it did want to spare one, the man who will be its carrier and living food reserve for the next few months.

Schiza backed away from the slaughter, her body trembling with fear. She could not ask the dwarves for aid for her companions as they were fighting the unknown monster to the death. Actually they were the ones who needed aid the most.

When she regained her ability to speak, she shouted for the innkeeper behind the bar.

Grog and his servants were finished with dressing up. They all wore chest plates, and held shields as well as brutal looking weapons in their hands.

"Innkeeper, sir! Aid my friends!"

Grog marched out from behind the bar flanked by two of his hulking men. He first glanced at the werewolf raging in the far away corner, then at the priestess. He waved to his men to follow him.

To the great shock and even greater anguish of Schiza, the innkeeper did not go to the aid of either Dragwaren or the dwarves but walked toward the stairs to the cellar instead.

Schiza was furious.

"My friends are going to die unless you kill the wolf-face! What are you waiting for?! Where are you going?! Kill it!" She ordered hysterically, while stomping her feet in rage.

Grog didn't even look at her.

"Leetss not geet ahead off oursselvess. The wereewolff and the back clook can weeit." he hissed between his teeth. Avoiding the furious woman he rushed down the stairs with his two bouncers.

"Lowly, Cowardly curs! Go, run away! Hide underground like the worms you are!"

The priestess of life had precious little time to look for

aid. She noticed the men sitting at the table in the corner. She could not believe her eyes. The four guests around the table were speaking calmly, laughing freely. They paid no heed to what was going around them.

Shouting over the noises of the fight, she asked them for help.

They however, were so involved in their conversation that they failed to notice her. Obviously, they had no intentions of getting involved in the events unfolding inside.

Schiza felt an instant hatred for them. She knew not who or what they were, she felt an honest disgust and disdain toward them.

As there was no one left to turn to, she picked up a chair, determined to use it in stopping or at least hindering the beast until her companions get their wits together.

The werewolf opened his enormous jaws. His saliva was dripping down to his chin. He aimed for the head of the elven wizard, and had already lined up the future victims. The young ranger was to be the next after the elf and then the man with the fu-manchu. When he was finished with them, he would target the guests laughing at the corner table.

That's when he noticed Schiza rushing toward him. He raised his gigantic paw. He knew that a single blow, even without his full strength is going to be enough to finish the woman. Then he will have time to deal with the others.

Schiza ran to her death bravely, heroically but at the same time needlessly. After all, she had no ways of harming or stopping the werewolf. All she could hope to achieve was a few seconds of reprieve for her companions.

Others found Schiza a selfish and stubborn woman. Someone only paying attention for her own interests, never caring about the opinions of others, and expecting to always have her way. She was capable of developing a lifelong feud with someone in a second. If Schiza found an inn distasteful then her party could not rest in it either. If Schiza got it in her head to finish a task, the others had to follow her lead and drop what they were doing, no matter how important a mission they were on. If Schiza found someone unsympathetic, she expected her companions not to befriend them. If Schiza liked someone then everybody had to be friendly to them. This is why many - those who didn't know her well - could not stand the priestess of life.

But true character shows itself in grand moments just like this one.

No matter how unpleasant Schiza was to her companions, she loved them enough to sacrifice her life for them. Thinking about her fellow adventurers lying there undefended, and her elven companion slaughtered without mercy she knew her duty. Sacrifice! Revenge!

With a firm, fiery temperament and blazing eyes she ran, she hasn't stopped or faltered not even when she came within an arm's length of the werewolf.

Suddenly the bloodthirsty howl of the werewolf came to a halt and turned into a whine. A terrible pain erupted in his nape. He stopped his attack and clawed at his neck. There was a dagger sticking out his nape. He grabbed the weapon and pulled it out then he threw it away with a roar. The skin on his hand started to blister.

A weapon forged from silver!

The beast backed away with fear then started turning around and around looking for the unknown attacker. Wolf-blood was pouring out of his neck in a thick stream.

The young ranger came to his senses and made a grab for the dropped dagger. The werewolf tried to prevent him from reaching it but another silver dagger shone through the air.

The mysterious killer was aiming for his heart.

The beast stumbled so the attack only hit his left

shoulder. The dagger scraped and burned his skin. He was howling with rage from the unbearable pain. He realized that he forgot something or rather someone.

The unknown attacker throwing daggers at him was none other than the man hiding in the corner of the ceiling.

The ranger stood up. The weak light of the oil lamps glinted off on the precious metal held in his hand.

The werewolf hissed and backed up. Then he decided to make a run for it. He pushed the ranger and the woman brandishing the chair out of his way and ran for the stairs. He left a long blood trail in his wake, rushing up the stairs. He disappeared from the sight of the people below, only his painful roars could be heard for a while.

The strongest and greatest warrior of the dwarven group feel fear for the first time in his life. He was hesitating.

Is it possible that their enemy, this devilishly agile black cloak can not be harmed?

Grunting, he gathered his strength for a single finishing blow. In this final attack he gathered not only his fearsome might but the experience and know-how of a hundred years of fighting. Snarling, he narrowed his eyes and struck as the veins bulged out on his arm.

The black death didn't back off, didn't even dodge just rushed right into the falling axe.

The handle of the weapon almost broke from the dreadful blow. But no matter how precise the strike, how furious the strength, it could not score a single scratch on the creature.

The black death jumped on him.

The dwarf roared. Letting go of his axe, he tried to tear his nightmarish foe off with his bare hands. Screaming, he pulled the cloak from one side to the other with fanatical haste. The black death enveloped him more and more, swallowed him until he was almost invisible. He was pushed down by a tremendous force and only his grim stubbornness prevented him from falling down. His robust barrel of a body held on - for now. His skin was burned and dissolved by the cloak. When his pain reached unbearable proportions he stopped the hysterical struggling, gathered his wits, and took a deep breath.

Shouting the name of the ancient God of Dwarves he asked Ballagar to throw him a glance from his blazing red eyes. Whether the god glanced at him or not, no one knows but the dwarven leader felt that He did, and acted accordingly.

With an enormous effort, he tore the black death off himself, and threw it two tables away.

The black death barely touched the floor, it was already on its way back to the exhausted warrior.

The dwarven leader cussed, and hoped Ballagar won't pay any more attention to him because looking at his own burnt, smoking skin the last embers of battle burned out in his soul. His warriors spirit, his own self-respect and his best men lost in this fight, the dwarf could only think of escape. Uncaring about his fame, losing his pride he did not care where he ran to, only that he got the furthest from here. He left two of his companions behind, but felt no regret. Even if he continued to fight, he would have achieved nothing. He would only die like the rest.

Instead of getting angry at their leader, the two remaining were grateful for his deed.

After all, the murderous creature left them behind and followed their leader.

Looking back, the leader almost died from fright. The cloak was barely three feet away. He had the misfortune of feeling the pain of the creature's touch before and knew that he did not have the strength of escaping the deadly embrace again and hoped feverishly that he did not have to try.

Tossing tables and chairs behind him, he was getting closer to the end of the room. He knew he wasn't strong enough to break through the thick wall of the inn, that he is going to die in a few seconds and even if he survives by some miracle he is going to fear black cloaks, sheets and rugs for the rest of his life.

Three shapes were hiding in the shadows next to the wall.

"Out of my waaay!" he shouted, and they stepped aside.

Although it seemed impossible, he still tried to break through the wall. The fact that outside an army of clerics, soldiers and fire mages were waiting did not bother him the least. It's better he is incinerated by a fireball, struck by lightning or pinned down by a dozen arrows than being digested for seconds in the horrid, disgusting false stomach of the black cloak.

Determined, he ran into the wall…

The inn shook. The wall cracked, but withstood the blow.

With his head swimming, the dwarf fell back onto the floor and lost his consciousness.

The three figures hiding in the shade did not move. They examined the dwarf lying at their feet, then glared at the dark cloak.

The black death loomed over them like a manifestation of doom, malice and devilish strength. It seemed to stretch out and elongate, growing to an enormous size. It looked like it wanted to devour the three guests and the dwarf in one go.

The faces of the figures standing in the dark could not be seen.

One of them was a large, fat albino man who weighing more than three hundred pounds in an ornate silk robe. Next to him, sticking to his side and clutching his arm was an emaciated, half-naked boy. He couldn't be older than twelve. A few feet further away stood a wealthy looking older man with his arms crossed. All his clothes were made from black baize: his tight pants and his form fitting dolman, with the stand-up collar. The dolman had silver buttons and he wore black boots on his feet. A dark sack was lying next to him.

The dwarf awoke with a loud cry, as if he was waking from a nightmare. He rubbed his eyes, trying to get rid of the stingy blood which was dribbling down from the wound on his forehead. Attempting to regain his sight, he could only make out faint, blurry shapes all around. He could not decide if he died, and got to the afterlife or if he was still alive. He hoped to have died, and not having to face his dreadful enemy any more.

Slowly his sight came back. Turning his aching head left and right, he examined the room.

"Where did it go?" he asked.

"Something must have frightened it" answered the black-clad old man looming above him in a calm voice. "It left the inn using the door leading to the inner courtyard."

The dwarf shook his head, unbelieving and uncomprehending. To say that the beast got frightened! What could possibly force a monster like that to retreat? Nonsense! What a load of crap!

Although it is true that he and his companions are alive and the black cloak was nowhere to be seen. The inn seemed surprisingly quiet. Half the clientele being dead had a lot to do with it. The people remaining in the room consisted of Behemor, Weevil, Yabbagabb, Zaislo, the dwarves, the adventurers, the three guests standing silently next to the wall, the mysterious figure hiding in the corner of the ceiling and a dog. The two lowland dwarves, the innkeeper and his bouncers went to the cellar. The other guests escaped upstairs or to the inner courtyard.

Corpses were lying all around the room, under the tables and benches sometimes on top of each other. Some crippled, some torn apart, a few burned by acid. The smell of disemboweled bodies and burnt skin could be felt all over the inn.

Chapter 6
Wolf hunt

"How come werewolves can only be hurt by silver weapons?" asked Yabbagabb from Weevil.

The goblin opened his mouth to answer but he was interrupted by Behemor.

"Not just silver. I tore one apart with my own hands."

"And once when a beast like that attacked me, I raised it above my head and snapped its spine before throwing it into a pit which I filled with soil. It was thrashing wildly, but couldn't move with a broken spine. " Zaislo added "A week later I got curious and checked out what was left of it. I know not whether it suffocated or died of thirst, but the filthy cur was dead indeed."

"Because of the metamorphosis of the compounds in the protoplasm..." Weevil was starting his casework on the resilience of werewolves but could not continue because of an angry, feisty woman stepping up to the table.

"I don't know who you are nor who do you think you are..." Schiza shouted while she flailed her arms wildly in the air "...but your the behavior you displayed is despicable!"

"What did we display?" a chastised Yabbagabb asked.

Schiza stomped. annoyedly

"Don't you dare interrupting me! I am the one talking now! You displayed nothing! You let the humans, the dwarves and everybody else die! You have weapons! You are warriors and you did nothing! Nothing! Nothing when my elven companion was killed. You did nothing as the wolf-face tore him apart. You sat here peacefully, drinking and laughing."

"Right, our booze is gone." Zaislo remarked.

Schiza slammed the table and looked into Zaislo's eyes. Hers were blazing.

"My elven companion died and you have the nerve to talk about booze?"

Zaislo furrowed his brows. It was obvious that he was getting angry. Schiza went on.

"Do you want to know the name of my elven companion?"

Zaislo cleared his throat, then spat on the ground instead of answering.

"He was called Timarkhausozar. A good and wise man. He liked nature and he liked people. He was a hundred and twenty for years old. And now he is dead! A hundred and twenty four years! What are you compared to him? Nothing, that's what!"

"I wouldn't talk like that if I were you milady." Weevil answered with excessive politeness.

Schiza however slammed the table again and continued to shout, beside herself with anger or actually being herself and angry.

"Cowardly worms, who do you think you are? Do you think that you will be left alive if you do nothing?"

"We made a pact." said Yabbagabb simply. "We will not interfere with anything."

"Pathetic curs!" hissed Schiza and tossed one of their cups off the table.

Zaislo made an irate growl…

Schiza did not stop.

"I hope that you will be the next who gets caught by the werewolf or the black-skinned monstrosity! In fact, I will pray to the God of Life for it!"

"But milady! A Priestess of Life doesn't use ugly words like these! Surely you are not speaking seriously" said the goblin cleric kindly.

"...and when the beast tears your limbs off or the black monster burns its mark into your skin then you will realize just how nice some aid would be! A pathetic, lecherous, filthy bunch, that's what you are!"

To his credit, Zaislo endured the abuse for a long time but this is where his patience ran out. Just as he wasn't bothered about his opponent being a mighty archmage, warrior or monster, he also had no reservations about it being a woman. He wasn't a knight or a nobleman after all.

He went and stood up from the bench to give the foul-mouthed lady an educational strangling after a few slaps.

"Enough now, shut your face!" he shouted at her.

If looks could kill, they would be both dead already. Their faces contorted by rage, he raised his fist up to Schiza's face, ready to strike.

But as Zaislo stood up from his place, he had a line of sight to the other side of the inn and noticed something.

"Oh, what a fool I am!" he said clutching his head, and hitting it a few times with his fists. What he noticed was none other but the huge barrel left at the bar, full of the widely renowned, savory tolkenauer red.

"For all the saints, how could I forget the free wine?" he asked shaking his head and no more concerned about the Priestess of Life "Damned innkeeper! Midnight is long gone! He forgot distributing the portions didn't he? But hang it, I forgive him! It was actually a good idea to wait with the portions. By now - gods rest the souls of my fellow guests - we need to distribute it among fewer people. In fact, what do you say about drinking it, just the four of us?"

He left the others without waiting for an answer.

"I was not finished! Don't you dare turn your back on me! Stop at once!" Schiza was stomping her feet.

Zaislo however did not care about her, he rushed to the bar with an excessive glee, half dancing and humming a buoyant battle tune. Behind the bar he noticed his bloody broadsword, which someone recently used to kill the bouncer called Talak. He bent down, and slipped it back into his scabbard, careful not to be seen, then covered the upper part of the scabbard with his cloak. Then he emerged from behind the bar and as the innkeeper was nowhere to be seen decided to serve himself. He pushed the huge barrel over and rolled it to their table.

Schiza had to jump out of the way to avoid being trampled by the man rolling the barrel.

Zaislo readily filled everyone's mugs while he himself lied under the barrel and drank from there. The Priestess of Life continued her angry tirades, but her words blurred together and seemed to come further and further away for the tavern brawler.

One of the dwarves was hissing in pain as he tried to get to the table. With his broken shin, every step was a challenge.

Schiza gave up the fruitless invectives and wasted no more time on the drunks. She rushed to the aid of the wounded. First she stepped up to her companions and examined their wounds. Relieved, she noticed that they are fine, apart from a few scratches. Then she ran to the dwarves and told them that she will heal them as well as she could with her magic.

The dwarven leader refused her help at first - for both his men and himself - but Schiza was adamant. She was as stubborn as any dwarf.

Finally the leader consented grumbling and mumbling through his teeth, even though he was wary of any manifestations of magic.

The Priestess of Life touched the warriors forehead with her soft, delicate hands and started chanting magical words. Her concentration was intense, she used all her priestly might. The wounds closed within seconds, bones mended and the acid-burnt skin started to heal.

The dwarf could not believe his eyes at first. Not only did his pain vanish but almost all the wounds he got in the fight were healed.

He stared at the priestess with narrowed eyes, full of suspicion and disbelief. He granted a curt 'Thanks'. Then he did something he has never done before. He offered his hand to a female human and introduced himself. He was called Dragar, Dragar the Trollslayer.

Schiza went on and healed the second dwarf. She got dizzy for a moment. Using concentrated magic was exhausting her. She wiped the beads of sweat off her forehead and. She could barely stand but she got herself together and treated the wounds of the last dwarf as well.

The stout dwarf with a child-like face was exceedingly grateful for the priestesses healing. His face displayed an enormous respect. He looked as Schiza as if she was the Goddess of Providence herself. She wanted to hug the long, muscular legs of the priestess but thought better of it in the last second. He did not want Dragar to think less of him. He felt he had to say some words of gratitude though so he made a remark in his deep voice:

"If you weren't so freakin' big, I would love to marry you!"

For a moment Schiza was shocked and outraged by the words but then she smiled a kind smile. She knew that she could not have received a bigger compliment from a dwarf.

Now that the dwarves strength has returned and they were ready for another battle again they wanted to act immediately. They got into a heated argument with Dragwaren's team regarding their next move. Schiza wanted to move the dead somewhere proper until they can be buried. But no matter how strongly she argued or reasoned this once she got overruled by the majority. They all voted against her, only the ranger abstained.

"The dead can wait." Dragwaren said. "Moving them can wait. Now we have a more important task." He drew a deep breath before continuing.

"We need to find that summoner and take back the heart of the dwarven warrior. That's the only thing we can dismiss the arriving demon with."

"Maybe we ought to destroy that black cloak first" Dragar the Trollslayer rumbled "as long as that abomination is inside the inn, we cannot have a moment's rest."

Swinging their weapons about, the two other dwarves agreed. They all wanted to avenge their fallen companions.

The shadow at the corner of the ceiling started to move, and a young man jumped down to the broken furniture, bottles and bodies torn apart. He arrived crouching and made no noise. Standing up slowly he made his way towards the people arguing. Both Dragwarens team and the dwarves failed to notice the man with the trousers of black velvet, fashionable dark shirt and black vest until he reached and addressed them.

"My lords and ladies, we should not forget about the werewolf, he is not a trivial opponent either."

"Who are you? How did you get here?" barked Kavak, the warrior with the fu-manchu.

The young man stood up straight.

"My name is Tifur! Settle for the fact that I am the one you could thank for being still alive."

As they stared at him with uncomprehending faces, Tifur continued.

"You can keep the silver dagger, no problem. At least until you kill the werewolf."

The mistrustful eyes of the ranger changed immediately, he looked at the stranger with an honest avowal now.

"You were the one throwing the silver daggers? Then we do indeed need to be grateful to you! You saved the lives of our entire group. What can we do to repay you?"

"Kill the werewolf. It's as simple as that. His presence disturbs me. To make things easier for you, I can provide you with two more silver daggers."

He was putting the weapons on the table as he said it.

Again, the party started arguing about who should do what and how until Dragwaren silenced them with his magically enhanced voice.

Then he summarized the tasks awaiting them.

"One team goes upstairs and kills the werewolf. Meanwhile Schiza will pray to her God for spells, creating magical hammers and I will ready myself for a spell to make an ordinary weapon magical. By the time you return from the upper floor the weapons to destroy the black mantle will be ready…

Let's not waste any more time! Everyone, do your jobs!"

Soon a small team has gathered at the bottom of the stairs: Tifur, Dragar, Kavak and Dagar's two dwarves. They were all holding silver daggers apart from Tifur. The young man had no weapons in his hands. He was the eyes and ears of the group. He proclaimed to be able to smell the werewolf's scent and to hear it's breathing from thirty feet.

At the moment however, the blood the beast left behind was proved enough to track it.

With slow, controlled movements and no breathing Tifur started ascending the stairs followed by the four warriors.

Dragwaren and Schiza sat down at a table and entered a trance. While they were meditating the young ranger stood guard. He looked eagerly at the people leaving, he would have liked to be there when they defeat the werewolf but he didn't want to leave Dragwaren or Schiza alone. The priestess prayed with closed eyes and an otherworldly look on her face. The ranger took pleasure in her angelic beauty. Only occasionally did he took his eyes of her, turning sometimes toward the stairs and sometimes toward the courtyard door.

Three guests were loitering not far away. The older man in black baize and the child was standing there silently. The silk clad guy with the pale skin was pacing nervously but he never got far from the kid.

The company of four at the corner table was drinking peacefully.

"I think I have begun to rot" Yabbagabb remarked absent-minded, turning his hand around. Dark, amoeba-like spots were growing on his palm and on the back of his hand.

Behemor also examined his arm and similar spots could be seen on his skin as well. Like a horse, he snorted angrily.

Zaislo climbed up from below the barrel and scampered back onto the bench. He laughed into the faces of his companions then - after noticing the signs of rot on himself - the smile froze on his face.

Weevil took a big gulp from his drink.

"Just stay calm, friends! Easy does it. The patriarch will arrive at midnight at the latest...and if he doesn't then I will get rid of this damnable rot. But now it would be too early. We can..not know...What is it we cannot know?"

He took another sip.

"Oh, right! We cannot know what else is going to happen today. I don't want to waste my magic on healing spells. When we can be sure that there is no more danger approaching and if the patriarch doesn't save us, then I will occlude your illness. It cannot be any trouble for me!"

"Another cup of wine?" Yabbagabb asked.

"Yes please!" the goblin mumbled, and held his cup out.

They were crouching there in the dim corridor stony

and unmoving as if they were figures on a painting. Tifur was about thirty feet ahead of the others, studying the junction and the open rooms, raising his head from time to time and taking long whiffs of the air. After a while he signed the warriors that they can approach. Although Kavak and the three dwarves tried to sneak as well as they could, they always made some noise. The old strip floor creaked under one or the others. Sometimes it was a weapon that clinked or a breath that came out too loud.

Tifur made them stop again and advanced on his own. He made no noise. The blood trail has disappeared, so he was moving at random Suddenly some small susurrus made him stop. The average man would have doubted if he actually heard something or if it was his imagination. Tifur was no ordinary man however. He was still very young, but his abilities were well known in his trade and that if he manages to reach the proper age, he is going to be the grandmaster of the Karavan Assassin's Guild.

Tifur carefully stepped through the half-open door and started to move into the dark room using his eyes and ears. He smelled the werewolf's scent but could not determine if the monster was in the room or has left it. He heard the faint noises again. They were closer this time. Whether they were made by the werewolf or something else, he did not know. He was not the type to get scared easily or to run away from his own shadow. Slowly, he creeped forward, ready for a lightning quick escape should it be needed.

There was a dresser standing in the corner and the noises were coming from under it.

Tifur listened and realized that under the dresser there is a man hiding, nervous and breathing heavily.

The warriors were approaching the room. One was holding a lantern. The light from the dancing flame infiltrated the room through the open door. Darkness gave way to a dim light inside.

"Come out, I won't hurt you!" the assassin said in a low

voice.

However, the man lying and trembling under the dresser did not move. His face was contorted by dread, his mouth opened to scream but only a gurgling whimper emerged due to the terror holding him by the throat. The assassin tried again:

"Calm down! No need to fear! There is nothing here to be scared of!"

If possible, the man squeezed himself even further under the furniture.

"You have nothing to fear, you are not in danger!"

As soon as he said the words, he started to hesitate. 'Is he actually in danger?' he asked himself, and then his body trembled.

He realized that the guest hiding there is not afraid of him but of somebody else. The assassin sensed this somebody standing right behind him.

Many would have panicked after this realization, many would have turned around to make sure of their misgivings, losing precious seconds, many wouldn't have been able to move at all.

Tifur was sure that it's the werewolf silently towering above him. He did not hesitate but trusted his instincts. As he started to move, his muscles tensing the beast gave a large growl behind him and snapped his jaws.

Tifur jumped on top of the dresser. The robust werewolf moved too slowly to get him with his attack. Still, the assassin could not celebrate yet.

The beast grabbed the dresser with both hands with the intentions of smashing it against the opposite wall.

That's when the dwarves rushed in followed by Kavak. They were third the size of the werewolf, but attacked him with the ferocity of a lion. Even though they could not wield their favorite weapons - axes, hammers or maces - they were able to make good use of the silver daggers. The black death defeated them shamefully in the last battle. The thirsted success. Now they had the opportunity to repair their damaged pride. They saw the werewolf as a warm-up exercise before the main battle. In spirit, they were already fighting the black cloak.

The werewolf tore out a piece of meat from the shoulder of one and clawed deep gashes into the face of another but did not manage to tear his head off. He also missed with his bite, Kavak jumped back from the sharp teeth.

The dwarves were running, swirling, turning, fell down and got up, tumbled and never missed an opportunity when they had the chance to wound the beast. Silver daggers pierced the legs, knees, groin, kidneys and stomach of the beast - the dwarves could not reach higher up. Although once, when he was trying to snap at them with his jaws, Dragar Trollslayer managed to wound his chest as well.

The werewolf was howling like a real wolf and the dwarves were yowling around him like a pack of hyenas tearing apart a defenseless, dying animal. So occupied was the werewolf with the dwarves that he was too late to notice Kavak's masterful attack.

The silver dagger pierced his heart!

He gave an earth-shattering roar. His vision blurred, the images of the room fading. He made two more useless attacks toward Kavak with his paws and then fell to his knees. With the last of his strength he tore the murder weapon out of his chest, then started to tremble and fell back. By the time he hit the ground he wasn't alive anymore. He wasn't alive for a while actually. Slowly, he began to change back. He took up human form again.

Kavak was twirling his fu-manchu, satisfied. This was something he did when he was especially proud of himself. He was glad that he managed to avenge the death of Timarkhausozar. His happiness only faltered once he looked at the corpse.

The face of the late werewolf showed endless relief and gratitude.

Chapter 7
The secret of the Yellow Serpent

The dog lying by the wall of the hearth in the corner of the inn stood up on four legs. He passed by the drunken figures.

"Hey, isn't that the werewolf?" Weevil chuckled.

"No, that's a dog."

"Teeny-tiny doggie-woggie! Is doggie-woggie hungry? Uncle Weevil will give you yum-yum, doggie" Weevil cooed and started sifting through his belongings.

"Love at first sight!" Zaislo quaffed "The dog and the dog-faced goblin. How touching! I'm going to puke."

Yabbagabb saw that he has fallen behind in drinking compared to his table companions. He started gulping down the tolkenauer red at a faster pace.

The goblin unearthed one of the magical druidic berries he was served as dinner from his backpack. He threw it in front of the dog.

The animal was obviously intent on ignoring the party but when it saw what they were trying to feed it its eyes widened. It leaned closer to the berry and sniffed it. 'I am on track' it thought. It looked up at the four figures at the table.

Yabbagabb leaned down and snatched up the magical berry lying in front of it.

"Don't eat it it would be too expensive for dog food! And after all, who ever heard of a vegetarian dog?" he said as he put the berry away.

The dog was looking at him with a grim face.

"Don't be mad!" Yabbagabb consoled him "If you truly want a wondrous berry, you should talk to the innkeeper. He was the one who got Weevil his."

'So the berry is from the innkeeper! Then he is the one I want' the dog thought, and started walking down the stairs to the cellar after the owner of the Yellow Serpent.

"That's one clever dog." Behemor remarked, and he was partially right. It was clever, but it wasn't a dog…

The two lowland dwarves were working busily. Thanks to their racial abilities, they could determine how deep they were underground, how likely tunnels were to collapse and last but not the least where it would be worth starting their attempts to escape. They felt along the freestone wall, paying individual attention to each crack.

At one point, they stopped. They both had the same impression: about a feet beyond the wall there was an empty space which could be a natural cave, a hall, or even another corridor.

The two dwarves looked at each other. They exchanged no words. One bobbed his head, the other nodded back and then - grabbing their pickaxes with both hands - they attacked the wall. The noises of their hammering were echoing along the corridor. They worked without a word. Recently every single one of their conversations ended with arguing, quarreling, cursing and almost fighting. They were angry for they should have already left Karavan behind. If they went according to plan and hadn't got stuck in the Yellow Seerpent then they would arrive at Piare from the Southern Connecting Grain Route about now. It would have only taken half a day's walk from there to reach the token of their enrichment, the treasure mine of their dreams.

They could not get it out of their head that while they are here breaking stones and all kinds of mad people were killing each other above their heads, lowland dwarves like them were hammering away at the walls of their gold mine. The worrying thoughts sent them to work even faster and even more determined. Fat drops of sweat were rolling down on their dusty faces. They did not rest. Their work soon bore fruit. They made a crack on the wall which they quickly enlarged. Soon it was large enough for them to squeeze through.

Thanks to their infravision the lowland dwarves easily navigated through the dark and needed no torch to see what they found.

Their eyes grew wide.

In the room they reached three feet poles were rising from the ground, half a feet from each other. They filled the room wall to wall.

The dwarves shivered. Not all the poles were vacant. Impaled humans, elves and dwarves were hanging from them. They must have been dead for a long time. Most of them were skeletons covered by scraps of clothing. Others just started to rot away. And there was one which - despite the four javelins sticking out of his back and the one from his head - seemed completely whole. He must have been the latest victim. A middle-aged man, wearing the white robes and green cloak of the Druids of Mongor.

The dwarves looked up. The ceiling was thirty feet above their heads. They saw four trap doors on it. Thats where the guests have fallen through, onto the poles.

Possessing an excellent sense of direction underground, both dwarves were dead sure that the guest rooms of the Yellow Serpent were above them.

The two miners looked at each other, shocked. They stood there at their wits end.

"Spike traps in the inn." one of them said.

"I would like a few words with the innkeeper" said the other.

"Sso be eet!" someone behind them said.

Horrified, the dwarves turned around, and they were not at all happy with what they saw.

In front of them stood the innkeeper and two of his bouncers. All three wearing chest plates and wielding weapons.

"Deedn't I warn you not to come down heer? Grog shouted at them pointing his crossbow at the first one second and at the other the next."

"What does this mean, innkeeper?"

"Are you bleend, dwarf? Or jusst thiss sstupeed?"

The dwarves raised their pickaxes. Then one of them said:

"If you let us leave in peace, allowing us to dig ourselves out and reach our new gold mine in time we could gain a great amount of wealth. In turn, I promise in the name of my companion and I that we will not report what we saw to the captain of the guard. The secret of the Yellow Serpent stays between us!" the dwarf offered.

A shifty smile spread across Grog's face.

"Thiss is a trulee generouss offeer on your part! But the captaan of the guard would keell you himsself if you told heem what you ssaw. He iss in eet ass much ass me afteer all! I pay heem a honesst royaltee. And the fact that I keel a strageer or two ssometimess with the trap-doored beds weell indeed sstay between uss. I mysself know the perfect ssolution for eet!" he said snarling and pulled the trigger on his crossbow.

The bolt embedded itself into the throat of the dwarf. The lowlander mumbled something about his gold mine and what would happen to it without him while coughing up bloody spittle then he collapsed. He was dead by the time he hit the ground.

His companion didn't need any more prompts. He stared grimly at the armed figures for a while, then he charged forward swinging his pickaxe. The sprang away in all directions to avoid the dangerous instrument.

The lowlander did not bother to pull the pickaxe back, he let it smash into one of the bouncers. Then he threw himself through the opening and ran.

"Get heem!" Grog shouted to his lackey, and threw himself after the lowlander as well, but not before instructing the wounded bouncer to cover the hole with something.

The lowland dwarf ran through corridors and wine cellars. His small stature made him run half as fast as a human. If he had just a bit longer to go he would have been caught. Suddenly a dog jumped in front of him, he could barely avoid it. He ran up the stairs leading to the inn. Behind him, Grog and his lackey followed, brandishing their weapons.

There weren't many in the room, but the presence of the guests calmed the dwarf down: the group drinking peacefully at their table, the meditating adventurers and the guests standing around silently. He stopped.

"Murderous innkeeper!" he wheezed, trying to catch his breath and then repeated himself at least seven times.

Grog appeared in the cellar door. It looked like he had no intentions of slowing down. Swirling his morningstar, he stomped toward the dwarf. He wasted no time and struck at him full swing.

The lowlander raised his hands in front of him in defense and shouted "bandit" then the metal ball smashed his skull in.

Grog sighed in relief, looking satisfied with his actions.

The drunk guests roistering in the corner were so occupied with their feast, they didn't even notice what happened.

The three figures standing there wordlessly showed no reactions either. No shock, no surprise. The continued to follow the events silently.

Dragwaren was concentrating deeply, he did not come to his senses from meditation.

Schiza was praying, her soul was occupied somewhere else.

The ranger was the only oan shocked by the unfolding events. He stepped up to the innkeeper with his hand on his weapon.

Grog put his morningstar away.

"Calm down rangeer! Don't be hassty in draweeng conclusionss. I weell tell you what happeneed…"

"Speak!"

"…The..the lowlanderss trieed to deeg themsselvess out of the eenn to reach theer gold mine beefore ssomeone elsse could reech eet. Me and my peeple preeventeed thiss and then they losst their mindss compleetlee and attackeed uss with their pickakssess. We had no choisse but to deefend oursselvess. What we deed wass sself defenss!"

"But he was running away from you!" the man pointed at the dwarf lying on the ground with his head bashed in.

The innkeeper rubbed his temples. He started to heavily dislike the fuss the man was making.

"Eet wass too big of a reessk. The two dwarvess were obsesseed, they wanteed to leeve the Yellow Sserpent at anee cosst. I ussed the onlee sure method to preevent eet from happeneeng. If theese monee-grubbing veermen managed to geet out, they would have reeleessd the plague upon my beloveed home town. What kind of lowlife sscum could do that? They could have caussed the deathss of their fellow men jusst for monetaree gain! How could someone bee sso ssoulless? I could never undeersstand and I never weell. What makess a man ssink sso low?"

He stood there and shook his head with regret.

"I deed what I deed. I couldn't have done aneething elss. I accept the ressponssibilitee in front of the God of Thruth and the capteen of the guard" he added and tried to remain serious but the edge of his mouth was turning up in a smile.

He hasn't managed to convince the ranger of his innocence or the rightfulness of his actions.

"With his last word the dwarf called you a bandit. Correct me if I am wrong."

Grog pondered this while rubbing his chin with his thumb.

"No you are not misstaken, honored rangeer. He musst have ssaid so. Thiss only confirmss that theess possessed peeple were completelee inssane. He musst have had a delussion about mee wanting hees gol mine and wanteeng to keel heem for it. But thiss iss ssomething we weell never know."

"It would have been enough to tie him up" the ranger sighed but then he waved in dismissal, signaling he was no longer interested. He had much more important things to consider.

Kavak and the dwarves had not returned yet. Maybe they aren't alive anymore. Maybe he is going to die soon and Dragwaren and Schiza with him. It was a depressing thought and it filled his heart with sadness. Rotting away alive, a bloodthirsty werewolf, a deadly cloak, a murderous innkeeper and an unkillable demon...good heavens! What kind of a place did he get stuck in?

The bouncer was picking at his wound. He hissed in pain. The skin was discoloured and ugly where the dwarf's pickaxe hit him. He was bleeding internally and at least two of his ribs were broken.

He got his act together and limped to the barrels. Grabbing an empty one, he pushed it away from the scaffolding and rolled it in front of the hole on the wall.

"What are you looking at, sickly mutt?!" he growled at the dog staring into the hole. "Your ribs will be broken soon too, unless you move the hell away!"

The dog shifted its gaze from the druid impaled on the pole and looked the bouncer in the eye with a sinister growl.

"Get out you ugly mutt!" he snapped at it again and raised his boot to kick it.

The dog quickly jumped away from his foot. The he changed shape!

The bouncer could not believe his eyes. Within ten seconds a druid wearing a green robe and a white mantle stood in the place of the dog. He looked almost exactly the same as his friend on the pole.

"I am called brother Floraus, a member of the druidic order Starry Night. You could have at least make the effort of burying poor brother Benetius" he chided the bouncer with an emotionless voice then he rushed him swift as the wind.

Huge, dreadful tiger-claws grew in place of his hands and his skin thickened into bark. He would not have needed this protective spell. He struck his victim with such speed that he didn't even have time to grab his weapon or to cry out in fear or pain. Brother Floraus tore his head off with a single, determined swipe of his tiger arm.

Chapter 8
The black death

Slowly, the survivors gathered back at the inn.

The victorious wolf hunters returned in the company of eight guests. They have been hiding upstairs until now. The dwarves boasted about their heroic battle against the werewolf. They could hardly wait to get their magical weapons and move against the black cloak.

Meanwhile the dog appeared on top of the stairs leading to the cellar. It stalked up to a table in an unhurried manner and laid down. No one cared about it's reappearance.

Schiza and Dragwaren finished their meditations almost at the same time.

"We killed the werewolf!" said one dwarf thumping his chest.

"Did he suffer a lot before his death?" Schiza asked hoping for a positive answer. The murderer of Timarkhausozar had to suffer a lot.

"He whined pathetically once he realized his end has come. He suffered a long, agonizing death." Kavak lied, for he knew what it could be like when his Priestess of Life is dissatisfied with something. "The dwarves fought like madmen. I would not have been in the place of the werewolf."

The dwarven warriors stood straight and proud nodding in agreement.

"But now we would go and tear up the killer of our comrades" Dragar Trollslayer brayed "Are the magic weapons ready?"

Schiza chanted arcane phrases instead of answering.

Her spell resulted in three see-through warhammers appearing, all glowing with a faint glimmer. They floated motionlessly above ground.

"Go on, grab it!" the priestess beckoned them.

The dwarves displayed little enthusiasm. They only obeyed reluctantly. Dragar was the first to touch the ghostly weapon with his thick, hairy index finger, then he quickly pulled his hand back.

Schiza smiled.

"Be courageous, great warrior!"

"I am not afraid!" the dwarven leader grumbled angrily, and to prove his words true, he grabbed the weapon determinedly.

He felt nothing unusual. It was like holding a regular warhammer.

"Try it!" he ordered one of his fellow warriors, giving it to him. The dwarf turned it around in his hands, satisfied.

Seeing the confidence of his companions, the third dwarf also took a warhammer.

"Whose weapon should I turn magical for a short while?" Dragwaren asked.

The dwarven leader instantly offered his battle axe. There were no objections so the elven wizard performed the incantation with strange hand gestures and a few mumbled arcane words.

Dragar almost dropped the axe when it was suddenly enveloped in a pale green aura of light.

"Are you certain it is useful against the black filth?" he asked, unsure.

The only certainty is death or maybe not even that. Take the weapon and try it yourself!

Dragwaren's answer did little to calm the dwarven leader down.

"One warhammer left. Who goes with the dwarves?" the wizard asked.

"I will!" Schiza replied.

The ranger started protesting immediately.

"Schiza, it's too dangerous! Please think this over! Kavak should go instead! Let's leave this to the warriors!"

"I conjured the warhammer. I am as proficient in using it as any fighter. I will go for sure! And anyway, don't tell me what to do! Who do you think you are? You are not my father. I have had it with you breathing down my neck all the time!"

The ranger sighed and replied with:

"I care not. I will go if you will."

"You have no enchanted weapons!" Schiza laughed scornfully into his face.

"I will take yours after you have died." came the grim answer from the ranger.

"We should not waste any time while our companion march on the black cloak." Dragwaren began "We need to continue looking for the dwarven heart. Can we go on with the search, innkeeper?"

"Or do you want to kill someone first, innkeeper?" the ranger asked. He pointed out the dead lowland dwarf on the floor to his companions and in a few words told them about the events that unfolded in the inn.

Grog shot him a murderous look, and answered with a simple:

"I deed eet for the good of the ssitee."

Dragwaren quickly took up the initiative again.

"Let's not concern ourselves with that now! We have a more important task. Let's search the belongings of the dead first. Perhaps our summoner is among the victims of the werewolf. If we don't find him there, there is but a dozen of us left. We will be done with the search in no time."

The two teams said their goodbyes. Schiza, the ranger and the dwarves went to take on the black death. Dragwaren's team wished them good luck and made them promise to be careful and return safely.

"Have a good rampage!" Kavak with the fu-manchu shouted after the dwarves as they left the room through the door to the inner courtyard. "And have a good time arguing and driving each other crazy!" he added to Schiza and the ranger.

Then, together with Dragwaren, Grog and the bouncer he began sorting through the torn apart, mangled, crippled, disemboweled corpses which were producing a stomach-turning smell. Only the innkeeper was more distraught than him and the elven wizard who was worrying about his companions.

He had a good reason.

He was only a little worried about the servant he left in the cellar who failed to return - he was always a slow worker. He will still woe the day he was born after he had the opportunity to talk to him. But he was more worried about what happened to Talak. The bouncer was stabbed in the back by someone in the outhouse. It surely couldn't have been the werewolf or the black cloak, they wouldn't have used weapon. But then who? And why did they kill him?

With a sudden idea, he ran to the bar to see if the murder weapon was still there.

The broadsword was nowhere to be seen.

He did not show his surprise but concealed it cunningly. Someone took the weapon. If the owner was foolish enough to reclaim it then they will find it during the search and he will be unmasked. If only everything was this simple! But not everything is so simple in life. It was a shame he had to kill that lowlander in front of the guests. He had no choice of course. He would have been in bigger trouble would the lowlander had the opportunity to gossip about the secret of the Yellow Serpent. Actually, he would only feel truly secure if no one was alive by the end of the quarantine apart from him and his men. He should kill all guests and then blame it on the werewolf or the black cloak. Yes, this is what he has to do! He will get rid of all guests at the right moment. Although there are some quite experienced adventurers among them, killing them shouldn't prove too difficult. He has the proper "tool" for it. The commander of the city watch will receive a small fortune again for his silence and cooperation.

After he managed to put his plans in order and come to a definitive decision he continued to sort through the bloody intestines, clothes and equipment happily.

"Don't be so hasty Schiza! Let the dwarves take the lead!" the ranger whispered while scanning the looming shadows of the bushes and shrubs.

The Priestess of Life payed him no heed, she led the group. The ranger would have liked to drag her back next to him by force but he quickly abandoned the idea - it would have done no good. Inside he was steaming, cursing Schiza's governor priests and teachers for being unable to break the spirits of the wild woman. Were he in their place, Schiza would have become a polite and obedient female for sure.

He had a hard time accepting that he cannot keep up with the girl. Him, who became famous by taming a werebear. It took him three years of course.

He was the patient sort.

While he gave three years to the werebear, he allocated five to Schiza and only one of them has been gone yet.

The ranger did not know that Schiza couldn't really be impressed by any sort of discipline.

While spending her time at the monastery, the priestess slept on a stone slab and whipped herself whenever she had the time, to keep the malicious spirits and evil demons away from her soul.

They were being as stealthy as they could. They had a feeling that no matter how silent they moved, the black cloak cannot be surprised. The monster will be able to detect them from afar with its special senses. Their stealthiness was simply a way to detect the small, telltale noises in time and so to prepare for the attack of the monster.

"Where could it be?" one of the dwarves asked nervously. He did not care for this game of cat and mouse. Although if asked, he could not have decided if he thinks himself the cat or the mouse.

"Anywhere" the ranger answered grimly. "It could be that black stone-thing next to the bush there. It is possible that it folded itself and hid in a hollow tree. It could be under our feet or maybe the black sky above our heads is not what it seems."

After this revelation, Schiza suddenly looked up to the sky, the dwarven leader intently knocked on the ground with his weapon and another dwarf was examining the large black rock.

The black cloak however did not reveal itself.

The went on excitedly, circling around the outhouses. Then they decided to turn back and go toward the left corner of the inner courtyard. From there they planned to go right first then left from there to continue their careful examination.

As they left the path and stumbled toward the side of the courtyard among the thick shrubbery in the dark of the night, suddenly the Priestess of Life gave a panicked shriek. Something touched her shoulder! At the same time she jerked forward and turned her head back. That's when she realized it was the ranger who touched her with his hand.

"You must have gone mad!" she cursed him. "Do you have any idea how much you scared me?"

"I am sorry Schiza, it was not intentional. I saw that

you were looking everywhere, but you did not notice that...thing in front of you."

What the ranger called a "thing" was a two feet high pile of garbage composed of human remains. Shriveled, shrunken, acid-burnt limbs, smashed up skulls, flesh-connected intestines were waiting to become the home for maggots and the feeding ground of worms in a bloody horror show.

"I thought I would notify you, so you would not mess up your shiny new boots." the ranger made his sarcastic remark with a grim face.

Schiza only spared a single glance for the disgusting, stomach-turning pile of human flesh. She almost threw up.

"By the flaming axe of Ballagar! What horrors?! It's a terrible sight! They had been had, badly..." one of the dwarves stuttered.

"We are on the right track" Dragar Trollslayer was elated seeing the bloody pile, and grabbed his weapon more firmly.

"These are the remains of the guests who ran to the garden from the werewolf. Let's avoid it, and continue. The smell they emit is horrible."

They reached the tall freestone wall of the Yellow serpent. They took up a formation side by side and then started to move next to the wall, slowly and observantly.

No matter their concentration, their silence and their expectations for being ambushed from any direction, even above they still could not do anything when the attack came. They were surprised by the monster.

The dwarf with the childish face felt as if the sky itself had fallen. In a second the already dark night got even darker for him.

The black cloak fell down from the branches of the tree above them, like an autumn leaf. It clung to the dwarf, coiled itself around him squashing him and preventing him from breathing. It left no time for the others to save him, devouring him in a second and digesting him instantly.

Dragar Trollslayer roared; his shout echoing through the entire city quarter. He rushed forward flanked by his last remaining warrior and the Priestess of Life.

The monster rose and stretched out. It was black as the night or perhaps even darker. Eerie and mysterious. And this frightening thing was trying to devour Schiza.

The ranger was hesitating at the back, not knowing what to do. Without an enchanted weapon he had precious few opportunities. He thought about searching for the hammer of the dead dwarf, that's when he noticed the hellspawn picking Schiza as its next victim and in fact already looming above her. His heart started to beat faster. He had no time for deliberation.

He had no intentions to either. He was strangely satisfied with his fate.

He jumped from the ground. Soaring above the head of the priestess he flew toward the dark mass with an enormous leap.

He felt lucky. Only a select few are given the opportunity to die for the woman they love. His unexpected move will distract the monster. He dies, Schiza lives. He was filled with endless joy - he could not have given a greater gift to his priestess. And on top of it he will have the last word, Schiza won't be able to scold him for his deed. He only hoped that his sacrifice won't be in vain. That his beloved will escape and think about what happened; about a man sacrificing himself for her, about how she will become more because of it, about how she now has a duty to him and to the world to continue doing things he considered important and that the one who dies now has to live through her from now on.

With these lofty thoughts, the ranger smashed into the hellspawn. As his legs touched the soft and extremely tough hide of the monster however, he was already leaping again.

The black death turned away from the woman, lunging after the ranger by twisting its entire body inside out. As its dark sheet of a body twisted around it seemed to be a huge constrictor snake in the middle of molting.

The exceptional reflexes of the ranger were on par with the speed of the monster. He managed to reach the tree he wanted before the monster reached him. He only grabbed one of the branches for a second before his momentum took him on. His sandals were trailing smoke as he flew on toward the next branch. The soles of his footwear were completely destroyed by the acid even though it was a second at most while he was stepping onto the dangerous hide of the monster with his sandals.

He pulled himself up with acrobatic movements as high as his body could be supported by the thin branches. When he could not climb any further, he looked down. The monster was almost flying toward him. Through the whistling of the wind and the rustling of leaves he heard the angry shouting of Dragar Trollslayer from below. The dwarven leader was roaring at him to lure the monster down, to bring it to him and how he will tear it apart and make it into a large dossal if there is anything left.

He also heard the sharp, excited voice of Schiza - urging him to flee. The voice, so wonderous to his ears calmed him down. The monster creeping up on the trunk of the tree was almost there. They were half a feet apart. For a second he pondered, marveling at being still alive. Then he smiled and let go.

He threw himself to the ground...

"Hyhari-hyari-hyari yay! Hoi-hoi-ho-hoi-hoi!" Yabbagabb sang after becoming so drank that he no longer knew where he was. He was glad to see the other three figures next to him shouting as well.

"Hyhari-hyari-hyari yay! Yay! Hoi-hoi-ho-hoi-hoi! Hoi! Hoi!"

Yabbagabb laughed in Weevil's face for the goblin appeared to him as a caroling dog. He continued to sing.

Their bursts of song echoed through the inn. It

suppressed the sounds of battle from the courtyard.

The innkeeper and Dragwaren's crew shot them hostile glances, but said nothing. As they did not find what they were looking for at the corpses, they continued by searching the guests and going through their belongings.

The goblin suddenly stopped singing and looked into Zaislo's eyes with a serious, drunken-stiff face.

"You really slayed twelve dragons once?"

"...hoi-hoi-hoi...of course! Not even once! Three or four times!" Zaislo laughed. "Let's see how many dragons that is. Twelve and twelve and twelve and twelve. You must be some kind of genius to add all that. Must have at least a merchant to do it. Hey, city scum! Is there merchant-breed among you? One who also mastered the big numbers. You are silent? Whatever! I killed many dragons."

"Even twelve seasoned warriors would have a hard time against a fledgling dragon. I find a single warrior slaying twelve completely impossible." said the goblin unbelieving.

"Are you saying, I'm lying?" the alcoholic tavern brawler saw red. He would have punched the goblin already, if only he could have decided which one to attack.

He saw two of him thanks to the excessive amount of alcohol.

"No matter how much you try with your mirror-image spell" he scowled threateningly "if I want to beat you up, I will find which one of the two is real.

Weevil gave a happy laugh for he was seeing more of Zaislo as well.

"My god...Zaislo! One is already too much of you. Stop multiplying! I would rather believe you slaughter dragons by the dozen."

"Well...you better!"

Yabbagabb did not like the goblin retreating. Wine made him pugnacious.

"How many fingers does a dragon have?" he asked,

turning to Zaislio.

The tavern brawler looked back uncomprehending.

"You are asking me?"

"Yes."

"I don't get it. What do you want?"

"I wanted to ask how many fingers a dragon has. Obviously you, who slaughters them by the dozen can answer this simple question."

Zaislo seemed to be hesitating for a second. He croaked, and then nodded self-assuredly.

"Sure. Of course I know...how the hell wouldn't I know how many fingers a bloody dragon has. Sod off with your stupid questions!" he grumbled annoyedly before falling silent.

Then they just stared ahead of themselves without a word for a minute.

"How many fingers?" Yabbagabb asked again, breaking the silence.

"Who?" Zaislo grunted.

"Dragons of course" the fighter mage replied readily.

"Dragons?" Zaislo wondered, as if he didn't know what to do with the question "Do you want to know about their hands or the ones on their feet?"

"Dunno...tell me both!"

Zaislo had enough of beating around the bush.

"Five and five."

Weevil started a lengthy, whining laugh and it seemed he would never stop.

Zaislo hit the table angrily.

"How should I know how many fingers a bloody dragon has? I never counted. I am a warrior, I can't even count."

Weevil was tearing up from laughter.

Behemor, who so far has been sitting and drinking without a word suddenly spoke grimly:

"Weevil should not drink any more. We can only trust his clerical knowledge if the patriarch won't heal our sickness. And you need a clear head for magic. I do not want to rot away alive."

"Come on! No need to worry" Yabbagabb said "the patriarch will come to us and if he doesn't, our goblin friend will perform the healing spell even with a hand tied behind his back. Right Weevil?"

Weevil started laughing so hard, he almost fell off his chair.

His companions looked at each other uncomprehending, then continued to drink.

The ranger gave himself to the fall. The monster lunged to grab him but it could not reach him. He hit dozens of branches as he fell. The world was going blurry…

He thought he heard Schiza's scream from somewhere afar. It made him shudder and pulling himself together he suddenly came back to reality.

He was lying on the ground at the trunk of the tree. The black cloak was down as well. It was advancing toward his companions. It crawled over a large rock which melted away hissing beneath it. A dwarf jumped in front of it to strike it down with the magical hammer, but Dragar Trollslayer pushed him aside - he wanted to be the first one who manages to wound the beast. His battleaxe - glowing with green light - sailed through the air to slice the black death apart. Dragar scored a deep wound on the monster with his weapon. As he saw the skin splitting and the ooze beneath it spurting and flowing - possibly it was the creature's blood - an enormous joy was radiating from his satisfied face.

"Finally, finally, finally!" he shouted almost mad with glee. "Now you die, you bloody rug!"

He struck again and again as if possessed. He would have only needed some sort of death rattle showing the beast's pain and fear for his joy to be complete.

The black death made no sounds. It showed no signs of fear or pain. It trashed around like a fish out of water to avoid the dangerous weapon. In the meantime it hit the dwarf with one or two parts of its body.

Dragar Trollslayer did not care about his wounds. He was not interested in the skin of his arm - where the monster hit him multiple times - cracking or boiling.

He struck and he struck and then he struck again as if he was chopping wood.

Schiza tried to attack as well but the monster threw her back at least seven feet away with a well-aimed hit. The priestess hissed in pain as she fell to her knees. Looking at her blemished skin she started to curse madly. She cussed the hellspawn as loud as she could. She stood up and joined the fray again with the magical hammer in her hand.

The ranger - even though he felt he had no unharmed body parts left - stood up from the ground. He could barely believe he was able to stand. Each step meant horrible pain for him. Slowly and unsteadily he limped toward Schiza to pull her away from the monster. But he did not have enough strength left to do that. He also had a feeling that Schiza won't stop fighting on her own accord. He stopped and pretended to feel dizzy.

"Schiza, help!" he whispered, falling to his knees.

His pretense got him what he wanted. The Priestess of Life disengaged from the fight and rushed to him. Caring not about causing him unbelievable pain, she grabbed him firmly.

The ranger hissed in pain but endured it with gritted teeth. He was too proud to cry out.

Dragar's last remaining dwarf however must have suffered a serious wound since he gave a full on animal roar.

Schiza stopped, letting the ranger go.

"Go back to the inn! It's not far from here. You can find the way on your own!"

The ranger, pretending to have no strength to walk, fell to his knees but the priestess didn't care about him anymore.

"The dwarves need me greatly!" she said and left him behind.

"Use your protection from evil!" the ranger cried after her because he had no other ideas to keep Schiza away from the monster. That spell would provide little protection but she would at least keep away from the fight while she casts it.

He got on his feet again and started advancing toward the black cloak as well. He began searching for the magical hammer where the dwarf with the child-like like face met his end. Finding the glowing weapon couldn't prove too difficult, provided it did not disappear yet.

Schiza wasted no time on her spell of protection against evil. He stood between the two dwarves and the monster to inspire them with her courage.

Dragar Trollslayer was getting cocksure.

"Let's jump on it before it escapes!" he shouted and immediately leapt onto the creature.

The black death did not feel like it was losing. It didn't look like it wanted to flee at all.

The dwarf tried to pin it to the ground while the undulating body jerked wildly beneath him.

Dragar Trollslayer felt a burning pain in his legs. His boots and clothes started to dissolve together with his skin. Despite all this he held himself firmly and tenaciously as a rock among the waves of an angry sea. Of course a rock would not have growled as wildly as he did.

The four corners of the black cloak rose, and it would have enveloped him had his companions not interrupted.

Schiza and the dwarven warrior leapt almost simultaneously to be riding on the back of the twitching hellspawn a second later.

The black death could not deal with their combined weight. It could neither devour them nor could it throw them off. The three adventurers clung to it as if they were the dangerous parasites instead of it. It twitched and lashed out with its biting, burning skin.

The two dwarves struck again and again with their weapons. Schiza likewise. The cloak retaliated after their every attack. A burn wound on Dragar's skin, a cut on the monster, a hit on Schiza a strike on the cloak, a horrid wound on the dwarf a hit at the hellspawn….and so on until exhaustion. As long as there was strength left in the arms wielding the magical weapons they rose and struck.

They were bathing in a sea of acid.

The body of the black cloak broke through at one point and only after three or four attacks did Drgar realize that he was hitting the ground below instead of the monster.

Schiza was blemished by dozens of wounds but she held on with firm fanaticism while shouting like an amazon princess.

The monster was moving slower and slower. It was weakening.

The dwarf fighting alongside his leader smiled at the priestess - he was keyed up by the thought of the impending glorious victory. He brushed thick beads of sweat out of his eyes to see the results of his rampage better. That was when the monster tore his head off with a powerful blow.

The head flew into the thick bushes and undergrowth.

This was the last act of the black death. While turning grey from black, it became motionless in a singular second.

Seeing the change, Schiza leapt off it and got rid of the acidic fluids burning her body by rolling around on the grass.

The ranger who up until now was searching fruitlessly for the weapon of the dead dwarf limped to her and started wiping her skin with a clean piece of cloth he took out from his pocket.

Schiza endured it without a word.

Dragar Trollslayer could not believe the creature died, he continued to beat it for a solid ten minutes afterward. He stumbled off the acidic pulp with the last of his strength and fell next to the priestess and the ranger. He kept his eyes on the remains of the black death as if he was afraid it would rise again.

They said nothing. They were too tired even for talking. They sat silently next to the corpse until they got themselves back together a bit. Then they rose, helping each other up and slowly walked toward the courtyard entrance.

Chapter 9
Diego de la Moota

"I will ask you again. Open your bag." said Kavak to the fat albino man. He wanted to remain calm and make his request a polite one but it seemed recent events became a big burden on his shoulders and did not leave him unscathed. He was trying not to think about the upcoming serious challenges of the next few hours. Against his will, panic was starting to overcome him.

What if they don't find the heart of the dead dwarf? What if they find it but Dragwaren's power proves insufficient to banish the demon? What if they manage to banish it? Will the Patriarch of the God of Protection come to their aid or will they rot away until their muscles shrivel and their limbs fall off?

He was having a hard time breathing and tried to hide the shaking of his hands from the others.

The man he was asking wasn't at the top of his game either. Fat beads of sweat were rolling down his forehead. He was trying to get rid of these unpleasant bodily emissions by wiping with his paddle of a palm frequently, but to no avail.

"I don't want to open it" he replied feebly.

Kavak gave an annoyed sigh.

"Run, boy! Bring me a glass of water!" the fat man growled at the child standing next to him.

The boy, looking about twelve years of age did not obey his command. He turned toward the warrior and narrowed his burning eyes.

Kavak stared into them unbelieving.

What a young child! Has no hair on his chin yet! How come he is showing no signs of fear? In fact, there seems to be hatred and deep contempt emanating from his gaze. Is this child normal?

"Who the hell are you?" he barked at them.

"My name is Golak! I am a spice merchant" the fat man anxiously replied before glancing at the boy for a second. Then he went on sputtering: "I left my men and my wares at the serai of the Southern Gate, only taking this boy as a general dogsbody with me. All right, let it be as you want, I will open the bag."

He leaned over to the warrior, whispering into his ear:

"But I will only show it to you, and trusting in your honor, I am asking you not to tell anyone else about what you find in there."

As he said it, he opened the bag a crack while carefully covering it with his body.

At first Kavak didn't believe what he saw was not an illusion. He looked first at the merchant then at the bag with wide eyes. Then he could not take his eyes off it until the man closed it again.

"You understand that I am anxious and I don't want others to learn about the contents of the bag?"

Kavak nodded like someone swallowing a whole apple then went on dazed.

The bag was filled with fist-sized rubies shining blindingly bright!

Kavak was unable to apprise the value of the jewels but he know for sure that even if the treasures hiding in the bag could not buy Karavan, they were easily worth a smaller city.

That's when Dragwaren and Grog stepped up to the noble looking man dressed in all black.

The older man was shining one of the silver buttons on his dolman with a soft cotton handkerchief. His stature was commanding respect. He was unusually calm compared to the other guests.

"I would ask you to show us the contents of the bag at your feet!" said the elven wizard turning toward him.

The man did not even look up, he continued polishing the button on his dress. His long, silver hair was hanging in front of his eyes, covering half of his face.

"I am hoping to avoid it" he finally said with a low, meek tone "I am but a simple clerk, serving my country, king and people. I was in a hurry to the wedding of my half-brother when - like you my brethren - owing to this unfortunate turn of events I was cursed to waste my precious time like a convicted criminal behind the crumbling walls of this decadent city, which at the same time has az ancient and noble past."

Slowly, very slowly he raised his head and looked the elven wizard in the eye.

"I hope, I do not offend you or invoke your wrath by making the impolite suggestion that it is unnecessary to waste the time - of which we have so precious little left - on the search of a simple bag which obviously would not contain any other objects than the necessary equipment for a journey taking multiple days, such as: hygiene supplies, a change of unmentionables, some food and of course my simple, meagre, modest but heartfelt wedding gift to my beloved half-brother and his kind betrothed. Continue doing your duty noble elven sir, searching the objects of another person; my bag requires no more attention."

The man surely had a way with words! And by that I do not mean his eloquent sentences but the magical power coating every single word of his. A type of charm which of course none of the people present would notice. Apart from Dragwaren who was the target of the spell.

The alert elven mage noticed the mental attack on his person and was resisting it with all his strength. He was dealing with the power of an enormous will. The man, pretending to be a simple clerk was launching a harsh and powerful attack by focusing his magical energies. He was trying to break his will and gain control over him. It was a type of charm or perhaps a command spell but created from far more powerful essences than those Dragwaren knew.

The elf however was a powerful wizard even if it did not show on the battlefield.

He was wise, completive man with a vast knowledge of the world who only became an adventurer a few years ago. He had a strong force of will and a rock solid character. He resisted the command spell, though with some difficulty. The stranger only managed to unveil himself. Dragwaren now knew he was up against a magic user.

"I would still have a look at the gentleman's possessions" he said while signaling Kavak to be ready for an attack.

A kind smile spread through the face of the elderly man in black despite the failure of his command spell. Judging by the ridiculous and pathetic level of fighting the elven wizard put up against the werewolf he would not have believed him capable of resisting his mind magic. He underestimated his abilities. No worries though - the fiasco did nothing to dishearten him.

"Obviously I could not bare if I stupidly caused a conflict situation with my foolish behaviour so I am going to overrule my previous decision right this second and will provide the bag in question for searching."

He bent down and put it into the innkeeper's hand.

Grog felt it. He found it light as if filled with some spongy material. He untied the knot and looked into the sack, opening its mouth.

His whole body started shuddering. He was frightened and dazed by what we saw.

He stumbled back.

The bag was empty and full all at once. It was tiny and enormous. He was holding a bottomless sack in his hands! Its insides were the cosmos itself, dark space, a black hole swallowing everything. Another dimension!

The smile of the black-clad man twisted into a demonic grin for a second. But only a second.

"If perhaps the good innkeeper had a change of heart and would forgo the opportunity to examine the contents of the sack I would ask him to close it and give it back to me. If he would want to search it some more I wouldn't hurry him for the world but make it quickly, bravely and at his own risk. The latter I find important to mention for using extradimensional sacks is far from safe for inexperienced laymen."

Grog stared at the magic item, unsure. The mouth of the sack was like a window opened to a dark, unexplored and - at first glance - lifeless world.

The innkeeper shuddered again. He would not reach into this hellish item for all the treasure in the world.

The black-clad man was already extending his arm to take back his lawful possession but Dragwaren proved quicker.

"I am fortunate to know about practical magic items such as this" the elf said. "I would root around inside a little if you are offering my good sir."

The man nodded with a friendly smile - the elf could do as he pleased.

The elven wizard has never held a bottomless sack before but he has heard and read plenty of these items. For example that no matter how terrifying they look at first glance, they are completely harmless. At least the sacks themselves are although the items inside might not be safe at all.

Dragwaren looked at the smiling elderly man but could

read nothing from his face.

Before he reached into the sack he activated all the sensory magics he acquired during many decades which made it possible for him to notice traps and potentially unpleasant dwellers of the strange extradimensional world in time.

It was a strange feeling when his fingers, hand and finally his whole arm disappeared into the magic item. It felt as if he had lost his arm for real. A curious experience! The extradimensional space of the bottomless sack had its own rules which differed significantly from the common laws of the material world.

As if his hand was extending into infinity, it soared through space with an incredible speed. He left his eyes closed in the meantime, using his mind fortified with the magic sensors to search through the dark.

The guests were looking tensely at the wizard's antics. Many were imagining what would happen if he would find the dwarf's heart in the sack.

How would the owner of the sack react?

The black-clad guest continued to stand there meekly and smile in the face of the threatening looks of Grog, Kavak and the bouncer.

Tifur, the would be assassin-grandmaster creeped behind his back with a tiny dagger in his hand.

Dragwaren suddenly felt two things at the same time. There was a small object hiding in the far corners of space which might have been the heart he was looking for. The other one was a tiny creature moving with extreme speed.

Dragwaren reached for the object he thought was the dwarven heart with his hand. In the meantime, the creature he discovered started advancing toward him.

He tried to identify what it could be. He concentrated…

An astral scorpion!

He started to shake with fear. The creature was tiny but carried a deadly venom in its tail and it was getting closer and closer to him by the second. If the see-through little beast reaches his arms he failed. The sting of the scorpion would kill him in an instant.

Despite all of this, he did not retreat. He grabbed for the object, concentrating as hard as he could. He would have no opportunity for a second try if he misses. Perhaps he should not have attempted the this first one either.

He reached for the object.

He proved dexterous but it was mostly his luck that made him succeed. He grabbed the thing without knowing what it was. He would have time looking at it once he escaped and pulled his hand out of the bottomless bag.

He began pulling his arm back, lighting quick. The astral scorpion was getting dangerously close. It raised its tail to strike.

Dragwaren gritted his teeth and lines of worry started appearing on his face. Still, he proved faster than the murderous creature. He pulled his hand out of the sack in the last second.

The scorpion could not follow him, it could not leave the extradimensional space. It could only exist inside the world of the sack.

The elven wizard opened his mouth for a sigh of relief but his breath got caught in his throat. Though he was expecting to find the item he was looking for, it was another matter coming face to face with the truth like this.

He was holding a reddish-brown heart in his hand, covered by dried blood…

"Was it this you wanted to give as a wedding present to your half brother?" he asked cynically once he regained his composure.

Most of the guests stood paralyzed. Some were murmuring words.

"Demon summoner!"

"Warlock!"

"Dwarf-killer!"

The smile has disappeared from the face of the black-clad man. It showed no emotions right now. It did not betray the enormous disappointment he felt. The elven wizard should have been dead. Instead he found the heart and managed to get it out of the bag despite the astral scorpion. The elf has surprised him for the second time today. He would not believed there was anyone else capable of avoiding the attack of the scorpion apart from himself.

He carefully folded the piece of cotton he was using to clean his silver buttons and then put it in his pocket unhurriedly.

"I am patiently waiting for what comes next." he said calmly.

Kavak drew his sword slowly. Grog raised his morningstar. The bouncer in the back was reloading the crossbow. Tifur stepped closer to the demon summoner so he could cut his throat if necessary.

The other guests did nothing.

One of the four drunkards at the table started to speak.

"I want to order!" Yabbagabb shouted, waving at their direction "I am getting hungry!"

Dragwaren - holding the heart in his hand - stepped away from the black-clad man.

"Why?" he asked "What reason you have for summoning a demon? Especially at the cost of a dwarf's life?"

The summoner answered:

"The veil is lifted! It is time to leave this farce behind. My heart is heavy with grief when I think about the dishonorable death of our poor dwarven companion, the one I dared to slay in his sleep under the cover of the night but his death was that of a martyr's, serving a higher purpose. His death will save our lives. Sacrificing him was the price for summoning the demon lord."

"What do we need a demon lord for?"

"Your question suggests a keen mind, my elven friend! I will answer it promptly, honestly and openly but I must warn you that my answer will only add to your sorrow. I am, of course not actually a government official but a magic user like yourself. I am a warlock! Far be it from me to brag or try to toot my own horn but I have to say I can read time as if life was no more than a mere book where I can turn the pages back and forward as I please. This sentence might have come out as a bit much and perhaps there is more poetry than reality in it, but it is true that time sheds its mask sometimes and allows me to see a few images. One of these images showed up this morning. Half an hour before the rooster crows, which will be in about an hour the army of fire mages lining up in front of the inn will start to chant. Using their combined power, they will conjure up an enormous fireball, a firestorm, a cloud of flame-wraiths which will destroy the inn. The Yellow Serpent, the people within, even the neighboring buildings are going to turn to ashes in the fragments of a single second. The city has sentenced us to death!"

"Thiss iss impossible!" the innkeeper replied shaking his morningstar threateningly. "In tweentee hourss at mosst the patriarch of Alamadaar the protector weell come to uss and ssave uss from thee infecteeuss plague."

"The images do not lie" replied the warlock calmly "In an hour and a half the inn will be destroyed. The question is whether or not we reside in the inn at the time or not. If I guess correctly, none of us is an archmage, supreme sorcerer or high priest so no one can cast a teleportation spell or has the strength to break through a blockade made by hundreds of fire mages, clerics and archers. That's where the soon to be arriving demon lord will come to our aid."

Dragwaren looked at the warlock who had a smug smile on his face. He shook his head in denial.

"We are facing the wrath of a demon lord because of some ambiguous prophecy? What makes you think sir, that you can control the demon?"

Before the warlock could answer, Yabbagabb

interrupted them with a shout.

"I want to eat something before my disease-rotten and fire mage-spell-charred body is devoured by a demon!"

Yabbagabb was so drunk he actually had no idea what he just said. All he knew was that he was hungry and he wanted to eat.

The black-clad warlock has already been standing straight with his chest puffed and his shoulders pulled back but now he stood even taller.

"I don't have a habit of introducing myself with my full name but now I feel the procedure is necessary to prove it to you beyond any doubt that I possess the power to control a demon lord and I have the unfolding events in my control. My name: Diego de la Moota, count of Peredon, lord of Valpurg, the grandmaster of the Black Knights of Kreto, warlock of the Thirteenth Circle, carrier of the Belmie's death magic...or as simple folk know me with elegant simplicity: the Exarch of the Devil."

Local guests jumped back after this introduction as if bitten by a snake. The name Diego de la Moota was far from unknown for them. There hasn't been a more horrid evildoer since the dawn of time. The smallest child of the late count of Peredon has murdered his entire family then spent his days mastering the dark arts, keeping his lands in terror until the royal army conquered his castle. He managed to escape and disappear and was only occasionally heard from since then.

"I have a chance, not even a small one to press the demon lord into my service for a short time. I was the one who made the black death flee when it was chasing the dwarven leader and foolishly tried to attack me. The black death sensed my dark power and knew who it was up against. It wasn't a coincidence that it fled to the gardens."

Those among the guests who still believed in staying alive up to this abandoned all hope. The demon lord is going to kill them - either by its own accord or at the orders of the warlock. They did not even think about fighting Diego de la Moota.

"We will not make deals with demons." Dragwaren said disdainfully. Then he added: "Nor with warlocks. Tie him up, innkeeper!"

The innkeeper looked at de la Moota and the warlock looked back at him. He nearly died of fright from his gaze.

"I won't go aneewhere neer heem!" he said shaking his head.

Dragwaren put on an angry face.

"At least bring us some rope and rags for stuffing his mouth with! Kavak will deal with the rest."

"Gladly" said the warrior with the fu-manchu, twirling his mustache "I will tie you up, you weasel."

The warlock grew sad.

"I am sorry, sir elf that we can't reach common ground with this. I thought us being on the same side, united by the common goal of escaping the confines of these walls. I am thoroughly exasperated to be denied, excluded with my helping hand pushed away crudely...just like my family did...the peredonians, pathetically obscurant, orthodox doctrines, senseless principles, the morals of the foolish and the weak."

A single tear appeared on de la Moota's face. He did not wipe it, just let it flow down on his wrinkled face.

"Please give me the heart back and let me handle the demon!" he tried one last time.

But Dragwaren shook his head.

"I cannot. We need to find another way to escape. We cannot use the help of a demon."

"Why not?" the warlock asked, calmly.

"As you said it yourself: senseless principles, foolish morals. But these senseless principles and useless morals give a meaning to our lives, we cannot live without them. Were we to deny them, we would be denying ourselves. An individuum can only live as long as it preserves the purity of its soul. If it strays from the path it becomes lost, destroying itself."

He fell silent, the after half a minute he added:

"You won't get the heart back. If the demon arrives, I swear I will to send it back to hell!"

"Is that so?" the warlock asked, barely audible "Is that so?" he hissed again before lowering his head and stooping forward, making his white hair fall in front of his face.

"God is my witness, I tried everything to prevent bloodshed. It always ends like this! They force my hand again and again to kill. It always makes me wonder if I am a bad person or just a victim of circumstances. Why do I feel like I have no other course of action left. Do they like losing their lives? I don't think so! I don't understand. I don't understand any of it. It's a mad world. I cannot follow your way of thinking, sir elf. Of course it is possible the fault is mine, but I do not feel that way. I have to kill you like everyone else in this inn. Foolishly, I expected you to wait patiently until I managed to exert control over the demon! Who knows? In good humor, bolstered by my own success I might have let you live. But it is all the same to me in the end. If you are in such a hurry to die, let's get it over with! Let's make your executions the next item on the agenda!"

Right then the door to the courtyard opened, and Schiza, the ranger and the dwarven leader entered the inn.

All one of the guests had to say was that the man right there is the demon summoner, he was the one who killed the dwarven warrior. Dragar Trollslayer needed nothing else, forgetting the wounds he got in the previous battle, he charged the warlock like an enraged bull.

Diego de la Moota began to cast a spell.

Tifur slit his throat.

It was a masterful strike. The sneak attack was executed precisely, perfectly and on such a high level it even surprised the one who did it. Had the grandmaster of the Assassin's Guild seen it, he would have surely considered retirement and giving up his place for the young talent.

It was a quick, silent, merciless attack so quick that it

was undetectable by the naked eye. The cold edge of the blade slit the warlock's throat from ear to ear.

There was only one thing that might have made Tifur dissatisfied. There was no blood pouring from his enemy's throat.

The throat wound of Diego de la Moota regenerated in the blink of an eye, there wasn't a single tiny scar betraying the recent cut. The assassin didn't even manage to prevent his target from casting a spell. The warlock finished his deadly enchantment without a hitch.

Green fog erupted from de la Moota's mouth, fanning out into the room.

Dread spread onto the faces of the guests. They fell down,one after the other donning a mask of death. Everyone perished in the deadly cloud unless they had the strength to resist the poison. They didn't even need to breath it in, the substance was absorbed through the skin.

One of the guests was running toward the table of the drunks where the mist was thinner, while twitching with cramps.

Yabbagabb and his three companions were in a merry mood. Curiously, they turned toward the man, who was twitching with katatonic movements, his skin peeling from the poison and screaming in agony.

"Finally someone shows their face around here!" Yabbagabb said crankily "Run along and open the windows fast! The air is a bit stale here...Oh and bring me something to eat! I am ravaged by hunger! I will settle for some pheasant stuffed with chestnuts. What about you?" he asked, turning to his companions.

Zaislo answered after some hacking up and swallowing.

"Prickled boar's haunch with blueberries!"

"Roasted trout" Behemor grunted, staring ahead with empty eyes and licking his lips with a dumb smile on his face before becoming horrified about the nonsense - and the alien to the situation they were in - he was speaking.

"I am just a little string bean of a goblin. I am quite full after all that meat and druidic berries. Maybe I will have a few morsels from your plates."

The man nominated as waiter however had no intentions of serving them. He shook his head angrily, groaned, mad from the pain, drooled and then collapsed. He was slowly dissolving.

"Simulant!" said Yabbagabb disdainfully "Afraid of hard work, are you?"

The deadly cloud evaporated within seconds, leaving terrible devastation in its wake.

Schiza and the ranger could barely stand, though it was most likely due to the fight against the black cloak for they were quite a long way away from the poisonous cloud.

Kavak and Dragwaren had wounds all over their skin, feeling a piercing pain with every single move but it could have been much worse.

Grog's skin turned to an ugly colour, he could barely breathe and was at his weakest. Had one of his ancestors been anything other than serpentfolk, providing him with serpent's blood in his veins, granting some immunity from poison, he would have been dead for sure. He turned a table over, and was covering behind it. His vision was blurred. The images of the inn were swimming in front of his eyes, out of focus. He thought about using his 'secret implement' but then decided against it. He waited. Let the guests thin out and weaken even more. Then he will use the 'secret weapon'. His time will come.

Dragar Trollslayer, who waded into the deadly cloud like a madman could only thank his extraordinary constitution for escaping unscathed. Battleaxe in hand, he continued to charge the warlock without delay.

The innkeeper's bouncer, the fat albino man and the young child was almost in the same place when the deadly cloud struck. Still, although the albino who introduced himself as Golak and the bouncer fell to the ground - and while they remained conscious it wasn't sure they would survive in the end - the young kid resisted the spell entirely. He stood firm during the murderous cloud. Then he spared a glance toward the fat merchant and advanced toward the warlock with steady steps.

Father Floranus lurking in the shape of the dog has chosen his place well. The poisonous mist did not reach him.

After the shocking realization that the warlock stayed upright and continued with his spell as if nothing happened even after having his throat slit, Tifur wasted no time being amazed. He owed his survival to his quickness and determination many times over. He hasn't stopped contemplating now either, he turned tails and disappeared among the upturned furniture and piles of corpses. Only for a second was he dazed by the deadly cloud. When he came to his senses and saw the chaos conquering the room he decided to go on with his mission. The guests aren't paying him any attention now so he can finish what he came for. He couldn't very well do anything else. He could not harm the warlock.

He took out a blowpipe and a tiny dart which still gleamed with deadly poison. He aimed at his victim…

The spell from Diego de la Moota made Behemor, Weevil, Yabbagabb and Zaislo cough a few times but had no other effect on them.

Other then these however there was no one else left alive in the inn. They were killed by the deadly cloud.

Dragar Trollslayer ran through the room like a charging rhino. The dwarven leader waded through the bloody piles of corpses then buried his axe - still burning with green fire - into the dwarf-slayer's head with an enormous force.

He had an easy time doing it for Diego de la Moota did not move a muscle. The warlock was a bit disheartened about so many people staying upright after his poison cloud attack. But then a smile broke out on his face and he was pondering another spell with a happy face. His skull caved in with a loud crack as if it was a chicken bone.

Dragar had great difficulty pulling his battleaxe back

from his enemy's brains. Then he watched astounded as the hit he scored on the warlock's head closed in a heartbeat. He lowered his weapon, blinking rapidly and shaking his head in disbelief. The wralock was able to survive his wild charge without a scratch?

Even though he could have rushed him, or grabbed his arms to prevent him from casting spells that require somatic components he didn't. He lost his taste for battle as well his heart and ceased his attack. He saw no point in continuing the fight as not even his magical weapon was enough to harm the killer of his companion. His foe possessed a frightening ability to regenerate.

The events have made Kavak, the ranger and the Priestess of Life unsure as well.

Dragwaren started hastily casting a spell to identify the protective auras of the warlock. He detected no less than four of them! There was one that protected him from normal missiles, one from magical ones. The third aura was a prepared spell. If he got into trouble he could conjure a burning fire shield around himself which would set everyone and anything ablaze in his vicinity apart from himself.

What made him activate his identifying magic though was the desire to learn about the warlock's fourth defense. 'It's a kind of regenerative skin spell' Dragwaren concluded. It healed all wounds - whether they were caused by common or magical means - immediately. The extremely powerful defensive spell however had a single weak point. It was only able to absorb a set number of attacks. About twenty or thirty of them.

"Go on attacking him! He is only protected from the first few hits!" said the elf, encouraging his allies to fight.

With his face falling, Diego de la Moota noted that he was being assaulted again. By five people no less: Dragar, Kavak, Schiza, the ranger and the young kid.

'Pathetic bunch' de la Moota thought. And with that

little kid among them to boot? How ridiculous! What could the tiny squirt want? Or is he not so ridiculous after all? How could he have survived the poison cloud? But who cares? There is no justice in this world. Were there ten times more of them, they still wouldn't have a chance!

Still, he did take the fight seriously.

"I wouldn't like you to weaken my defensive spell. Wasting my protection on the weakly hits of a child when it could parry the blows of a demon lord. It's not right!" he said. Chanting a few words he flew up into the air where they could not reach him. Because he was protected against projectiles and magical missiles, he was almost invincible for his enemies. He started chanting a longer spell.

"Do I see it right, is there only one dwarf left from seven?" asked Yabbagabb from Zaislo, shaking his shoulder.

Zaislo's answer was a humongous burp which could easily have meant both yes or no.

"He is alone" the goblin nodded firmly.

"It's not a bad thing, adventuring on your own" Behemor mumbled with closed eyes. "Rambling alone in a forest at night, below the tree branches as the evening wind caresses your face, the leaves rustling with a low, melancholic hum and you are made to wonder by the mythical shapes on the darkened sky. It's just you and nature and the only thing filling the void is your own mind, you are the creator of the world and of yourself in it, the only one you can count on. Brute force, stamina, dexterity, quickness and cunning...no need for anything else. When you walk alone in a dark forest, you will see the world differently, you will think differently, you will change and become a different man. If you desire tranquility, you will find a peace of soul, if you suffer from an oppressive lethargy, you will be possessed by a rebellious spirit, if you want to forget, you will, if you want to remember, you will.

If you want to cry without anyone else seeing you, the trees will cry with you, if you want to laugh, the moon will smile at you. If you die among the trees of the forest, you will die happily."

"A barbarian does not speak so eloquently." Weevil whined "I wanted to tell you before."

"Just because I am a barbarian, I can have a silver tongue. Not all barbarians are thick morons."

"You are right. And not all goblins are stupid!" Weevil hit the table "But look over there! Does that old man think himself a bird?"

Diego de la Moota was possessed by a mad fighting spirit. With twisted, contorted, scowling-smiling face he spit out his deadly spells shouting at the top of his lungs at the dregs standing below him helplessly and impotently.

The air suddenly grew cold. An icy burst of wind flew through the room, a premonition of the warlock's ice-dome spell.

An amorphous cloud of ice materialized around the adventurers. Those who were able to, tried to run out of it. Growing into a huge dome of ice, the ice cloud fell down on the guests with a mighty rumble.

Dragar go out of the way with heavy steps. Kavak quickly ran out of the spell's range. He escaped with a few superficial cold sores. The young boy proved even faster than the mustachioed warrior. He avoided the danger zone without a scratch.

Schiza and the ranger were in the middle of the spell. They tried to run away but they couldn't get away in time. They came under the ice dome…

Dragwaren was forced to back away by the chilling wind and the bone rending cold. He stopped after a few steps. He raised up his shaking hands to form a spell but he was not speaking the magic words yet.

He had a single counter-magic spell and this made him

hesitate.

Should he save Schiza and the ranger by dissolving their icy prison? Or should he dispel the flying enchantment of Diego de la Moota? Schiza and the ranger are going to die if he doesn't help them. The walls of the dome were thickening, they could not get out from there anymore. The gigantic ice block could be broken neither from the inside nor from outside.

The features of Schiza and the ranger were becoming blurry as the ice thickened around them. Dragwaren could make out less and less from the silhouettes of his adventuring companions. Not being able to look them in the eye made the heartrendingly painful choice easier.

Were any of his comrades in his place, they would have acted differently for sure. None of them would have hesitated to use the counterspell to save the lives of two friends. The rules of camaraderie, the invisible bonds which bound them tightly would have made them to set their companions free. They would not have pondered about the situation, they would not have seen in their righteous fervor that they are making the wrong decision.

Cruel fate only gave them two options. They could decide on the bad one or the worse one. Would they have disabled the ice dome, they would set Schiza and the ranger free, true, but Diego de la Moota would remain in the air where he could not be reached and cannot be wounded. Therefore this decision would have sealed their fate. The warlock was chanting without stop and sooner or later his deadly spells would have reached everyone.

There was only one other option. Disabling the flight spell of Diego de la Moota. If the warlock falls to the ground, the others can engage him again. If they can dismantle the protective aura of the regenerative skin in time, they can finish him off easily. With his death, the ice-dome he made should perish as well.

Schiza and the ranger only had to somehow endure for a few minutes. If they are lucky, they can survive. They have to survive!

Carrying the heavy weight of his decision, Dragwaren disassembled the invisible threads of Diego de la Moota's flight spell.

The warlock was in the process of chanting chain lightning which would have burned all his enemies to a crisp when the world turned upside down around him. No matter how hard he slapped with his hands like a wounded bird or tried to keep himself in the air by pure concentration, the flight spell dissolved off him and he fell down helplessly, right at the dwarves feet.

Dragar Trollslayer struck him, frothing at the mouth and then threw himself on him.

De la Moota wasn't wounded by either the fall or by the dwarven battleaxe, but the unexpected turn of events made him mess up several magical phrases so his spell did not go off.

Following the example set by Dragar Trollslayer the young boy also pounced on him.

Kavak was trying to break the ice wall holding two of his companions hostage, uncaring about the horrid cold around the ice dome.

"Attack the warlock! It's the only way to make the ice spell disappear!" shouted Dragwaren but Kavak, had already realized this himself and his sword was on its way toward Diego de la Moota's head.

In the safety of his cover, Tifur took aim at the bouncer covering next to the albino. The man, weakened by the poison cloud was in the process of reaching for his crossbow.

The young assassin already managed to kill the bouncer Talak in the outhouse without anyone seeing him or arousing any suspicion toward himself. Now - using the chaos - he had the opportunity to send his second target to the underworld. He shot his deadly poison dart at him. His mind, was already occupied by the main target, the innkeeper of the Yellow Serpent. He wanted to leave him for last. He wanted him to know why he had to die and whose weapon it was that brought his demise when he killed him.

The Whispering Shade, the largest assassin's guild in Karavan has sentenced the innkeeper of the Yellow serpent to death because he and three of his men had murdered and robbed the guests sleeping in the inn without the guilds permission - or knowledge up until now. In these parts of the city even a simple picking of pockets without the acknowledgement of the Whispering Shade was considered a capital offense. The Whispering Shade allowed no competitors to live. It sent Tifur as its executioner.

In spasmodic concentration, the warlock uttered his next spell.

A tiny speck of light appeared next to him, turning into a seven feet-tall multicolored tornado in an instant. The chaotic vortex made of pure magical essence surrounded the summoner. The gust grabbed the raging dwarf, the mustachioed warrior and the silent, emotionless child.

De la Moota stood up with his chin raised high and a haughty expression on his face. He swept his attackers off him as if they were mere specks of dust on his clothes.

The whirlwind scattered his enemies, smashing them into the walls of the room.

De la Moota gave them no time to react. Before they could have recovered, he dismissed his useful, but not especially destructive vortex spell.

He turned all his attention to his next one. His chanting made the ground crack as dark, rubbery tentacles writhed forth from the depths of hell, flailing furiously and striking horrific blows.

The demonic, dreadful spawn surrounded the child within seconds. Dragar Trollslayer was caught by the leg and restrained, Kavak was being pummeled by them and they started to strangle Dragwaren.

It seemed Diego de la Moota has won the battle. His enemies was destined to die a slow and painful death.

Diego de la Moota cackled devilishly and allowed himself some time to marvel at the sight he created before casting his next spell. In the meantime, he put his battle-disheveled clothing to order.

Schiza and the ranger were making weak attempts to break the rock solid walls of their prison.

The freezing air was needling their skin, made their every breath painful and their muscles stiffen. It robbed them of their determination, slowly murdering their fighting spirit.

They fell to the ground in the middle of the dome, right next to each other.

The ranger grabbed Schiza's trembling hands. He was squeezing it so tight as if his life was dependent on it.

With his heartrendingly sorrowful eyes, the Priestess of Life stared at the ice wall becoming thicker and thicker.

"I do-on't wan-na d-die...N-not l-like th-this" she said, shivering "I do-on't w-want y-you t-to see m-me die."

Schiza was fighting with her full heart and spirit to keep it together, to die with dignity and show no fear. But she was fighting a losing battle against the dread that was overcoming her. She couldn't help it.

"S-save me!" she demanded of the ranger. "A-are y-you such a p-pathetic l-loser? C-can't y-you h-help me? W-why h-have I a-agreed to a-adven-turing w-with y-you? I c-could h-have j-joined s-so m-many o-other g-groups. W-why d-did I c-choose y-you? I h-hate y-you!"

Her last words she wanted to shout into the ranger's ears but she was only capable of a faint whisper.

The ranger squirmed as if hit. The cruel words of the priestess cut deep into his very soul. He didn't want to live. For the first time, life was hurting him badly. He fulfilled Schiza's every single request and demand during their adventures and now when her priestess needed him the most, he could not do anything for her.

Broken, he nodded along. He was thinking that Schiza was right, he was truly a pathetic nobody.

The goblin cleric, Weevil was somewhat sobered by the cold gust of wind conjured by the warlock. He saw the young man and woman imprisoned under the ice dome. Then he shifted his eyes away from the dying couple and looked at his companions. Behemor was staring into nothing dreamily with a zombie's face. Yabbagabb was sitting there in a sort of melancholy calm, turning his wine cup up and down in his hand. He was trying to trap a cockroach under it. Zaislo was laughing together with the warlock. Weevil took his eyes off them and returned his gaze to the two people imprisoned under the ice dome again.

He was assaulted by a feeling of melancholy. Seeing the young couple broke down walls inside him, walls which held old memories at bay. Deliberately forgotten images of his youth broke through the mists of time like a cascading river: monsters breathing acid clouds or frozen storms. Spreading chasms which swallowed cities. The great dragon-swarming of the North Sea. The crowning of a goblin king. Crying and suffering faces, showing themselves for an instant and then vanishing. The show of torment and misery took a long time before silence and emptiness came to the land of remembrance he conjured inside his soul. Then a sudden gust of wind swept the fog away and unrealistically sharp images appeared in front of him: the ornate bedroom of a castle. A young knight with a beautiful woman in his arms is inside. A woman who resembled Sciza but of course wasn't her. The knight, when his lips touched the woman's velvety ones trembled. And this young, male body not only trembled but also became blurry and vanished into nothing. Inside the bedroom of the castle the young man turned into a goblin, with deep lines etched into his face. It was him! He, the goblin twenty years ago. The woman saw her gallant knight turning into an ugly goblin and screamed. Young Weevil noticed that his knight's mask vanished from his body and the woman he loved more than anything in the world, who he would have done anything for came face to face with his true form: an ugly, naked goblin. It was the kiss, the elated, arousing, burning sensation that distracted his concentration, breaking his illusion spell and destroying his magical disguise. Driven by the screams of the beloved woman, bodyguards broke through the door, charging at young Weevil with their shields. They rushed him off his feet and started kicking him. First he didn't even defend himself as they broke his nose and his yellowish goblin blood started pouring from his mouth. He crouched down, his whole body trembling. He begged his beloved for mercy with lowered eyes but the lady was too disgusted to even look at him, sobbingly she screamed at her bodyguards to destroy the monstrosity as fast as they can.

'Monstrosity! Monstrosity!!!' even now, after twenty years Weevil trembled remembering the way he felt then. He remembered the horrid rage that swept over his soul. He remembered as he - despite many of his bones being broken - raised his arms, pointing his fists at the ceiling and sputtered a curse at the castle.

Anyone looking out from one of the windows of the castle would have seen blinding light, then - as if a titan rushed past nearby, or the earth itself woke from its sleep - the walls of the ancient castle started to shake. Lightning struck with destructive force where young Weevil pointed, blowing apart the marble foundation, piercing the castle to its cellar. The first lightning bolt was followed by another and then many more. Thunder roared with frightening force. The young goblin cleric mumbled a few more words, than in the same position he was lying with his broken body he rose and without moving, full of melancholy he flew out of the window, his head lowered as the castle fell to ruin behind him. For a second he heard the prayers and dying screams of the hundreds of people inside - guards, footmen, basement dwellers - then the nearby mountains shook from the noise of the blastwave. The bastions and towers buried all the appeals from the people of the castle beneath them…

This was what Weevil remembered. These were the dark shadows from his past that haunted him as he looked at Schiza. He was blinking back tears when he thought about how he caused the death of his beloved in his blind lust for revenge and despair ,bordering on madness. He thought that even though the past cannot be changed, even if he cannot raise his long lost love from the dead, he must do something for this woman, resembling the only love of his life so much and fighting for her life.

Weevil, goblin cleric suddenly rose and stepped in front of Diego de la Moota.

His drunken table companions ignored him.

Only Yabbagabb mumbled something about their pact and how you should not interfere in anything because he always interfered in everything and it never did him any good.

Weevil immediately started chanting a monumental spell.

The warlock turned toward the goblin, curiously.

"A new opponent! I was just starting to get bored. Although it is a grand overstatement to raise this little waster to the level of an opponent." he said, smiling. Cracking his fingers, he started his own litany.

He spoke the components of his spell with a disturbing speed. The goblin cleric was still only at the middle of his own spell when a four-inch wide lightning bolt erupted from the extended hands of Diego de la Moota. The ray of energy hit Weevil's body with an unerring accuracy. The lightning pushed him back to his table where he collapsed and lied there unmoving.

Shaking his head, Behemor reached down for the goblin and sat him back next to him. They all looked at his smoking clothes and sooty face. Zaislo started to laugh at the sight of his comrade's weary appearance.

"He deserved it! Why does he always have to on, heckling and yakking. I am surprised no one killed him yet for his annoying demeanor!"

Sorting through his vine-addled thoughts Behemor spoke:

"This is no laughing matter, Zaislo. Even though I think it was the vine that knocked him out and not the lightning spell, that changes little. Our cleric is in no shape to the eradicate the sickness ravaging our body."

Zaislo's mood turned sour and tried to bring the goblin back to consciousness. His healing knowledge amounted to a few loud smacks to the face.

Diego de la Moota did not waste time with the company at the table yet. The tentacles bursting forth from the ground started to venture off so he concentrated his attention on them for the moment.

Schiza and the ranger had minutes left to live.

"T-take my hand!" Schiza asked the young man.

The ranger has been holding the girl's hand for a while now, she just failed to feel it, so frozen and numb did they get in the inhuman cold.

The ranger touched her with his other hand as well. He was stroking her frozen body slowly and gently. Her hand, her arm, then with a feather light touch he felt along her lips with his fingers.

A tiny teardrop emerged from Schiza's eye and ran at most a few inches before freezing onto her sad face.

She started to cry.

"S-so many th-things, s-so m-many things I s-still wan-ted to d-do, s-so many things I wan-ted f-from life, s-so m-many th-things I have n-not tried y-yet! S-so many p-places

I h-haven't v-visi-ted, th-there are s-so many won-do-rus and i-nint-er-es-ting things in t-the world, w-why d-do I have t-to die? I wan-ted to d-do s-so many th-things yet! E-eating drake-meat in Rath-hk! T-travel to Moar! S-see the end-less des-sert, the en-or-mous s-sand wyrms. K-kos-mar, the Is-land of B-bliss...s-so many th-things..I wan-ted to s-see the world...f-find t-rue l-love...I wan-ted a ch-child..."

The ranger embraced him. He hugged her as strong as he could as if it could save her, but he could not save her from the embrace of the ice.

Schiza collected all her remaining strength. She embraced him as well and looked into his eyes.

The ranger felt hot in her gaze.

Schiza saw happiness in the man's gaze reflecting her despair and something else...being at peace with life and death.

They will take their steps into the unknown together!

Schiza knew not what she felt, but it was a good feeling. She never felt herself closer to the ranger. The two of them...together. Clinging to each other. Warming each other with their hot breaths...becoming one being!

Then the ranger froze. He kept looking at her with his eyes radiating happiness and a kind smile. Schiza discovered the gaze of the God of Life in his beautiful eyes. And then she knew: there were worse things than death. Death is a necessary state of being, everyone goes through it. Death is what gives life a meaning. Death is the only certainty in life. Everyone is equal in death. You fool around in the world until you know the thousand forms of happiness and suffering and then you die. Not dying would be the most horrendous curse of all. She went even further: the moment of death is the happiest moment of your life. True freedom! A release from all the burdens and problems of life.

The moment of the most beautiful celebration has come for her!

Sciza, Priestess of the God of Life stopped crying, stood straight and died as if death was a beautiful gift after the false pretense of a hard life filled with pain…

Tifur missed the shot.

The bouncer slipped and fell back. The poisoned dart embedded itself into the neck of the fat merchant behind him.

The bouncer stood up angry, not knowing how lucky he was. He only found out that something had happened when he glenced at the albino man.

The fat merchant was dead a second after the poison entered his bloodstream. He lay on the ground in a cramped position with glassy, bloodshot eyes and white foam spewed forth from his mouth.

"What the hell?" the bouncer cursed. Not noticing the tiny dart in the victim's neck, he thought the merchant died to an after-effect of the warlock's poison cloud.

Tifur put another poison dart into his blowpipe. He leaned out of cover, shot then retreated to the shadows.

"What the hell?" the bouncer cursed again. He felt a tiny prick on his neck. He grabbed the small dart and pulled it out. Nervously he looked around the hall. He felt dizzy. His hands fell down weakly. Letting go of the crossbow, he collapsed.

'Two dead' Tifur noted. He did not know that thanks to father Floranus he could have crossed out the third bouncer as well and only Grog the innkeeper remained on the list of targets.

Wisely, he stayed in cover and waited for the events to unfold…

Diego de la Moota was chanting. He summoned lightning again. The bolt blew Kavak, the warrior with the fu-manchu apart.

Dragar Trollslayer was raging. He could not escape the hold of the tentacles and this made him sunk deeper and deeper into madness.

Diego de la Moota must have sensed something about the abilities of the young kid for while Dragwaren was being strangled by a single tentacle and the dwarven leader by three, he sent twelve of them for the kid. Despite all of this, he was not sure twelve tentacles are going to be enough to keep the creature masquerading as a young child prisoner.

Father Floranus creeped out of cover in the shape of the dog. He believed he had to enter the fight despite the danger of being discovered. He cared nothing about the struggles of these people. But - seeing the events unfold - he knew that if the warlock wins this battle, he will spare neither his nor anyone else's life . It's better if he helps the others. He will make things a bit harder for the old demon summoner.

He sneaked up behind a column where he could not be seen. Changing back to his human form, he started conjuring.

The smile vanished from the face of Diego de la Moota and bitter tears emerged from his eyes.

His favorite tentacles withered and died in half a minute.

He didn't understand how it could have happened.

He could not speculate for long however, for the dwarf, Dragwaren and the kid all rushed at him once they were free of their bondage.

The warlock gave an annoyed huff.

'It is time to invoke a serious spell!' he thought. Belmie's death magic was the first thing he thought of, but he thought better of it. For these insects? Unnecessary! It would be wasteful!

He decided on something else. He tried the same spell he used on the elven wizard before the battle. Using pure concentration he invoked a domination spell. This time he chose an easier target.

While he was concentrating, the dwarven leader

embedded his battleaxe in his left shoulder, Dragwaren struck his heart twice and the person who looked like a young boy hit him with such force that his face broke. Despite all of this, his will remained unbroken and his wounds healed in seconds - he managed to activate his spell.

Dragar Trollslayer stopped. He was hesitating and felt extremely foolish. He had no idea who his enemies were among the men around him. He knew something was amiss and he sensed the presence of magic in the air which angered him a lot. He remembered that the elf next to him is a magician and immediately he concluded that he must have fought him thus far. With a tiny, firm nod he reassured himself. Hesitating no more, he struck his battleaxe into the head of the surprised Dragwaren.

The last thing the elven magician, Dragwaren saw was the conspiratorial wink of Diego de la Moota then everything went dark.

The dwarven leader who fell under the control of the warlock felt his situation weird and bizarre. His spirits were low and he felt ill at ease in his own skin without knowing why. The fight went on around him. He thought the next logical step for him to take would be destroying the young child.

Diego de la Moota nodded in agreement and this reassured the dwarf. Dragar Trollslayer striked the kid with his weapon.

Father Floranus called on nature's help against the warlock. After he stealthily murmured his long invocation, he shifted back into dog form and came out from behind the column.

Through the cracks of the tavern floor where de la Moota's demonic tentacles emerged not so long ago, now mustard-yellow vines slithered through, resembling large venomous snakes. They were controlled telepathically by the druid. Emerging from beneath the earth by the dozen, they creeped toward the warlock.

Diego de la Moota noticed the first vine when it had already coiled itself around his leg with such strength that is stopped circulation and it almost tore his limb off. Before he could react, a throng of vines creeped up on him, enveloping his body and preventing any kind of movement. Soon there was so many plants covering him that it was impossible to tell who the greenish tentacles are hiding.

The warlock tried to disengage but with his bound legs all he managed was to fall to his knees. Seeing that this is no laughing matter, he used pure concentration to activate his prepared firewall spell without hesitation.

After that, he looked like a gigantic burning torch. The dark red flames blazing around his body destroyed the druid's vines with incredible speed without causing him any pain or harm.

By the time he stood up, only some grey ashes and charred vines bore witness to the existence of the plants.

He dismissed the firewall spell, for maintaining it cost a tremendous amount of energy. Conserving magical essence would do him good.

Angrily, he began scanning the room. He saw no living creature apart from the drunken revelers at the table and a dog. He used a spell to detect invisible creatures but it did not reveal anyone else. Then with a sudden stroke of inspiration he realized who could be behind the attack.

Even though he himself was not able to use the entangle spell, he was a scholar of all kind of magic and was able to categorize this spell as well. To summon and keep the vines alive was a spell requiring serious skill in the druidic arts.

This meant that there was a druid in the inn who so far hasn't revealed himself.

A second later he knew who it was. Taking the shape of different plants and animals was a common practice in the druidic tradition. Smiling, he turned toward the dog:

Now, that I discovered you, you will become quite dogged soon my dear sir! I have always viewed your kind of magic with great interest! With your grandiose spell you have provided an exceptional show of the magical skill of your order. I salute you! It does you credit! I have to confess it not only surprised me but also provided me with some amusement. But now allow me, a feeble soul to demonstrate the magical strength of warlocks!

Diego de la Moota begin his most horrendous and frightening ritual - the starting lines of the thousand-times-cursed death spell of Belmie.

Father Floranus knew himself, his abilities and limits well and from what he has already seen he could asses the power of his enemy realistically. Wisely, he realized that he would have to get extremely lucky to achieve victory over the warlock in an open battle of magics. So he decided it's better not to attempt it. Staying in dog shape, he made a run for it.

He had no idea that his only chance of survival was to escape the area of the death spell's effect before the warlock finishes chanting the magical words of the liturgy.

The descending battleaxe of Dragar Trollslayer's was easily avoided by a quick sidestep from the youth. Grumbling, the dwarf raised the weapon for another attack.

The child showed no signs of surprise. His expressionless face did not show if he was especially worried about his ally turning on him. With a stoic calm he acknowledged that he has another enemy to fight. He attacked Dragar Trollslayer while constantly keeping his eye on Diego de la Moota. Before the dwarven warrior could do anything about it, he already touched him three times with his small, soft hands.

The first touch made Dragar Trollslayer's barrel of a body tremble. The second, hitting him on the shoulder was strong enough to break his bones and bend his short legs, forcing him to his knees. The third touch hit him in the chest. The kid barely touched him with the tip of his finger, soft as a feather. Dragar Trollslayer's ribs broke to pieces. A piercing pain erupted in the lungs of the dwarven leader, he could not breathe, fell back and died of his injuries before he could realize what just happened.

The kid stepped closer to the warlock without sparing another glance for the collapsing dwarf.

Seeing what the child is capable of, Diego de la Moota let the druid go and used the death magic of Belmie on him.

It should be noted about the death magic of Belmie that is one of the most effective anti personnel spells in the world. De la Moota got it from the archlich Belmie as a reward for his services.

Seven years ago a knight called Promicus, the Grandmaster of the Millenial Imperial Order was still alive. Many great potentates fell by the hands of de la Moota. The warlock remembered this one only because of all his enemies, this knight was the one who could resist the death magic of Belmie the best. Instead of falling to his demise as most people would when encountering such a spell, Sir Promicus only fell deaf to his left ear and lost the use of his left arm. He could not enjoy resisting the dark spell long however. It took de la Moota a dozen spells, but he defeated the knight in the end.

The death magic of Belmie was activated.

I had no effect on the child however.

The warlock felt dread.

Suddenly, seven untraceable attacks hit him. His regenerative skin spell could barely absorb the amount of damage he suffered. The protective aura was weakening, it only had power left for countering a few more punches.

The dumbfounded face, shock, surprised mumbling and groaning of de la Moota was soon replaced by mad rage.

"For all the devils in hell, the scythe of Arwan, the guts of Reschtrach, blood of Belmie what substance can resist the deadly words of an archlich?"

The kid didn't even blink. He delivered another batch of successful attacks. Diego de la Moota had two ribs and his left thigh bone broken, his kidney torn off, both his eyes gouged out, his skull smashed in and his spine broken in four places.

A second later, all his injuries were healed but he wasted no more time on useless chatter by then.

When his regenerative skin spell is gone, he won't be able to cast any more spells.

The kid continued his maddened assault without a stop.

Diego de la Moota sputtered out two spells before the last threads of his defense would dissolve. The first one he used to fasten himself to be able to move with incredible speed. The second summoned magical daggers into both his hands, glowing with greenish light. He cast no more spells. He was ready for a duel.

Diego de la Moota being not only a warlock of the Thirteenth Order but also a grandmaster of the Blackguard Order of Kreto and therefore an exceptional weapon master.

Ironically, he made a bow before the child but then when the kid almost tore his head off with a single swipe of his hand, he abandoned property, goofing off and taking things light as his face became emotionless just like his opponents and began concentrating only on the fight.

They fought as if they weren't human. They moved as quick as lightning bolts from the sky.

The person looking like a child clawed at the warlock with his left hand and tried to tear his heart out with the right.

Diego de la Moota struck forward with both his daggers, intending to stab him in the neck, then severe his head by moving both daggers crosswise.

It was a well practiced movement, many an enemy have

lost their lives like this, the boy however was too fast and too experienced a fighter for the maneuver to work.

The kid dodged, even the nearest dagger missing him by several inches. He only ran into a small cut, when the warlock pulled his weapons back moving them sideways. Even this only happened because he did not care about defending himself, he wanted to go through with his attack - tearing off the warlock's head and tearing out his heart all at once.

The quarter-inch cut struck the kid on the neck. It seemed serious at first glance but the wound did not bleed!

The warlock didn't seem interested in this new turn of events. His face did not betray his emotions, even though he was very glad with what he saw.

An average warrior would have been frightened, noticing his enemy had no blood running in his veins. Diego de la Moota was filled with endless satisfaction by the fact, something he hid quite well.

The reason the kid has no blood running in his veins is that he is undead. And this is the same reason he was not affected by the death magic of Belmie. And here he was, foolishly thinking he found an enemy of such power that they resisted the death spell easily.

That's not the case! He is dealing with a simple undead. Maybe a vampire. It matters not! He will soon destroy it. His only regret now was that he wasted his frighteningly powerful death spell on a corpse.

The young kid missed his attack on the heart, all he managed was tearing off a single button. The strike of his other hand however managed to hit his enemy right on the mark and even though he could not tear the head off, he did have a quite sizeable chunk of meat in his hand when he pulled it back.

The warlock grabbed at his missing half a face angrily. His skull was showing beneath the skin. Only for a second though, his regenerative skin spell healed the wound. But the, the protective aura evaporated. From now on, Diego de la Moota thought all his actions through twice. A reckless attack like the previous one didn't even enter his mind.

He was always using one dagger to keep his foe at bay, while trying to inflict small wounds with the other among the flailing arms. He was a more experienced fighter than the undead child but even with his spell of haste, he seemed sluggish next to his opponent.

Experience however did win over quickness - at least for a single slice.

De la Moota wounded his foe on the stomach. He adopted a defensive stance with both daggers to see the effects of his assault. He examined the long cut. Silently, he congratulated himself. Then he watched for signs of the wound starting to regenerate. Either his magical daggers were powerful enough to prevent self healing or the undead child possessed no regenerative capabilities - his wound obviously did not heal.

Diego de la Moota continued to fight with an elevated confidence. He hit his enemy with his daggers three more times. He had a hard time doing it. The child proved to be incredibly quick.

De la Moota was beginning to tire. The undead knew no such feeling.

The warlock suffered a tiny hit. His first actual wound! He felt no such shame in years! The beast clawed him on his left hand. He shook it angrily.

He decided not to play any more games. He would rather take a risk and try to finish off his opponent right now.

He attacked with both daggers and inflicted two new wounds - although both nonlethal - on the child's body. Then he stabbed again and again. The undead retaliated without success. He leapt, crouched and flailed like a whirlwind but was unable to outplay or counter devilish fighting ability of the warlock.

Diego de la Moota was starting to dance a maddened

dance macabre around him with his two daggers glowing with ghostly light.

Behemor, Yabbagabb and Zaislo were still in the process of trying to wake Weevil up. Father Floranus ran to the cellar from de la Moota's death spell and has not returned yet.

The innkeeper Grog was still crouching behind his table and was gathering courage to raise his head and look around in his inn. One guest however was emboldened by the sight of the first real wound on Diego de la Moota and decided to act.

Diego de la Moota was slicing and dicing his opponent as if he spent every day in his life cutting undead children to pieces. He committed himself fully to the slaughter. His disguise was gone, he was acting no more. He appeared as himself: a salivating, raging beast frothing at the mouth. He was growling, hissing, cackling and roaring…

…and then he was grabbing at his throat!

A shadow ran past him. Tifur, with his tiny dagger in his hand - for the second time today - sliced his throat from ear to ear. This time however, the wound did not regenerate. The blood of the warlock started to spurt. Dropping his weapons, he grabbed at his lethal neck injury. His animalistic rage was replaced by fear.

"Medic!" he groaned.

He stared at Tifur with huge, frightened eyes. The assassin ran past after his successful sneak attack for after previous events, he was unsure about a single cutten throat being enough to destroy Diego de la Moota.

The warlock looked at the kid with a grim face.

"Where is the healer?!" he whined "What are you standing around for, kid?! Call for help!"

The undead child hit him several times.

Right the first one made him fall to his knees. The next hit made his face unrecognizably broken, and after all the others one could not tell if he was even human. A bloody pile of meat, bones and guts was all that remained of

Diego de la Moota, count of Peredon, lord of Valpurg, the grandmaster of the Black Knights of Kreto, warlock of the Thirteenth Circle, carrier of the Belmie's death magic. He dissolved into the myriad of acid burnt, frozen, blown up and sliced up corpses.

Chapter 10
Endgame

"How come you have dozens of wounds and you are still not bleeding to death?" Tifur asked the kid suspiciously. "In fact, how were you able to fight so amazingly?"

"I am a psion." the child answered. "I provide my own magical energies. I use my mental powers to stop bleeding, increase the strength and speed of my punches and this is what allows me to look younger than I am."

The voice of the child was like his face. Cold and emotionless.

He said no more, and left the assassin to his own devices.

Tifur didn't care. Only know did he think about who he managed to kill. Diego de la Moota, the dreaded warlock!

He felt the need to sit down and drink something.

High on the rush of victory, he stepped up to the drunkard's table.

"Can I sit down?" he asked.

"If you have a chair" Zaislo grunted.

Tifur grabbed a three-legged chair from a neighboring

table and made himself at home.

Automatically, Yabbagabb pushed a cup of noble tokelnauer toward him friendlily.

"Don't go around giving it away hastily!" warned Zaislo. Then he shook the barrel, and merrily acknowledged that it had plenty of wine left. This made him calm down and able to concentrate on other things.

"Holy hell! It was a scary battle there!"

"You are telling me? I took part!" Tifur proudly stated "but what's going on with your goblin friend? He is not looking too well."

"Who are you calling a friend to this kobold-fart?" Zaislo took offense "there is nothing wrong with him. He took a lightning bolt to the face from the warlock. But the boy took it well. The same cannot be said about taking booze. He sort of knocked himself out a bit!"

Tifur took the cup offered to him. Before starting to drink the wine, he put a broad-bladed knife on the table. In answer to Zaislo's uncomprehending questions he explained that this is a simple security measure for him. The knife serves as a mirror. If someone were to sneak up on him from behind, he would see the attacker in time on the blade.

"Aren't you a little bit paranoid?" the other asked again "Whatever! Ummm...you do know though that wine is a company drink? It's no good drinking it alone." he warned the assassin then drunk with him. Yabbagabb did the same. Conjuring a cup, he filled it with wine then clinked his cup together with Tifur's. While the assassin was sipping carefully, enjoying every drop of the noble drink, Yabbagabb gulped greedily. From this point on, there was not much the fighter-mage was able to recall.

Grog's curiosity overcame his cowardice and since he hasn't heard any battle noises for a while he climbed out from behind his cover.

He was amazed by the sight of the latest destruction

but truth to be told there was nothing that could surprise him anymore. He long ago abandoned counting his monetary loss, he was at the point where he no longer cared who will live and who won't.

The last twenty four hours were character forming for him. Up until now he did have a certain amount of bad conscience when he murdered and robbed his guests using his trapdoor beds. The last few hours however he had to deal such horrid guests, monsters and villains that from now on he wanted every single creature stumbling into his tavern to meet his spike-trap.

At this time however, he was pondering something else. Any minute now, the number of unwanted guests could increase by one. Even though an important guest like a demon lord has never graced the Yellow Serpent in all its years of operation, he was not happy about the arrival of the infernal creature.

He walked among the tables, searching for the heart of the dwarven warrior. He saw multiple hearts torn out but the one he seeked was with Dragwaren's corpse. He picked the heart up, looked around in the room then approached the table of the drunkards. He turned toward the man wearing a crimson cloak with ornate symbols on the mantle.

"I think you a mageecian by your sstyle of dress. Are you?"

"Yuhh" Yabbagabb said, while his eyes were looking at different directions.

"Are you?" Grog repeated the question for he wasn't sure about Yabbagabb's answer.

The fighter-mage nodded furiously.

"In that casse, you are thee onlee persson left in the inn who could sstop the deemon. To mee it iss eequal if you baniss eet or make eet sserve you, jusst try to control eet! Do you undersstand?"

"Uhum, yeah!" Yabbagabb mumbled while rubbing his eyes.

With a weary sigh and shaking his head the innkeeper gave the drunkard the heart.

"Be careful with eet ass if it wass your own child! You need to use eet to sstop the deemon!"

"Aham, uhum, food!" Yabbagabb answered, then swallowed the heart.

The thin, slanted eyes of Grog widened to the size of tennis balls.

"What deed you do! You ate our lasst chansse! You have condemned uss all to death!" he exclaimed, still shaking his head.

"Food" Yabbagabb answered with innocent naivete as he tried to wipe the blood off his face but he only managed to spread it around.

Seeing the disgusting sight almost made the innkeeper vomit.

"Thiss dissgussting sspasstic ate the demon-controlling heart!" He shouted at the others. This made Yabbagabb laugh.

"My comrade is a true gourmet!" Zaislo cackled, and patted the fighter-mage's back.

Tifur was rendered speechless. He sat there unmoving.

Raging, Grog left them behind.

The twelve-looking child stood over the corpse of the albino man for a long time.

His face at this moment was anything but emotionless. His eyes betrayed a bestial fury. He smelled the corpse thoroughly, and his nose which wasn't human or capable of recognizing the scents of food or flowers, identified the characteristic scent of deadly poison.

Turning his nose upward, he smelled around the room. Then he started walking toward the table of the drunkards. He had an excellent sense of smell, even though this sense of his was highly selective in function. He was a vampire, just as Diego de la Moota suspected. A vampire lord of Goarra. A member of the Fighter Clan. And as such he could neither fly nor cast spells. He had no knowledge of enchantments or turning into a bat. But he was a fierce warrior. He loved the smell of blood and corpses. Even from miles afar his heart was warmed by these pleasant scents. He used to dislike poisons before. But ever since he died, he had a hard time finding scents that affected his distorted soul. His body became invulnerable against deadly poisons. Like a weird gourmet, he smelled poisonous substances for their scent and consumed them for their taste.

Smelling the air, he knew exactly there the scent of the poisoned dart were coming from. The vial in the side pocket of the upper vestment on the black clad man at the drunkard's table emitted the same scent.

As he approached the young assassin without making any noise and a murderous look on his face, he grew his canines into four inch long spikes and formed his nails into sharp talons - his mission was a failure so it was unnecessary to disguise himself anymore - and decided to kill everyone in the inn.

But first he is going to kill Tifur, the assassin.

"You truly won't intervene in anything?" Tifur asked, unbelieving from his table companions "were for example a monster sneaking up on one of us, would you not warn them?"

"You will soon get an answer to that, stranger!" a laughing Zaislo answered.

"I don't get it" Tifur said and spared a suspicious glance at his knife blade functioning as a mirror.

Then there was a loud crack, and the blood of the assassin was everywhere.

The vampire didn't go for anything fancy, he broke his neck and tore his head off in one go.

Tifur's caution was of no use. He could not see his assailant in the broad bladed knife. The vampire had no mirror image to see.

"Who are you and why have you killed this young man?" asked Behemor the boy grimly.

"My name is Kraschchah" the undead creature hissed into the face of the drunkards as he tossed Tifur's corpse aside. "I am a vampire lord! This pathetic human worm destroyed my life's work, the resurrection of the ancient vampire Bruddzaih. I spent forty years to collect all components of the ritual: Bruddzaih's left hand, the cave which is the source of magical energies, the stars alignment, the eleven conjurers - vampire lords, all of them- the resurrection scroll, all those material components, blood rubies worth fifty thousand gold and a proper sacrifice, a virgin albino man, born on the first day of the Bloodmoon and turning forty exactly on the day of the ceremony. And this pathetic human worm has killed the albino, the most important, indispensable component of the ritual. He destroyed my mission! He destroyed my reason to live!"

"Who the hell cares?" sighed Zaislo, tired and angry "blathering all this idiocy! Shut up and go to hell! I hate creatures who prefer blood to wine!"

This scolding was all the vampire lord needed. Roaring, he sliced with his hand ending in knife-sized talons to cut the alcoholic tavern brawler in half…

"Fuckeeng adventurrerss!" Grog cursed as he charged up with large strides from the cellar. "I weell sshow you! A meenute and you weel bee beggeeng for your livess!"

He wiped the sweat off his brows with his hand shaking from nerves.

"My poor old motheer! Shee alwayss ssaid: Dearr sson, sstay away from tavernss, don't go near them! And there I go, opening a tavern! Am I crazy? Why didn't I lissten to you, dear motheer!"

Father Floranus came up on the stairs in human form. His skin thickened, his hands ending in tiger claws.

Grog was so busy with his thoughts that he almost ran

into him. Seeing the druid made him grab toward his heart in fright. He thought it was the spike-tarp-bound father Benetius coming back from the dead to take his revenge.

Shaking, he pulled out his good luck charm, a four leaf clover made from metal, hanging on a golden chain under his tunic. He clutched it strongly to gain some moral support from it.

"Lady Luck why are you doing thiss to mee?" he pleaded to her.

The druid opened his mouth to answer but Grog had no intentions of listening.

Everyone in this accursed inn wanted to kill each other. The only thing he can do is get ahead of the others and kill everyone himself.

Undead, monsters, warlocks, demons - it was too much for him. It's time he showed something himself.

He threw himself at the druid, pushing him off balance. They both fell down the stairs.

The druid's head smashed into the freestone floor with a loud crack. A few seconds later he regained his senses, but Grog already disappeared into a side corridor by then.

"You cannot escape!" the father shouted after him, grinding his fearsome tiger claws on each other "As the executioner of the Starry Night Druidic order it is my honor to avenge our dead brother. The soul of father Benetius can only rest if his murderer follows him into the grave to serve him till the end of time!"

He turned into the side corridor. Stealthily, like a real tiger he began stalking his victim.

"Your fate is written! You chose it yourself when you killed father Benetius!"

He smelled the air. His senses, enhanced by magic told them where the innkeeper of the Yellow Serpent was hiding.

In the wall!

Behind the wall, he corrected himself.

He examined the cracks in the freestone carefully and saw that a secret door was built into the wall. He stroked the door. His tiger claws made a sharp, ear-piercing noise scratching the stone wall.

"Come out! Face the consequences of your actions!"

A rumbling noise came from behind the door making the whole corridor shake. Then Grog's voice came, also from behind the door.

"Feer not, good woodlander! I weel fasse the conssequenses! Just ass you weel have to fasse them for your foolish actionss! For I have to ssay it wass rather foolish of you daring to come heer alone."

Grog finished his speech with a loud laugh. There was no trace of fear in his voice.

Another rumbling noise shook the corridor. The walls started to crack in a few places.

Father Floraus stumbled back.

The wall he has been stroking with his tiger-clawed hand burst into his face. His thickened skin was of no use, the large pieces of rock wounded him severely and pushed him off his feet.

Everything was covered by thick dust.

By the time the dust settled, father Floraus already knew that he was dealt the role of the hunted in this game and not the hunter. He felt sorry for brother Benetius and cursed himself.

He failed!

He closed his eyes as the huge stone monster crushed him beneath its feet.

After reading the letter delivered a few minutes ago by the Alamander cleric twice, centurion Ibrak Farberg, commander of Oopolk morosely put it to the flame of the candle. He watched as the paper caught fire and burned.

The mission of the Alamandar grandmaster has been unsuccessful. The Protector Patriarch was undertaking an astral journey. After a lengthy discussion, the circle of leading clerics made contact with him, but his holiness had more important things to do than saving a few drunkards. He could be contacted for an audience in six days at the earliest.

Farberg could not wait six days. He has already risked a lot. He cannot endanger the lives of Kravan's citizens any longer. The center of the infectious curse has to be eradicated as fast as possible.

He sighed wearily. He looked at the remains of the burned paper and thought about the people stuck in the inn. Soon they will share the fate of the letter announcing their death sentence.

He shouted: "Lieutenant!"

The door opened and a young man entered the room. He stopped before centurion Farberg and stood at attention. He saluted.

The centurion returned the salute with a sloppy wave.

"Report!" he ordered in a weary voice.

"Sir, strange noises continue to emerge from behind the walls of the Yellow Serpent. Howls, shouting, the sound of explosions and according to the most recent reports a rumbling noise coming from underground. Permission to check it out with a unit, sir!"

Centurion Farberg waved his concerns aside.

"No need, soldier. Call the unit commanders of the fire mages together and relay my orders to them: the Yellow Serpent needs to be blown up without delay! I expect a united flame strike spell from them.Only ashes and dust shall remain, even from the ones hiding in the cellar. Order our troops to back off, evacuate the nearby buildings and call the sentries off the city wall! The magic of the fire mages results in earthquakes which can collapse other buildings. Do all you can for the safety of the citizens. That is all, lieutenant, dismissed!"

Even though Zaislo was so drunk he could barely see out of his own eyes, he had every nuance of tavern brawling in his blood.

He evaded the vampire's claws with a smile that looked more like a snarl, and he had his broadsword in his hands in the blink of an eye. He was beginning to get sleepy due to the alcohol and the long night so he was especially happy about the incoming thrilling exercise.

He was not even deterred by the fact that vampires can only be killed by magical weapons or wooden stakes driven through their hearts. He had neither but was not bothered. He had an optimistic outlook about most things - especially when he had enough to drink. He will sharpen a wooden skate mid-fight, that's all.

Behemor picked up his five feet long, rusty two-handed battleaxe from under the table in a languid move. The movement felt good for his back was a bit numb from all the sitting. He felt neither lust for battle nor fear, he wasn't even excited.

The goblin slept like a log.

Yabbagabb put his feet up on the bench, his elbows on the table and watched the show as if he was in the theatre. He understood precious little of the whole thing.

The vampire aimed for Zaislo's heart. His attack was interrupted by the noise of rumbling feet. Someone or something was coming up the stairs. According to the rumble, it was a large creature. Its steps shook the whole inn.

A stuffed gnoll trophy fell off the wall It almost hit Yabbagabb in the head.

Grog appeared on the stairs leading to the cellar.

"Bloodee heart-eeter, tavern-burneer, degeenerate mongreel, primeetive oafish brute and disgusteeng bloodssuckeer!" he adressed in turn Yabbagabb, Zaislo, Weevil, Behemor and finally Kraschchah. "You shall all die! Kill them, golem!" he ordered the monstrum lurking behind him.

"My deer old motheer alwayss said that if you have to open an inn, sson and if - thank the godss - it ees goeeng well and profeetable you sshould buy a protecteeve magic item from the profitss. A teleportation reeng that allowss you to sstreak if thingss go badlee. But Grog iss not one to jusst flee when there are a few dark cloudss on the horeezon. Who the hell needss a teleprottion reeng! Sstone golem! Thatss the sstuff! I onlee regret not beeing able to buy two! Grog will not run like a teene mousse from a cat. He protectss what's hiss!"

The golem started to approach the five remaining guests.

Kraschchah abandoned his plan to murder the tavern scum. He focused all his attention on the new enemy unlike Zaislo who did not care about the gigantic monstrum. Everything in the right time! First the vampire then the golem.

He broke a chair's leg off and started to sharpen it with his broadsword.

Behemor gave a huge yawn.

He didn't feel strong and determined enough to fight the innkeeper's pet. He went under the stairs leading to the upper level with a cup of wine - the stone golem would not fit there.

Yabbagabb looked at Weevil. Seeing that the goblin didn't move an inch, he decided not to do anything either.

The vampire lord hissed like a snake, only much louder. He raised his arm and pulled it back before rushing head on toward the golem. He wanted to destroy it with a single, lethal strike.

For a long second they were running headfirst into each other then when there was almost no distance left between them, he jumped into the air.

He put all his strength into this single strike.

The slow golem could not dodge. It was hit on the head. The stone skin started to crumble on its face and after a moment of hesitation it fell forward, burying the vampire under itself.

Kraschchah tried to jump aside, panicked but the

collapsing behemoth fell on him.

Yabbagabb clapped, satisfied.

Grog's face fell.

You couldn't tell who survived. Did any of them survive?

The golem started to move but you still couldn't tell if it was moving itself or if the vampire was trying to squeeze himself out from under the heavy body.

Then the golem rose from the earth just like the statue Sleeping God on Karavan's main square two years ago to the great fright of the people.

Zaislo stopped his chiseling. There was no need for it anymore. He expanded his knowledge about destroying vampires. If you don't have a magical weapon or a skate burying them under a four ton stone golem will do.

It seemed like the most effective method too. Kraschchah looked like a badly made gigantic meat pancake.

But now the alcoholic tavern brawler had to ponder what to use destroying a stone golem.

Images of ballistae, catapults and battering rams carried by dozens of people filled his wine addled brain.

To hell with the vampire not winning this fight! He would have had a so much easier time with him! After all it is easier to put a wooden stake together than it is a catapult.

What if he were to kill that miserable innkeeper? Sadly the golem would still fulfill the command. No, no. He will not change the order. First he will destroy the golem, then it will be time for the innkeeper.

It wasn't him however whom the stone golem started to approach. It targeted the peacefully drinking Yabbagabb…

In the middle of the pentagram, painted with blood on the wall of the upstairs room the corpse of the dwarf nailed there started to twitch. A long tear appeared on his chest. Dark, foul sulphurous gases emerged from the wound.

A hand, dirty with blood and ripped entrails reached out from the dwarf's gut. It wasn't a human hand, it wasn't even of this world. It did not belong to a mortal - it was made for destroying mortals. It's fingers ending in long, sharp claws, the hand was one and a half times as large as an adult humans. It was sitting on a sinewy, long arm. Then the creature's shoulder appeared. The dwarf blew to pieces. The monstrosity emerged.

With a long, blood-chilling growl, unable to be produced by a human throat the demon lord announced his arrival to this lowly world.

The earth shook.

Yabbagabb was trading glances between the charging golem and the sleeping goblin.

"A new table companion is coming" he was mumbling to the goblin.

Then he stared at the ten-feet tall, stocky sone colossus. He couldn't do anything. He was too drunk to run away and he had no chance beating the golem. So he did not move.

Taking advantage of his last seconds, he poured another cup of noble tokelnauer into his mouth.

"See you in hell, Yabbagabb! Man, you got properly wasted there!" he heard the goodbye from Zaislo.

Yabbagabb answered the words of the alcoholic tavern brawler with a kind smile, and he raised his right arm up. Turning his palm away from himself, he closed his fist, with only his middle finger pointing toward the sky. This was a common gesture with him. It was something he did when he wanted someone to go to hell, when he was very happy, when something amazed or exasperated him and when he faced death. Grim features appeared on his face.

Lady Luck has left him. Despite all the funny adventures he gifted and amused her with. Or did she?

He wanted to gather his thoughts but at the moment it was not working out for him. He looked around in the room to see if he could find something that would work against the golem.

There were no effective weapons or tools around. He cannot count on his table companions either. Weevil is asleep, Zaislo is laughing at him, Behemor is tired and passive. They can go, climb into a troll's arsehole! Boorish oafs!

The gods help those who help themselves, that's what they all say, but where is the solution here?

He defeated plenty of dangerous adventurers, powerful fire mages, watchful tyrants, even a lesser demon with cunning and tricks and just a bit of luck. Why would he fall now? But what could he do? Where is the solution? Where is Lady Luck now?

And then the answer and the solution entered his brain, blowing his mind - before the golem's foot could - like a bomb.

A sly smile appeared on Yabbagabb's face. Then it vanished because he was so drunk he actually forgot his life-saving idea.

"Don't fuck with me!" he whimpered.

The golem was ten feet away.

Where is Lady Luck now? Why doesn't she help him? Did he insult her in some way?

And then he remembered the solution again!

Lady Luck was looking down at him from the medallion of the Yellow Serpent's owner with large, sparkling eyes.

Yabbagabb glanced at Behemor.

"Hey, Behemor! Behemor, our favorite innkeeper is a follower of Lady Luck! Look at the medal he is wearing! A four-leaf clover! A symbol of Lady Luck!"

Behemor came out from the alcove under the stairs. Sleepiness left his eyes in an instant.

"Do you see the medal?"

Muscles were starting to twitch on the barbarian's arm. Yabbagabb went on:

"This is a filthy Lady Luck follower! Look at his eyes! The man is an obsessed fanatic!"

Behemor started frothing at the mouth.

"Cursed Lady Luck fanatics! Will you never just give out?!" the barbarian shouted and swinging his battle axe high in the air he charged at the innkeeper.

"Give my message to the dirty bitch! I will murder her clerics and followers until I exterminate all of them! I will make her stop spreading her false words in this world."

The last sentence he shouted, completely beside himself with rage. Veins were bulging out on his face, his head was becoming fiery red and his whole body shook with anger. His brain was consumed by berserker rage!

This wasn't the same Behemor who was slouching under the stairs a minute ago. He shed his civilized skin off. He became an animal. His muscles filled with dreadful power. His spirit was enveloped by a dark cloud. He knew no fear, no pain and no mercy. He only felt desire - to destroy, to kill!

"Back, goleem!" Grog shouted, seeing the barbarian thundering toward him, obviously insane. "Leave the heart-eeter! Keell the rabeed bruteesh oaf!"

The golem stopped, two feet in front of Yabbagabb. His shadow fell on the fighter-mage. It turned around, and with its raised fists- which resembled hundred-pound stone balls - knocked the barbarian down as he was rushing past it.

Behemor fell back with a thunderous rumble, hitting the inn's floor.

Yabbagabb hissed. He felt he would meet the same fate soon.

Grog snarled, and nodded, satisfied.

Zaislo spat but did nothing else. He was still pondering how he should go about destroying the golem.

Behemor moved...he raised his head!

"By all the saints!" Zaislo said, unbelieving. "He survived what a man cannot!"

Grog was backing away, astonished.

"On your feet, you pansy!" the alcoholic tavern brawler shouted at the barbarian.

Behemor roared like a lion. As if he found the hit on him lacking, he smashed his forehead into the floor three times. His blood was pouring into his eyes by the gallon. This was how he stoked his battle rage then he stood up from the ground.

The innkeeper was shouting in despair:

"What are you waiteeng for, you usseless pile of sstoness? He iss jusst a man! Keel heem alredee!"

The golem attacked again, using the same move as before. This time however Behemor wasn't caught unaware by the strike. Raising his oak-like arms he caught the creature's fist. Continuing to roar like a lion, he managed to keep the two hundred pound stone ball in the air.

"Keell heem!" shouted Grog.

"You are stronger Behemor!" Zaislo encouraged the barbarian. "Play with it for a while, then finish it!"

The barbarian stepped aside, twisted the arm of the colossus with an incredible strength and elan then letting go of it, he used a straight kick to make the unbalanced golem fall over. Before his foe even hit the ground he was already leaping onto it with his battle axe in hand. He hit it's head with four amazingly powerful strikes, making half of its face fall of but unable to take it out of the fight. It stood up and then made two jabs at the barbarian, first with the right hand and then with the left. Behemor dodged the attacks, in fact he retaliated instantly. The golem weighing four tons stumbled back from the coming hits. Behemor took it head on. He jumped up and headbutted his enemy.

Either Behemor's head was harder than stone or perhaps it was Grog who bought faulty merchandise from the mage order of Edo but what was left of the golem's head burst into tiny pebbles.

The headless monster continued to flail around, causing a frightening amount of destruction in the inn's furniture. Suddenly its slab of a hand struck the barbarian dancing around it.

Behemor flew across the room with a broken face. It was the wall of the yellow serpent that ended his flight. He had the opportunity to study the inn's floor again. Keeping his battleaxe in his right hand, he picked up a warhammer lying on the floor with his left, then stood up and charged again with the anger of a raging storm, the power of a roaring waterfall and the fanaticism of an orcish army marching to war.

The golem which finished off father Floranus, executioner of the druids with ease and buried and splattered Kraschchah, the vampire lord beneath it using only its weight proved to be a weak and helpless opponent to Behemor driving himself into a berserker rage. The barbarian's strikes were raining upon it by the dozen from left and right alike. The alternating battleaxe and warhammer were making a rhythmic noise.

Grog had enough of what he saw. He didn't need to be a fortune teller to know how the fight will end. Still, he could not believe his eyes. He worked his whole life to buy the golem. It cost him forty thousand gold pieces! He made himself believe that the golem was going to be capable of defeating the demon lord and then a simple barbarian smashes it to pebbles. The stupid oaf wrecked his life's work.

Thus far the barbarian was occupied by his fight with the golem, so Grog was able to escape from him. Without hesitating he ran up the stairs and along the corridor.

He had to hide somewhere. The room where they killed the dwarf had a secret alcove. He could wait out the end of this madness there. If he survives this day, he is going to have a change of careers. He should have listened to his mother from the beginning.

He stepped inside the dark room and closed the door.

He smelled a sulphuric smell. There was something under his feet that made a squelching noise. He bent down and touched the floor. He found small shreds of meat, it was all that was left of the dwarven sacrifice.

What happened to this one?

He felt hot steam on the back of his neck.

He turned around.

Even though he couldn't see the demon itself, only the blazing eyes, he knew that things went wrong a long time ago. His life should have been different.

His last words were: "My poor old motheeeeeer!"

Then the demon lord tore his head off.

With a clumsy final strike, Behemor broke the golem to pieces.

Yabbagabb stumbled closer to the pile of stones and took a pebble as a souvenir.

Meanwhile, the barbarian was furiously searching for the innkeeper.

"Where did the hireling of the luck-bitch go?" he snarled at Zaislo who was just about to congratulate him for his amazing victory over the stone golem.

"I was astonished by your primitive fighting style!"

"He has to be around here somewhere!" Behemor growled and went on upturning the tables one after another to see if he was hiding under them.

Yabbagabb helped him pushing them over.

Weevil opened his eyes.

"What's with all this noise?" he whined "Stop making it please, my head is about to burst!"

"Drink!" Zaislo grunted at him "That will make the headache go away."

Weevil took a large sip from the tolkenauer red.

His headache was gone in an instant. On the other hand he started to feel dizzy and sick in the stomach. He could not remember what happened. His last hazy memory was singing together with the others and talking about dragons.

"Did something happen that I should know about?" he asked, uncertain as he looked around. Piles of corpses, broken furniture, vines, black tentacles cut in half, the remains of a splattered vampire and a stone golem broken apart...

"What happened?" he asked the same question again.

"No idea." Yabbagabb mumbled.

"Nothing interesting" Zaislo summarized the events. Then he added:

"There is only the four of us left. The innkeeper is gone and the others are dead."

Weevil was shocked by the news. Suddenly his memories returned: Diego de la Moota's fight with the guests of the inn, the lingering agony of the ranger and the priestess of life Schiza under the ice dome.

He turned where the ice prison was supposed to be, but it wasn't there. The warlock was dead and his dark magic has vanished with him. He wasn't interested in what happened. He turned his head away so he didn't have to see Schiza among the dead. He threw up... He heard Zaislo laughing at him.

He stood up, drank from the wine barrel then wiped his mouth.

"What is the point to all of this? What is the point in living?" he asked bitterly.

"To feast, to fight, to bed women" Zaislo winked at him.

"Nothing! There is no point to it" Behemor growled as he turned another table over. " except perhaps trying to send as many worshippers of Lady Luck to their demise as possible before we die ourselves."

Yabbagabb said nothing. He never cared for such questions.

Weevil was not satisfied with the answers.

"I will answer my own question. I see now that I have to answer even my own questions."

He took a swig once again, climbed up on top of the wine barrel, collected his thoughts and then delivered the following speech while waving his hands around:

"I have come to recognize two type of intelligent species. The first consist of those who care about nothing, the second of those who try to find a meaning to life. The first type lives without a care, the second type set goals for themselves. The mission for the second type is to serve. Deeds become meaningless if their sole purpose is fulfilling selfish desires. Securing the future for their children is enough for most people. Others offer their every act to the service of a God. Thus their existence gains a purpose. They live, they fight to make their faith and emotions toward their God expand into infinity. And they are right to think and do so. After all, no matter how little of a speck of dust they seem compared to the Gods, they are not. They are parts of them. They are mighty! Faith makes them mighty. It's the power of faith that determines how much someone will become part of a God he believed in at the moment of their death when they merge with Them. This is the life of the faithful. But what meaning has one's life who doesn't truly follow any god, who is a prisoner to their own desires and gives a free reign to all his emotions?

Of course, it still has meaning" he added, easing up a little "If we examine the problem on the level of society. Those who follow no God but still believe - believe in the power of the community. They think themselves a part of a community. They procure descendants, recreating themselves to sow the seeds of continuity.

They fight for progression. For the world is progressing - even when a few lifetimes aren't enough to notice the change. I talked a lot about this with a six-thousand year old demon. I learned from him that if magic was not there in a noticeable quantity in our world, our knowledge and society would develop much faster, we would get to know ourself and our environment much better, we wouldn't limit the advancement of science and would become more mature."

He paused for a second to think.

"I see you don't care about this at all Zaislo. Of course there are those who belong into a type that cares about nothing. This is an enviable position as long as one can enjoy it and won't get fed up with it after some time. But sooner or later everyone will get fed up." he said, glancing at the alcoholic tavern brawler.

Zaislo did not like the look the goblin was giving him. He answered angrily:

"I cannot preach with a zeal like yours. But you can also only do it because you don't use your pecker enough. You live out your suppressed carnal urges in long, useless and meaningless speeches."

Weevil climbed down from the barrel.

"You are right Zaislo. I have never slept with a goblin woman."

"For all the saints, I wouldn't have done it with those either!"

"Only with the orcs!" Yabbagabb giggled.

This moment the starting accord of flame strike spell's erupted from two hundred throats. The prayer of the Alamandar priests that they chanted for the salvation of the guest's souls that were trapped in the inn could not be heard among the song of the fire mages.

Tired from upturning tables, Behemor stumbled back to his place and sat down next to the goblin. His berserker rage was gone.

Morosely, he examined his companions.

The sickness was spreading more and more on them. The dark spots on their skin grew to palm-sized blotches. The first ulcers and carbuncles were also starting to appear in Yabbagabb and Zaislo. The rotting process was speeding up.

The silence was broken by a fearsome roar coming from the room upstairs. The group knew the demon has arrived.

The only remaining question was if it will be the deadly disease that kills them, the spell of the fire mages or the demon lord.

Zaislo stepped up to Weevil and said.

"There is no point in waiting any longer, goblin. The guests of the inn are dead, don't spare your strength any longer. If you are indeed as powerful as you said then it's time to heal us and open the gates to the planes or whatever. I say let's get the hell out of here!"

The goblin turned to Zaislo with his all-knowing melancholy eye.

"Power" he savored the word "am I as powerful? And if I am? What does it matter? Power if a horrid curse which weighs down heavily on your shoulders, bends your back, drives your soul to madness and makes your journey into death harder. A powerful man leaves more behind than a miserable wretch - and this is what makes dying painful for him. Everything he fought for, all he gained by his own sweat and pain: his belief in himself, his power and his wonder he sacrifices when he makes his final goodbye to the world. Power" he savored the word again, with deep hatred "Stupid is the man who desires power!"

"What moronic rambling is this again for god's sake!?" Zaislo was shaking his head. "Can you help us, or were you lying through your teeth this whole time?"

"I am powerful. Perhaps the most powerful goblin cleric in the whole world. But I made myself seem stronger than I am. I was not born a man and therefore I hate myself. Humans - I lied when calling them stupid, I was only envious - are worthy of admiration. I am amazed by their beauty, their diversity but mostly by their intelligence which - and believe me, I know - is as fascinating and endless as the universe.

As a goblin, I could never become such a mighty cleric

as I would have been able to as a human. I have reached the limits of my race and there is no way up. I can never become as powerful a cleric as I wanted to be."

He didn't say, but he thought: 'I can never have enough power to raise my dead beloved from the dead.'

"So this means?!" Zaislo asked threateningly, obviously irritated.

"I can neither cure nor teleport you" the goblin sighed "I am sorry."

For a long moment, Zaislo looked silently into the air. Then he stood up from the table and pulled out his broadsword.

Yabbagabb did not react to the goblin's statement. He was picking the abscess on his left arm absent-mindedly, making it sprout a pus-like secretion onto Behemor's chest.

The barbarian either didn't notice what the fighter-mage was doing or he did not care about Yabbagabb using him as target practice.

"I knew it" he grumbled "I knew we were all going to die. As unlucky as I am it could not have gone any differently. Accursed Lady Luck!"

The demon appeared on top of the stairs. His hooves hit the steps with sharp clops. He hissed as he drew a breath between his needle-sharp teeth, then exhaled it through his huge nostrils as steaming hot mist. It moved with slow, coordinated movements.

Yabbagabb found it so amusing that he could fight a demon lord that he could not stop rejoicing. He was making loud hoots.

Behemor's lips pointed downwards. He stared ahead of him gloomily.

The goblin jumped between the demon and his companions from the bench.

"We will not surrender without a fight!" he shouted "Get up, and let's show him who we are!"

"We are cattle driven to slaughter" Behemor

murmured.

"Speak for yourself!" Zaislo growled at him.

Just a second ago the alcoholic tavern brawler was planning on knocking Weevil out but he was impressed by the goblin's spunk and decided on slaughtering the demon instead.

The demon lord stepped off the last stair and looked his victims in the eye.

'Four heartbeats worth of time' he thought. 'Not more.' that will be enough for him to finish them off.

"What are you looking at, pig head?" Zaislo addressed him "Did you get a cramp in your leg or are you afraid? Come on closer! Don't make me go there! It won't hurt, I promise!"

"It's not even a pig head!" Yabbagabb corrected him "pigs have no horns. Such hideous, ugly bent stub of a horn you can only find on mentally retarded cows "

This once, Zaislo did not mind having his words corrected.

"A cow then." he agreed with Yabbagabb. Examining the demon better, he nodded in agreement. "You might be right, it is just like a large, mentally retarded cow."

"A really fat, large, mentally retarded cow!" Yabbagabb continued.

"Yeah a fat cow."

"Fat cow with wings."

"Angry, fat cow with wings. What shall we make of this, friends?" Zaislo was asking as he continued to examine the monster more closely, which considering its fearsome muscles, sharp, deadly claws and teeth, its hooves capable of trampling castle gates down, huge horns, terrifying tail and angrily flapping wings - they rose with the taking of each breath and lowered when it exhaled - didn't actually resemble a cow all that much.

"Sausages" Yabbagabb answered in a completely natural voice.

"What?"

"Sausages. We should make some sausages."

"What sort of sausages?"

"Demon sausages!"

The demon lord had enough of the one sided conversation. He bellowed at the top of his voice and lunged at them to tear them to pieces.

There are few creatures posessing greater power in the known universe than the demon lord attacking Behemor, Weevil Zaislo and Yabbagabb. Were it a hundred Behemors a hundred Weevils a hundred Zaislos and a hundred Yabbagabbs opposing him stone cold sober and with a clear head, they would still had no chance of winning.

The demon's hand struck at Zaislo's head.

Suddenly a gust of wind swept through the room. A large whirlwind was conjured up from nothing between Zaislo and the demon. It pushed the alcoholic tavern brawler off his feet while tossing the demon lord about twenty feet back.

The wind vanished in an instant. A figure wearing a black cloak appeared in its place. Even though all black cloaked figures look pretty much the same, the four adventurers still knew that the man towering above them is the archmage who visited the inn yesterday and gave a quest to the other company.

"I already had seventy-eight of my adventures start with a wizard in a black cloak appearing in a tavern to commission me with some sort of quest." Yabbagabb began. "Although only on four of the seventy-eight had the wizard arrive by teleportation."

The archmage Pentelor was surrounded by fifteen feet wide rainbow-coloured bubble which now enveloped Behemor, Weevil, Zaislo and Yabbagabb as well.

Once he regained his momentum, the demon lord lunged at them again. But as he reached the outermost aura of the rainbow sphere, he had to draw his hand back with a pained groan. The magical sphere burned his skin which was resistant against almost every kind of fire.

The demon lord however was not only possessing and extraordinary physical strength but also a tremendous amount of magical power. He immediately dismissed the outermost layer of the rainbow sphere with pure concentration. Thus the radius of the protective sphere decreased by two feet, but it was still over ten feet wide.

Pentelor glared at the adventurers and as if he was speaking to revolting, disgusting worms he talked down to them:

"The mission is the same as yesterday. To acquire the fiery-red medallion of the death knight. Do you accept or not?"

Zaislo got up from the ground. Looking at his face, it was obvious he was planning to do something insane. He wanted to charge the wizard with broadsword in hand. A demon lord wasn't enough for him, he wanted to take on an archmage as well. The slap he received yesterday from the magical hand was a painful point in his memory. He swore right then that he would get his revenge on the wizard and heal his wounded pride. He raised his broadsword up in the air.

But Behemor noticed in time what he was trying to do and proved to be quicker. He immobilized Zaislo from behind.

The bones of the alcoholic tavern brawler were rattling in protest. The barbarian held him so tight that he could barely breathe. He twitched and threatened for a while but as he ran out of breath he could only wheeze.

Behemor still didn't let him go.

"What happened to the previous company?" Weevil asked the wizard, not paying the interlude any attention.

"They died..."

"You should have entrusted the task to us in the first place" the goblin reprimanded him "we accept the quest as long as you immediately remove the disease plaguing our bodies."

"And our oath?" Yabbagabb turned to them, his face serious. "We made an oath. No adventuring for us."

"By the God of Knowledge Yabbagabb, please come to your senses! Our bodies are being devoured by an unknown disease, there is an army of fire mages prepared to execute us, a demon lord is waiting to hold a wake over our corpses and once again you drag our stupid oath into this. Well be assured that I will never take any more idiotic oaths ever again and I am not going to keep this last one. Oaths are for breaking them with a clear conscience if we were ever stupid enough to make them. Life creates enough obstacles as it is there is no need to add to them by making up more artificial barriers. I advise you to forget our moronic oath, I will break it anyway, accept this quest with or without you and get out of here!"

"All right, all right." Yabbagabb mumbled.

The goblin turned to the archmage.

"Are you able to cure the disease?"

Pentelor snapped his fingers and all four of them were healthy again at once.

"Wow!" Yabbagabb exclaimed, surprised.

The raging demon tore another aura down.

"Maybe we should get going" the goblin offered. And he was not at all interested in why the wizard wants the fiery-red amulet so much, why he doesn't get it himself, who the death knight is or if there is a map or some information about the place they are going to. He was not interested in any kind of forward payment or the treasures the death knight has apart from the medallion. He was only interested in one thing: to get away from here, the further the better!

Pentelor started chanting a teleportation spell.

Weevil stood there grim-faced and silent, preparing himself to the upcoming quest.

Yabbagabb stuck out his tongue at the demon lord and made annoying grimaces.

With a sudden move, Zaislo freed himself from

Behemor's grasp. First he looked like he was going to attack the barbarian then that he would assault the archmage or try his luck with the demon lord. But he cared not for barbarian, mage or demon. He rushed toward something else. In the last second he lunged at the barrel of tolkenauer wine and then he was teleported away with his acquaintances.

They left the demon lord and the hundreds of mages, clerics and warriors of Karavan behind. They will be better off without them…

Thus the Quest ended. You know parts of what followed Horius, my friend.

The demon lord survived the spell of the fire mages and attacked the hundreds of shocked mages, clerics and warriors. By the time he finished them off, a relief army numbering in thousands led by centurion Ibrak Farberg and the captain of the city guardhas arrived. The demon broke down several communal living towers. The guard captain died right in the beginning of the battle under the rubble but centurion Ibrak Farberg had the honor of being trampled under the hellish monster's clumsy hooves. In the end the rampage of the beast was stopped by the Alamander patriarch actually returning in time, the archmage of the city and the archangel named Aubal, summoned by their combined effort. The three of them managed to banish the demon back to its hellish home.

The four surviving characters of the tale arrived at the tower of the death knight. Weevil and Zaislo argued about who the leader of the group should be. Behemor was caressing his battle axe. Yabbagabb straightened a bent nail of his spiked club on the freestone wall.

Before starting their quest, they drank every last drop of the tolkenauer wine then the drunkenly searched, looted and destroyed the tower of the death knight. They slaughtered dozens of monsters. They cared little about whether they were hostile, seemed friendly or were attempting to tell annoying riddles. They put all of them to the sword. They reached the death knight drunk as skunk, crawling on all fours. They attacked him at once. By the end of the battle, a fistful of ashes, a few bone fragments and a fiery-red amulet were all that remained of the knight.

Pentelor must have felt the demise of the death knight, for immediately after his defeat he teleported into the room. This was when Zaislo took his revenge for a certain slap. He killed him with a single, delicious strike.

How did he defeat the archmage that easily?

While they were fighting their boring battle with the death knight, they had a chat with the host and learned from him that the provider of their quest had not dared to get the medallion personally because the knight had a crossbow and a bolt which was made to destroy archmages.

Zaislo used the weapon to shoot poor Pentelor in the head, then returned to his companions, statisfied. Behemor, Yabbagabb and Weevil noticed nothing of this interlude, they were busy with the treasures of the death knight.

Weevil and Yabbagabb used magic to identify the magical items. Behemor had a special ability to sense the magical potential inside items. Lacking either, Zaislo used the expressions on his companions faces to tell how much each one could be worth.

Dividing the loot took a long time. There were magical items they could not agree on at all and the argument was not far from turning into a battle.

By the end of the process they were so angry with each other that they had no intentions to go on adventures together anymore. They each went on their own way in No Man's Land.

They never met each other again nor have they heard from one another. After a while, they couldn't even recall the names of the other three adventurers they once shared drinks in the Yellow Serpent...

ABOUT THE AUTHOR

Cal Dorne has published five bestselling science fiction
and fantasy novels in his native Hungary. He lives in
Budapest with his lovely wife and two amazing children.
When his family is asleep he rubs his fingers on his black
skull necklace and moves to sit in front of the otherwordly
glow of his word processor.